"I Had the Wrong Impression of You.

"I thought you were harder, that you'd had plenty of men, that you didn't care about anything but your job. I figured that you'd be the perfect casual affair. Smart, sexy, great in bed—but last night I realized I was wrong. When I find the right woman I'll get remarried," he said stiffly. "I want someone who puts me first, the way I'd put her first. Someone who wants a family. I can't see you pushing a stroller, Katie. You're just not right for me."

"Not right for you? What you're saying is that I'm not good enough for you!"

Dear Reader:

There is an electricity between two people in love that makes everything they do magic, larger than life. This is what we bring you in SILHOUETTE INTIMATE MOMENTS.

SILHOUETTE INTIMATE MOMENTS are longer, more sensuous romance novels filled with adventure, suspense, glamor or melodrama. These books have an element no one else has tapped: excitement.

We are proud to present the very best romance has to offer from the very best romance writers. In the coming months look for some of your favorite authors such as Elizabeth Lowell, Nora Roberts, Erin St. Claire and Brooke Hastings.

SILHOUETTE INTIMATE MOMENTS are for the woman who wants more than she has ever had before. These books are for you.

Karen Solem
Editor-in-Chief
Silhouette Books

Interested Parties

Brooke Hastings

Silhouette Intimate Moments
Published by Silhouette Books New York
America's Publisher of Contemporary Romance

For Phyllis, Lynda, and Marty,
and in memory of Teri

SILHOUETTE BOOKS, a Division of Simon & Schuster, Inc.
1230 Avenue of the Americas, New York, N.Y. 10020

ISBN: 0-671-43074-2

First Silhouette Books printing February, 1984

10 9 8 7 6 5 4 3 2 1

Books by Brooke Hastings

Silhouette Romance

Playing for Keeps #13
Innocent Fire #26
Desert Fire #44
Island Conquest #67
Winner Take All #101

Silhouette Special Edition

Intimate Strangers #2
Rough Diamond #21
A Matter of Time #49
An Act of Love #79
Tell Me No Lies #156

Silhouette Intimate Moments

Interested Parties #37

Chapter 1

KATHARINE ANNE GARVEY HAD WATCHED DR. ANTHONY M. Larimer many times over the past eight days, even if only on a television screen, and each time her body had reacted with an aching warmth she preferred to dismiss. Now, sitting in the State Department auditorium in Washington, DC, listening to the secretary of state and waiting for Larimer to take his turn to speak at the jam-packed news conference, she was feeling a buildup of that same unfamiliar feeling. Anthony Larimer, the hero of Odessa! she thought with a tiny shake of her head. The events of the past few weeks suddenly seemed incredible.

It had all started a week ago Monday, when the FBI had arrested a Soviet cultural attaché named Alexei Borlin in San Francisco, charging him with espionage. Two days later, a group of armed Soviet university students had stormed into the Black Sea retreat of a top Communist party official, disturbing a dinner party he was giving in honor of a visiting American string quartet. For the next eight days, the host and his family had been held hostage along with the members of

the quartet and the other American guests; the students had
permitted everyone else to leave.

The students' initial demand had been for an investigation
into the host's "anti-Soviet activities," which consisted of
overly friendly relationships with westerners. Holding the
Americans had apparently been an afterthought, a way to
force the United States to release diplomat Alexei Borlin.

The Soviet government's official reaction to the villa sei-
zure had been mild, a gentle denouncement in the state
newspaper with no subsequent police action. Across the
Atlantic Ocean, American president Eli Hendrickson had
called for a quick resolution to the situation, while Secretary
of State Clemenger had announced that he was using "all
available diplomatic channels to secure the timely release of
our citizens."

Those citizens were now home, but no thanks to Secretary
Clemenger, who sat among them at a table at the front of the
auditorium. Kate listened with growing shock as they told the
press and the American public about their experiences in
captivity and of the slowly escalating tension that had eventually erupted into angry arguments with the Soviet students
and stomach-turning instances of physical brutality. Accused
spy Alexei Borlin was back in Moscow now, the charges
against him dismissed. A major Soviet espionage ring stretching from California to Washington, DC, had been broken
wide open. And the man who'd received most of the credit
for these feats, Anthony M. Larimer, was due to speak next.

When he walked into the room and sat down at a microphone, the effect on the audience was electric. The jaded
Washington press corps bolted up and collectively snapped to
attention. On paper, Kate supposed, Anthony Larimer was
impressive enough—a former Peace Corpsman and State
Department expert who now taught political science at the
University of California at Berkeley—but his academic credentials couldn't begin to explain why people responded to
him so dramatically.

Studying him, Kate understood why her boss had sent her

clear across the country to attend today's news conference and White House reception. Television cameras could never quite convey the essence of a man, so Kate's assignment was to watch him in the flesh and take his measure. She wasn't a journalist but a top-flight political consultant who represented a number of influential Californians, people who believed that Anthony Larimer might make a first-rate candidate for the United States Senate. If, after watching him in person, Kate concurred with that opinion, she would approach him about running.

As she listened to his brief, evasive answers to the reporters' questions, she realized that, far from putting anyone off, Larimer's manner only added to the aura of authority and mystery that had come to surround him. She wasn't immune to the magic; in fact, her physical reaction was so embarrassingly intense that she had to remind herself that she was in Washington on business.

After repeatedly dodging questions about Alexei Borlin and about his own role in breaking up the Soviet espionage network, Larimer finally agreed to give further details of his discussions with Vladimir Rvanski, the students' leader. He declined, however, to comment on the specifics of his talks with President Hendrickson, merely stating that he'd sought to convey the urgency of the situation in Odessa to the president. Of course, no one in the room believed that that was *all* he'd done.

When the questions turned personal, the temperature in the room seemed to drop ten degrees. A California features reporter asked Larimer when his daughter would be returning to Berkeley from her grandparents' home in San Diego, and he lazed back in his chair, nailing the woman to her seat with an icy stare. Until that point he'd paid little attention to the audience, but now his eyes raked the room, colliding with Kate's and sending her pulse rate soaring.

For some reason his look made her nervous. When his eyes lingered, traveling down her body and then returning to her face, she was tempted to look down. She didn't. He smiled slightly, making her feel like she was sitting in a sauna. By the time his eyes resumed their journey around the room, her face was flushed.

"I'll be happy to respond to questions about my role in the Odessa negotiations," he finally replied, "although I hope you appreciate the fact that there are things I simply can't go into, for reasons of national security. As far as my family goes, my daughter left my brother's house to go to San Diego to stay with my parents because reporters found her and wouldn't leave her alone. I'll be going to San Diego in a day or two for a short visit with my parents before taking my daughter home with me. I'm not sure I understand this fascination with my personal life, because it's really very ordinary; I feel very strongly that I'm not a public figure, and I won't answer questions that invade my privacy."

Kate could have explained the public's fascination with a single word: charisma. It wasn't solely a matter of looks, although Larimer was a handsome man. It wasn't even a matter of charm; he'd exhibited exactly none of that today, although in the past he'd shown flashes of humor that had left her both amused and aroused. It was sheer personal appeal, the ineffable aura he somehow generated. The women in his classes, she thought in bemusement, must all fall in love with him.

She'd never lacked self-confidence, but after Larimer's firm little lecture she was unsure of her ability to talk him into running for dogcatcher, much less United States senator. He was obviously a very private person. The only positive note in his whole performance was that brief smile he'd given her, but admiring her as a woman didn't imply that he would respect her as a political professional. And, first and foremost, Kate Garvey considered herself a political professional.

The thought took her back to the first time she'd ever laid eyes on Anthony Larimer. She'd been a dinner guest at the Beverly Hills home of her boss, William Dorset, but the social part of the evening had bored her senseless. When the dinner party had finally broken up and Bill Dorset's wife had started to tease Kate about her habit of wandering off with the men to talk politics, Kate had freely admitted where her real interests lay.

"When I was growing up in Washington," she said with a smile, "the men went to one room after dinner and the women to another. I always wound up with my father, not my mother, and things haven't changed since."

"How is he?" Emily Dorset asked, referring to Henry "Hank" Garvey, the senior senator from Connecticut.

"Just fine. Naturally he's concerned about losing the chairmanship of the Intelligence Committee if the Republicans take control of the Senate in November, but I told him we'd do our best to prevent that by trying to elect a Democratic senator from California this fall."

Emily and the two remaining women went off to the master bedroom to inspect some fabric swatches while their husbands and Kate started down the hall to the game room, where Kate took her usual seat on the couch. She was thirty-two but looked younger, a tough, savvy pro who had the delicately innocent features of an angel. Five feet six inches tall, with a slender body that curved in all the right places, she had curly blond hair that fell to her shoulders and baby-blue eyes that missed very little.

Bill Dorset sat in a leather chair to Kate's left. Forty-five years old, handsome and urbane, he'd once been a state senator. Politicians liked him because he was quicker to listen than to talk. He was now the president of William Dorset and Associates, probably the most influential and effective political consulting firm in California. Because of the company's efforts, the Democratic candidates for statewide office in most of the western states were currently in power, including George McClure, who sat to Kate's right on the couch.

McClure, a year older than Bill Dorset and graying nicely at the temples, with only a few extra pounds on his six-foot frame, was in the middle of his second term as governor of California. He was an intelligent, decent man, and Kate was proud that she'd helped elect him. The last man in the room, who had sprawled his considerable girth into a modern leather and steel chair, was the only one of the three who

looked and acted like the public's notion of a back-room
politician. His name was Vince Collier, and he was Governor
McClure's chief of staff and most trusted aide.

The four of them promptly picked up the discussion that
they'd started well before dinner. The subject was next June's
primary election, which was about five months away. The
Democratic party had two major problems. The first was the
incumbent junior senator, a former Olympic athlete named
Jack Handlin. He was up for reelection, but a combination of
limited intellect and ability and a messy divorce had landed
him in hot water with the voters. Although he was a fellow
Democrat, Kate and her colleagues invariably referred to him
in the most scathing of tones.

Handlin's one saving grace was that he had enough common sense to know when he was in trouble. After twenty
minutes of political strategizing, Governor McClure finally
decided to dangle the prospect of a lucrative statewide
appointment in front of Handlin's nose and pray that he'd
grab it.

That left the second problem, the man who was almost sure
to be the Republican senatorial candidate in the November
general election. Congressman Bob Woodruff of Orange
County in Southern California was a smart, smooth politician
whose expertise in the areas of taxation and finance had
earned him a national reputation. He'd be darned hard to
beat.

After fifteen minutes of further conversation, Governor
McClure lazed back on the couch and announced, "If I'm
going to go to the considerable effort of ridding the Democratic party of Handlin, it would be nice to replace him with
someone remotely qualified and electable. You know who's
interested—and not interested—as well as I do. We've gone
over this before, and the plain fact is, no one wants to take on
Bob Woodruff." He glanced at his watch. "Let's drink some
brandy and watch the news. I want to find out what's
happening in Odessa."

A police show preceded the late-night news, and the final
credits were rolling as the picture came on. Kate fetched

herself a soda while Bill Dorset poured out three snifters of brandy and carried them to his guests. Kate had discussed the Odessa crisis with her father only the night before. His position as chairman of the Senate Intelligence Committee gave him access to classified information, but he didn't share it with Kate. Instead, he'd merely remarked that American high officials were convinced that the students' actions were government instigated and that their first demand, concerning the Soviet party official, was mere window dressing. The Soviets wanted Alexei Borlin back, but nobody could figure out why they were suddenly so determined. After all, the FBI and the CIA had had three days in which to induce the fellow to spill his guts, and if he hadn't talked yet, he probably wouldn't. If he had, getting him back would be too little too late.

The local news anchorman, who looked suitably grim about the situation, stared into the camera and announced in an important tone, "There's been a surprising new development in that drama being played out in Odessa. Stay tuned for details on the eleven o'clock news, next on TV-Three."

News teasers were one of Bill Dorset's pet peeves. "Beverly Hills invaded by aliens," he grumbled. "Details at eleven."

"How could they tell?" Vince Collier asked ingenuously.

"No Gucci handbags," Bill informed him.

After a promo for some fading singer's upcoming special and a public-service announcement for a medical charity, the anchorman reappeared. "Good evening," he intoned, telling his name to those in the audience who couldn't read it on the screen. "It's now ten o'clock in the morning in Odessa. At this hour, the Black Sea villa of Communist party deputy secretary Yuri Spelnikov is still under the control of a group of armed Soviet students. Mr. Spelnikov and his family, American ambassador Charles Whitlaw and his wife, the members of Boston's Back Bay String Quartet, and at least six other Americans remain inside. Vladimir Rvanski, the students' leader and spokesman, has again demanded that the American government return Soviet diplomat Alexei Borlin, arrested three days ago in connection with the disappearance of top-secret documents from the Lawrence Livermore National Laboratory in California. In addition, labeling Deputy Secretary Spelnikov an 'enemy of the people,' Rvanski has called for an investigation into his relationships with western visitors."

The camera drew back from a close-up of the anchorman's face to focus on a photograph of a large villa, which was projected onto the wall beside him. The house was lavish but stark, surrounded by gray skies, bare trees, and a brown lawn dappled with snow. After a moment the picture changed to show a pair of adolescents staring sullenly into the camera, rifles poised threateningly on their shoulders. They reminded Kate of insecure little boys who were trying to prove to the local bully that they weren't afraid of him. As the anchorman continued to read the news, a third slide appeared on the screen, and this time the camera moved in for a tight close-up.

The man in the photograph was thirty-five or forty years old, with dark eyes and rather unruly brown hair that curled over his collar in the back. Kate wasn't usually affected by a man's looks, but this one was special: toughly handsome and a little too grim-looking. She wondered if he made his living with his body rather than his mind and doubted if his prominent brows, firm jaw, and rather thin lips had made the acquaintance of a smile lately. She found it hard to tear her eyes from his face.

"In a startling new development," the anchorman explained, "student leader Rvanski has requested that American political science professor Anthony M. Larimer fly to Odessa, apparently to serve as a liaison between the students and the American government. Dr. Larimer, traveling in the Soviet Union to research a book on Soviet foreign policy, was taken from Moscow to Odessa earlier today. He arrived several hours ago."

A brief film clip of Larimer's arrival at the villa was shown next. The Soviet government had permitted a sizable group of western journalists to cover the Odessa crisis, but the tape offered little enlightenment. Reporters were shouting questions at a stony-faced Anthony Larimer as his black limousine slowly passed them by and then continued through the high iron fence surrounding the villa. Kate could see him shake his head and managed to lip-read his answer: "I'm sorry, I have no comment right now."

"Who is Anthony Larimer?"

During the dramatic pause that followed the newsman's rhetorical question, Vince Collier inserted cynically, "Local boy makes good—at least for a day or two. They must be eating this up in Berkeley."

The anchorman continued, "Dr. Larimer, thirty-nine years old, is an expert on the Communist bloc and the author of two major books, a highly regarded study of Soviet policy toward other Communist nations in the 1950's, and a Pulitzer prize-winning book on American-Soviet relations in the 1970's. He speaks fluent Russian, as well as a number of other languages. After graduating from Stanford University, he spent four years in the Peace Corps, serving in several different Asian countries, then earned his doctorate at Georgetown University in Washington while working in the State Department as an expert in Asian affairs. He is currently an associate professor of political science at the University of California at Berkeley."

A well-kept but ordinary suburban ranch house flashed onto the screen. There was a blue station wagon in the driveway but no other sign of occupancy. "Dr. Larimer, a widower, lives in Berkeley with his daughter, Jessica, fifteen, and his niece, Kristin, a junior at the university. According to a neighbor, earlier today the two young women left to stay with Dr. Larimer's brother in Palo Alto. Neither the White House nor the State Department has any comment on Larimer's involvement in the crisis, although at this hour the President continues to insist that under no circumstances will he release accused spy Alexei Borlin. For a complete summary of events in Odessa, stay tuned for a special report following the news."

Bill Dorset lowered the volume of the television set, softening the impact of an annoyingly peppy diet soda commercial. "I read Larimer's book—the one that won a Pulitzer. I have to admit it put me to sleep in a couple of places, but on the whole it was impressive. Do you know him personally, Vince?"

Vince nodded to Governor McClure, who proceeded to answer the question. "Both of us know him. After I submitted the budget last year, a faculty committee from the University of California asked to meet with me about UC budget cuts. Larimer was on the committee."

"Larimer—that name rings a bell." Kate quickly made the right connection. "Any relation to Howard Larimer of your San Diego campaign committee, Governor?"

"His son. Believe me, Kate, I was very polite to him. He can be charming and persuasive, but he wasn't particularly interested in hearing my standard speech about the state's fiscal problems. I got the feeling that he has a less appealing side than the one he was willing to show me—an arrogance and lack of patience with people who aren't as smart as he is."

"Which makes you wonder how he's going to cope with Vladimir Rvanski and his pals," Vince Collier remarked. "You can't tell me that the Soviet government isn't pulling the strings here. They haven't done anything but wiggle a finger under Rvanski's nose and tell him he's a naughty boy. They're letting foreign newsmen swarm all over Odessa. The only question is, Who's the central issue here? Yuri Spelnikov or Alexei Borlin?" He looked straight at Kate for an answer.

"They want Borlin back," she said. "Spelnikov is just a red herring." Realizing the unintentional pun, she smiled and added, "So to speak."

"But spies are supposed to self-destruct," Vince drawled. "Bite down on little red pills or something."

"Maybe he didn't have the chance. My father told me that no one can figure out why the Soviets want him back so badly. After all, we've arrested their people before and they never set up a phony hostage situation to get them back."

"Very true. Why don't you ask your father to phone Kevin O'Neal for us, Kate?"

The question came from Governor McClure. Kevin O'Neal had been the director of Central Intelligence for the past thirteen years. He was a Washington fixture by now, a man who seemed to know everyone and everything. He was also brilliant, unusually low-key, and unfailingly loyal to whichever administration happened to be in power. Those factors explained his ability to keep his job when every political rule said he should lose it. As chairman of the Senate Intelligence Committee, Hank Garvey knew Kevin O'Neal quite well. The two men were friends by now, and as a result, Kate had met Kevin on numerous occasions over the years.

"I've told you everything I know," she informed the governor, her face a little flushed. "My father doesn't pass on classified information to me, but even if he did I wouldn't spread it around. I'm only free to repeat—"

George McClure smiled and interrupted with a wink. "Now don't start lecturing me, Kate. I was just teasing you. If you were the kind of person who leaked all over the place, I wouldn't trust you. And I do."

Kate, blushing hotly by now, started to get up. "I'm sorry I overreacted. I guess it's been a long week, and it isn't over yet."

"Stay another few minutes." Bill Dorset gestured for her to sit back down on the couch. "I want to toss out an idea."

Kate obediently settled back into her former position. It *had* been a long week, but then, every week was a long week. In the months before the November election there had been no such thing as a day off, and now that the election was over, everyone was putting his energies into placating all of the nonpolitical clients, who'd been given less and less attention as election day approached. In addition to running three or four campaigns per election, Dorset and Associates handled public relations and legislative advocacy for a select group of private corporations, corporations that paid through the nose for the privilege of being represented by someone as well connected as Bill Dorset. Political work, though it turned a nice profit, was a labor of love compared to the more lucrative private lobbying contracts.

"What would you think about running Larimer for the Senate?" Bill Dorset sipped his brandy and glanced around the room, inviting an answer from anyone who cared to speak.

"When this is over," Vince Collier said, "he'll probably smell like Los Angeles on a bad day." He puffed on his ever-present cigar, thereby contributing to the pollution he decried. "The American public won't like the idea of sending Borlin back to Russia. We've labeled him a spy. No matter what kind of deal Larimer swings, that one fact will remain."

"Maybe," Bill answered, "but let's assume for the sake of argument that Larimer pulls it off in a way that satisfies the public. He's going to wind up an instant hero. You've got a smart guy with high name identification and a solid background in foreign affairs. Maybe he's a little arrogant and difficult, but so are most senators. He's served in the Peace Corps—that shows idealism. He's worked in the State Department—practical experience. He's fought to maintain the quality of higher education in California—a concern for the future of the state. He's from a politically active family and he's even a widower. With those macho looks of his, the ladies will eat him up."

George McClure looked dubious. "It's going to seem too opportunistic, this sudden celebrity running for the Senate."

Bill Dorset was quick to counter McClure's objection. "That's no problem, George. It's just a question of public relations. With the right kind of press releases, we can make him look *very* reluctant."

Kate was amused by Bill's persistence. Usually he let others do the talking until they happened to reach his own point of view. "Suppose Larimer really *is* reluctant?" she asked. "He might think he's got better things to do than run for the Senate. Who's going to change his mind?"

"Not me." George McClure started to laugh. "I'm the guy who refused three-quarters of the things that his committee wanted, remember?" He paused, still grinning, and then said to Kate, "How about you? I still remember my first campaign, when none of the Los Angeles television stations would sell me any more air time. You alternately bullied and sweet-talked them until they gave in. Given your talents, Larimer will be a piece of cake."

"I promised the TV people regular access to you after the election. I reminded them that the regulatory legislation they'd fought so bitterly would be reintroduced in the next session and that you'd voted against it. What am I supposed to bribe Larimer with?" She caught the teasing look in George McClure's eyes and shook her head. "Oh, no, Governor. I know I have the reputation for being tenacious, but I'd never go *that* far. I don't mix business with pleasure, even business as attractive as Dr. Anthony M. Larimer."

Governor McClure winked as if to say that he hadn't really been serious and changed the subject. A little while later Kate excused herself, thanked her hostess, and started back to the cottage she owned in the beachside town of Venice. She was surprised to find herself picturing Anthony Larimer as she drove home, but knew that the attraction would never last. She'd long ago learned that the only time a man could top her list of priorities was when she was trying to elect him to something.

There was a pair of color television sets built into a walnut cabinet in Bill Dorset's office, and the following afternoon Kate joined Bill for what would be the first of many crisis updates that they would watch together. The first major break came late Friday night, California time, when it was Saturday morning in Odessa. Via a special report they learned that Anthony Larimer had emerged from the villa to announce that Vladimir Rvanski had agreed to release the women hostages; in return, he said, President Eli Hendrickson would resume the shipment of food and medical supplies to the earthquake-ravaged Central American country of Moroguay. Hendrickson had cut off emergency aid less than a week after the earthquake occurred because the government of Moroguay was staunchly Communist, but television footage of starving children and newspaper articles about homeless families had convinced the American public that the presi-

dent had been too harsh. Kate considered Larimer's compromise to be a brilliant political deal. It allowed both Rvanski
and Hendrickson to pretend they were humanitarians.

Both Kate and Bill worked most of the weekend, so that
when the tape of Larimer's announcement to the press was
shown on American television, they were sitting side by side
and watching. Larimer walked slowly down the driveway,
apparently oblivious to the cold, and stopped a few feet short
of the eight-foot-high iron gate. After explaining the agreement he'd negotiated, he went on, "I've spoken with Ambassador Whitlaw, as well as with the other American hostages.
All of them are safe and healthy, although Mr. Sosnick, the
string quartet's cellist, has a moderate case of intestinal flu
and will be permitted to leave with the women."

Larimer looked very tired, which might have explained his
flat tone of voice and expressionless features, but even so,
Kate found him devastating. She was totally baffled by her
continuing physical response to him. The last time she'd
become this infatuated with a filmed image, she thought with
amusement, she'd been thirteen years old and had just
watched Clark Gable in *It Happened One Night*.

"I have a few brief comments about my role in this
situation," Larimer continued, "and then I'll take your
questions. I first met Alexei Borlin when I was serving in the
Peace Corps in Thailand and Mr. Borlin was a Soviet cultural
attaché. We became reacquainted about eight years ago,
when Mr. Borlin was assigned to the Soviet legation in San
Francisco. I was already teaching at Berkeley. I assume that
our acquaintance has as much to do with Mr. Rvanski's
invitation to come to Odessa as my expertise in Soviet affairs,
but I have no comment on Mr. Borlin's guilt or innocence. I
assume that the FBI arrested him on the basis of legitimate
and convincing evidence, and I've certainly pointed out to
Mr. Rvanski that Mr. Borlin will receive a rapid and impartial
trial in the United States." He paused, then nodded at a
woman reporter. "Yes?"

"Would you please outline your background for us?"

Larimer obliged, sketching out the same information that

Kate had already received via the TV news. He proceeded to answer half a dozen questions that bordered on the inane, but declined to divulge the contents of his talks with Vladimir Rvanski or any American official.

Only when the questions became personal did his patience appear to wear thin. Kate suspected he was trying to hide it, but a steely look flashed in his eyes and he straightened just a little too noticeably.

"Have you talked to your daughter?" someone asked.

"I was hustled out of a hotel room with very little time to spare, but I managed a call home and reached my niece. Now I'll ask *you* a question. Is everything okay at home?"

"Your brother threatened to turn the hose on a television crew," the reporter answered, smiling.

Larimer smiled back, genuinely amused. "Doug was never much of a diplomat," he said. "It's a good thing *I'm* here, not him." The smile left Kate slightly breathless. She'd majored in political science in college, but none of her professors had come close to affecting her like *this*.

"Is it true that the President plans to appoint you as his next national security advisor?" another reporter asked.

Exasperation flickered across Larimer's face. "No, that's not true. The President has a very capable man serving in that capacity now. I enjoy teaching and research and have no plans to give them up."

"We've been told that your wife's illness was very difficult for you, Dr. Larimer. How did you feel, knowing that she had only—"

Larimer cut the man off. "I'm sorry," he said curtly, "but I see no reason to answer a question like that. Is there anything else on the situation inside?"

Someone shouted out another personal question—something about Larimer's relationship with a fellow professor—and he looked as though he wanted to turn on his heel and walk away. But he stayed, enduring another ten minutes of questions before he excused himself.

Bill Dorset clicked off the set, remarking to Kate that Larimer had handled himself extremely well. "Not that it would matter to the women voters if he hadn't," he added, "if your reaction is anything to go by."

Although Kate blushed, she also smiled a little sheepishly. "Is it that obvious?"

Bill grinned at her. "It was only a guess, Kate. You looked very intent. I figured that for once in your life you might be seeing something besides potential votes when you looked at a candidate."

"*Potential* candidate," Kate corrected. "Although if he continues at the rate he's going, I intend to talk him into running. For a man who can't possibly be used to obnoxious reporters, thugs with rifles, and high-stakes negotiating, his performance has been superb."

"Just don't let any reporters hear you talking that way," Bill warned her. "Political consultants get enough flak about interfering in the political process without handing out free ammunition."

Much to the disappointment of Bill Dorset and Kate Garvey, however, the breakthrough on the women hostages was followed by a total lack of progress elsewhere. Larimer met the press twice over the next few days, becoming increasingly ill-tempered as the same questions were asked over and over again. He appeared to be confident about the eventual outcome, but smiled only once, when wearily remarking that he really didn't mind Rvanski's refusal to negotiate; what got on his nerves was being forced to endure hour after hour of bad propaganda.

Kate woke up Monday morning to learn that Larimer was on his way back to the United States to consult with President Hendrickson, but it wasn't until two days later that the crisis was finally resolved. As Anthony Larimer and Alexei Borlin boarded a plane for the Soviet Union, the White House released an announcement stating that the president had agreed to exchange Borlin for the American hostages. The president's press secretary refused further comment.

Those who criticized this arrangement—and there were many—were angry that America had knuckled under to Soviet blackmail. They suggested that a career diplomat might have protected the nation's honor where Anthony Larimer had clearly failed to. It struck Kate as unfair that the president escaped almost unscathed, but apparently his popularity was so high that even his bitterest opponents were loath to attack him.

As matters turned out, the public redemption of Anthony Larimer took less than thirty-six hours. Late Wednesday morning, as Kate and Bill watched on TV, an American Air Force jet carrying Larimer and the remaining hostages landed at Andrews Air Force Base outside Washington. A lectern and microphone had been set up for Secretary Clemenger, who walked over to greet each former hostage as he deplaned. Numerous microphones picked up their conversations, various versions of "Welcome home" and "It's great to be back." When all six men were off the plane, a security detail escorted them into a nearby building.

Anthony Larimer came off last. After the continuing public attacks on him, the tension was so thick that Kate could almost feel it. She watched in fascination as Clemenger put his arm around Larimer's shoulders and murmured something into his ear, the words much too soft for the microphones to catch. Larimer, who looked exhausted, shook his head, and this time Clemenger's comment was audible. "The President insists, Anthony. Let's get it over with."

When they stepped up to the lectern, the buzz of the crowd quieted dramatically. "I have a brief statement to make," the secretary announced. "On behalf of President Hendrickson and the American people, I'm relieved and pleased to welcome home my fellow citizens. Their detainment in Odessa constituted a flagrant disregard for international law, as did the action of the Soviet government in implicitly tolerating and even encouraging that detainment."

He paused for just a moment, giving Bill Dorset time to say to Kate, "That was hardly more than a slap on the Russians' wrists. Hendrickson must be mellowing."

Clemenger continued, "I would like to add that the American people and the American government owe their deepest gratitude to Dr. Anthony M. Larimer for his role in the negotiations leading to the peaceful resolution of this incident. The American government would like to make it clear that a thorough investigation of Mr. Borlin's activities has revealed absolutely no evidence that he was personally responsible for the theft of documents from the Lawrence Livermore Laboratory. At the same time, however, our conversations with Mr. Borlin and the information we received from a number of other sources enabled us to uncover and neutralize a serious threat to the effectiveness of United States intelligence operations. Dr. Larimer made a vital contribution to this effort."

The secretary proceeded to name two Americans arrested the night before on charges of espionage and three foreign diplomats expelled from the country that morning. "We're going to return to the White House now to brief the President," Clemenger concluded, "but you'll be able to talk to Dr. Larimer and the freed hostages at tomorrow's news conference. That's at noon at the State Department. Thank you."

The news conference was over now, Kate thought to herself, but the reporters were almost as much in the dark about Larimer's activities as they'd been ninety minutes before. As Larimer was hustled out of the room by security men, Kate stood up and stretched. Her father had of course been invited to the White House reception that afternoon, and since her mother was up at their house in Connecticut, recovering from the Christmas holidays, Kate planned to use her invitation. Having an influential father was very convenient at times, especially when it came to obtaining press credentials or access to exclusive White House functions.

As she walked out of the building, she told herself that, given what she'd seen of Anthony Larimer, the man wouldn't jump at the chance to run for office. Not only did he profess to enjoy teaching and writing, he clearly valued his privacy, and privacy was a commodity that politicians had precious little of. The wisest course of action would probably be to study his behavior at the reception before approaching him directly.

If he hated every minute of being in the limelight, it was useless to talk to him about running for office, but if he appeared to enjoy himself, she would try to find out where he was staying and drop by for a private chat. Otherwise she could ask for a few minutes of his time before he left the White House.

The thought of finally meeting him was a little too appealing for Kate's peace of mind, so she never would have admitted that her decision to change from her wool suit into a more feminine dress was motivated by anything other than a desire to be socially correct. The dress, which she'd left in her father's office that morning, was red silk printed with a leaflike white overlay pattern. It was saved from being a shade too sensual for afternoon wear by the matching jacket that covered the slender bodice.

As she strolled the twenty or so blocks to the Capitol, she kept her thoughts on Larimer the candidate rather than Larimer the man. Certainly he was wonderful raw material, she told herself, but he had some serious liabilities.

The University of California at Berkeley, where he taught, had been the center of the Free Speech Movement in the 1960's and as a result carried the taint of radicalism in many voters' minds. Indeed, the nickname *Berserkeley* was still common parlance. If Larimer ran, their first move would be to position him as a solid, moderate candidate, despite Berkeley's left-wing image. They could stress the parts of his background that identified him as a member of the Establishment, like his State Department experience, and tailor an image to match. He'd need a haircut and a suitable wardrobe —none of those tweed jackets with leather patches on the elbows or preppy little outfits like faded blue jeans with a beat-up corduroy jacket.

According to Governor McClure, the man was something of an elitist as well as an intellectual, two attributes that spelled poison at the ballot box. They could pound away on the theme that he was a family man, the sole parent of a teen-age daughter, a man who understood the economic problems of the average household.

And then there was the question of his speeches. Judging from what Kate had seen thus far, he'd definitely need the kind of coaching that she specialized in. The best political speeches both entertained and exhorted, making broad, general statements and accusations and backing them up with just enough numbers and facts to impress the audience. Larimer would have to learn to smile and hold his temper. He'd also have to stay away from the kind of painstaking detail and complex analysis that he evidently used in his books.

At the very least, Kate thought, he'd be a challenge. He was probably a babe in the woods politically when compared to a pro like George McClure, but if he was smart, she could teach him to play the game. She wanted the opportunity to try.

Chapter 2

No one was more surprised than Anthony Larimer when he found himself actually enjoying the White House reception in honor of the returned hostages. The past eight days had been so grueling that by all rights he should have wanted to avoid people, but he supposed that it was only human to savor the handshakes and congratulations of the influential. Besides, he couldn't deny that he found the attentions of the local ladies rather pleasant, even though he knew perfectly well that their admiration would have been equally effusive had he been a foot shorter and fifty pounds heavier. Power was the ultimate aphrodisiac in this city.

He could have taken his pick of them if he'd been so inclined, but the only woman who'd really caught his fancy was behaving in an unpromising, even puzzling manner. She seemed to be watching him but didn't come over to introduce herself the way all of the others had. It didn't make sense to Anthony, and his training told him that when something didn't make sense, it was time to start asking questions. He wound up his conversation with the vice-president's wife and looked around for CIA chief Kevin O'Neal.

The average person would have noticed that the two men seemed only to have nodded to each other in passing. In fact, with fewer than half a dozen words exchanged, they had managed to arrange a meeting in five minutes in one of the downstairs bathrooms. As Anthony reached that destination and shut the door behind him, the events of the past week suddenly seemed to close in on him all over again. He didn't really want to remember how agonizing it had been, but somehow he couldn't help himself.

The low point, he supposed, had been that first flight back to Washington. After almost four days with Vladimir Rvanski he'd developed a new admiration for the courage and skill of a good diplomat. Rvanski was tough, aggravating, and at times downright frightening. After the women were released Anthony had suggested every compromise he could come up with and gotten precisely nowhere. The only thing he could think to do was to go back home and talk with President Hendrickson, a man he rather admired despite his blanket refusal to release Borlin.

During that trip Anthony gave a good deal of thought to what he would say, concluding that he would have to be blunt, even aggressive, if necessary. There was a lot about the Odessa crisis he didn't understand. He'd played enough political games in his life to be thoroughly sick of them, and if people's lives were to remain in jeopardy, there had better be a damn good reason for it.

Secretary of State Clemenger met his plane, telling him they would be taking a chopper directly to the White House for a meeting with the president and CIA director Kevin O'Neal. The head of the FBI, he remarked, was still in California with Alexei Borlin, but he'd be bringing Borlin back to Washington that evening.

The secretary, showing a thoughtfulness that Anthony appreciated, had arranged a telephone hookup from the helicopter to his brother's house in Palo Alto. Anthony spent most of the flight talking to his sister-in-law and his daughter, who were coping as best they could with the unwanted attention of reporters.

The president was waiting in his office talking with Kevin O'Neal when they arrived. Anthony had first met O'Neal in Asia, when O'Neal had been his superior at the Agency. His membership in the Peace Corps had, of course, been a cover identity, although no one knew that except a handful of CIA colleagues. Anthony's life had gone in a different direction from Kevin's since then, but they'd become close friends over the years. Three or four years ago, when Anthony had reached for the phone in the middle of the night, needing someone to talk to, someone to share his pain with, it had been Kevin O'Neal who he called.

"Hell of a situation, isn't it?" O'Neal slapped him on the back. "I've briefed the President and the secretary on your four years with the Agency, Anthony. If Rvanski ever figures out that his Pulitzer prizewinning American professor used to be a CIA agent, his face will turn the same color as his politics. We're damn lucky you happened to be in Moscow."

Anthony shook hands with the president, then took a seat between O'Neal and Clemenger, opposite the president's desk. "On the other hand," he said, looking at Kevin, "maybe luck had nothing to do with it. You knew I was in Moscow, so you grabbed Borlin. You're going to have to explain to me *why* you grabbed Borlin, because if he's a KGB agent, then I'm Queen Victoria. True, he's done his share of skulking around the Silicon Valley, trying to promote cultural and scientific exchanges and swipe a little American technology here and there, but there's no way on earth he could manage to steal nuclear secrets from a secure facility. So tell me, Kevin. Was I supposed to be conveniently on hand as an unofficial negotiator, so the government wouldn't get its hands dirty when things blew up?"

Kevin grinned at him. "Very creative, as always, Anthony. But not even close. The fact is, we have very convincing evidence linking Borlin with the stolen documents. The arrest was legitimate. But over the next few days we gradually began to suspect he'd been set up. He talks like he's in the dark.

He's been more than cooperative. In order for you to really understand the situation, you'll have to listen to the tapes of our conversations with him, but the bottom line is that, without knowing it, he's feeding us information that contradicts other intelligence data. It doesn't add up and we're trying to figure out why. We checked on Rvanski's background, by the way. He's twenty-eight years old and he's been a party activist since he was in diapers."

"There's no question that Rvanski's in touch with Moscow," Anthony told Kevin. "The phone rings at least half a dozen times a day. I've tried every angle I can think of, but he won't budge on releasing any of the other hostages. He says Borlin is innocent."

Anthony hesitated, then looked at Eli Hendrickson. "Mr. President, when I was with the Agency in Asia, one of my jobs was to keep track of the opposition. We checked Borlin out upside down and sideways. He simply doesn't have what it takes to be a KGB agent and stay alive for very long. I know his type. He's a front man."

When the president nodded but didn't comment, Anthony turned back to Kevin O'Neal. "You say Borlin is cooperative but inconsistent. Maybe . . . maybe the Soviets were using him as part of a complicated operation—feeding him information, setting him up for an eventual arrest, knowing that when he talked, we'd reach certain conclusions. Erroneous conclusions that would undermine our intelligence capability."

"If that's the case—and we agree with your analysis—then something obviously went wrong," Kevin said. "Maybe we snatched him too soon, before they were finished programming him. We assume that they wanted us to have him for a little while—Rvanski waited a few days to make his move. But now they're afraid we'll figure things out. We were hoping you'd be able to buy us a bit more time. . . ."

"Rvanski's no fool. He knows I've been stalling. I got you twenty-four extra hours with a bunch of impassioned speeches about how holding women is uncivilized, but . . ."

"Here's to motherhood and apple pie," the president drawled.

Anthony couldn't help but smile. He'd heard rumors about Hendrickson's sardonic sense of humor, which the president exhibited only in private. "I figured you'd want me to stall as long as possible, so I wasted most of another day by proposing a whole set of options that Rvanski had to reject," he continued, "but by yesterday I had to get serious. Rvanski's making threats, talking about 'accidents.' He says he can't promise to control his people. I want to stress to all of you how tense the situation is. Rvanski may be a pragmatist, but his private army are true believers."

"I can't let Rvanski blackmail me into releasing a man the American government has charged with espionage," President Hendrickson reminded Anthony. "It would be political suicide, and I have to run for reelection in November. If Rvanski won't let the hostages go, we have to break this case wide open and *then* release him. Or we have to trade Borlin for the hostages *and* somebody damned important—that Nobel prizewinning novelist would be acceptable. Shchikovsky."

Anthony shook his head. "I've tried Shchikovsky. Rvanski gave me a solid hour on how he's an enemy of the Soviet people. The Russians will never let him out. You have to understand, Mr. President, that some of those kids with rifles aren't even old enough to buy a drink. Tempers are short on both sides, and when one of our people gets a rifle shoved into his back and makes the mistake of shoving back, he's going to get hurt or even killed. All of us in this room know that Borlin isn't a spy. Let him go and get our people out of there."

"You're panicking, just like the Reds want you to." Kevin shot Anthony a scathing look. "You should get out of Berkeley, Anthony. You've been playing schoolteacher for too long."

Anthony wanted to tell Kevin where to go, but old habits died hard. Even after all these years away from the Agency, one didn't curse one's former superior in front of other people. "You've had Borlin for nearly a week, Kevin," he answered. "Maybe you're asking the wrong questions, or maybe the answers you're looking for don't exist, but your ineptitude isn't sufficient reason to endanger the lives of six innocent people. Rvanski gave me until tomorrow at two. He says that if he doesn't get word that Borlin is coming home, someone may get hurt. He means it."

The conversation continued, the same ground being covered from every conceivable angle. Anthony heard a lot of talk about ensuring the safety of the hostages, but there was also an insistence on refusing to succumb to international blackmail and on defending the security of the United States. By the time the president brought the meeting to a close by promising to release Borlin if he thought the hostages were in imminent danger, Anthony was exhausted. His body told him it was the middle of the night and his patience had been worn to a frazzle.

"I'd like you to listen to the Borlin tapes," Kevin said as they walked to the door. "But first you have to stop in at the pressroom."

"I don't think I can handle it. I'll lose my temper."

Kevin dropped a reassuring hand on Anthony's shoulder. "You've done okay so far. More than okay. You've been superb, despite some unforgivable personal questions."

"I was less tired and less worried then, Kevin. Why do they ask me about Beth's death? Try to interview Jessica? What does that have to do with Odessa?"

"You know the answer as well as I do. You're famous. People are curious about you."

"Not now." Anthony said the words in a way that left no room for argument. Secretary Clemenger volunteered to brief the press, asking Anthony's permission to set up a news conference for noon the next day.

He agreed, then allowed Kevin to lead him out of the office and into a limousine that was waiting in an area cleared of reporters. Two identical cars sat nearby to serve as decoys, the window shades in each pulled down. As all three limousines pulled away from the White House, Anthony rested his head against the back of the seat, staring at the ceiling. "I don't even know where I'm staying," he said, "or what happened to my suitcase."

"You're coming home with me, and your suitcase is in the trunk." Kevin reached to the rear, opening up a compartment and taking out two beers. He held one out to Anthony, who shook his head.

"If you want me to," Kevin offered, "I'll get someone to take Jessica to your parents' place in San Diego. She'll have more privacy there, at least until they track her down."

"I'd appreciate that. Maybe I'm getting too old for this stuff." Anthony smiled because Kevin was twelve years older than he was. "I meant what I told the President, Kevin. The situation in Odessa is very bad. Rvanski knows we're stalling and he's leaning on us . . . hard. He probably figures that once he starts bargaining, we'll toughen our stance and refuse to return Borlin at all."

"So it would seem. Just relax, Anthony. I haven't seen you this strung out since Beth . . . " Kevin checked himself, saying instead, "Just listen to the tapes for me. Either Borlin's the cleverest liar I've ever come across or he thinks he's giving us the harmless truth. But when you correlate his statements with information from other sources . . ."

Kevin paused, then went on gently, "We need time to chase down all the leads, Anthony. If it hadn't been for the work you did thirteen years ago, we would never have broken the State Department spy case. I need the same kind of help now—help in figuring out what questions we should ask Borlin or how to phrase questions so he'll think it's okay to answer them—and help in getting the time we need to fit the jigsaw puzzle together. Can you buy me another day or two?"

"I'll try." Anthony sighed and closed his eyes. He owed Kevin far too much to refuse. "I'll have to convince Rvanski that the President's concern about the election is making him impossible to deal with—that he won't believe that Borlin isn't a Soviet agent. He's already figured out that I'm not the ivory-tower professor he expected, so it won't be easy to sell him on waiting, especially when my instincts tell me you're taking too big a risk. But it won't be the first time I've trusted your instincts ahead of my own. I'll try."

Anthony had not only tried, he'd succeeded brilliantly, spending hour after hour with Kevin and an elite team of counterespionage specialists until an unwitting Alexei Borlin led them to a spy network so potentially damaging that even Kevin O'Neal had paled with shock. He'd bluffed Vladimir Rvanski into waiting and then waiting some more, but as the clock left Rvanski's deadline further and further behind, his stomach had churned with tension and ultimately rebelled. If even a single American life had been lost, he would have felt personally responsible, so along with the listening and talking and stalling there was also a bit of heartfelt praying.

Given what he'd been through, it was probably absurd to worry about a slender blonde with curves in all the right places who was almost sexy enough to make him forget how tired he was, but he couldn't get her off his mind. By the time Kevin knocked on the bathroom door, Anthony was feeling much more relieved than he ever would have admitted.

"Alone at last," Kevin drawled as he stepped inside.

Anthony closed the door and locked it. "You know what people would say if they knew you'd followed me down here?" he asked with a grin.

"Not what you're thinking," Kevin answered. "They'd ask if you work for the Agency."

"I hope they don't. I've told enough half-truths over the past week to last me a lifetime. How much longer do I have to hang around here?"

"Half an hour should do it. Why? You seemed to be having a good time."

"It's not as bad as I thought it would be. To be honest, it's a bit of an ego trip," Anthony admitted. "But I'd rather be in San Diego with Jessica and my parents."

Kevin gave him a sympathetic look. "I know that part of it's been tough on you, Anthony, but you'll be able to fly to the Coast tomorrow. Why don't you come over for a quiet dinner with me and Liz tonight? We'll send the kids to a movie."

Anthony shook his head, thanking Kevin for the invitation. "I've sponged enough meals off your wife. Besides, I'll unwind better on my own—I need some time alone."

Feeling a bit defensive, he began to explain the reason for the clandestine meeting. "I'll tell you why I wanted to speak to you, Kevin. I may be getting paranoid, but I think someone in there is watching me. I first noticed her at the news conference. I even smiled at her—after shacking up with Rvanski for a couple of days, she looked damn appealing. I figured she was a reporter, but she's obviously not, since they're keeping reporters in the hall. She seems to know a lot of people, but for some reason she hasn't come up to introduce herself. She just keeps watching me instead."

Kevin frowned. "I don't like the sound of that. What does she look like?"

"Late twenties, medium height, blue eyes, and curly blond hair worn loose to her shoulders." Anthony was puzzled when Kevin began to smile, but he continued with his description anyway. "She's wearing a red dress with a white design on it. Not beautiful, but sexy and very pretty—almost angelic-looking. Maybe that's what worries me."

To Anthony's chagrin, Kevin had stopped smiling. He was now bending his head, his hand at the back of his neck, valiantly choking back laughter. "Okay," Anthony snapped, "what's so funny?"

It took Kevin a moment to control himself. "That's Katie Garvey, Hank Garvey's daughter," he finally managed. "I wondered who you were smiling at at the news conference. I must be losing my touch, because I didn't realize she was checking you out. When she came over to say hello to me, I assumed that she happened to be in town and had decided to keep her father company today. Her mother stays in Connecticut a lot of the time. She's in her early thirties, by the way, and single."

"A senator's daughter?" Anthony asked. "What is she, some kind of socialite?"

"Not exactly. Ever hear of Dorset and Associates?"

Kevin might as well have asked if Anthony had heard of Disneyland. "Of course I have. It's one of the biggest political consulting and public-relations firms in Los Angeles. Bill Dorset is close to George McClure."

"Exactly. And Katie Garvey is one of Bill's top assistants. The other is a fellow named Sandy Cohen, who does their polling. Don't let Katie's innocent looks fool you, Anthony. She's persistent, persuasive, and pragmatic. If she's here in Washington to watch you perform, it means that they're interested in asking you to run for something, probably the Senate. Rumor has it that Jack Handlin isn't going to run for reelection."

"Which would be a boon to us all." Anthony tried to make sense of the information that Kevin had provided. "Are you trying to tell me that they want to find out if I'm—*suitable?*" he asked. "That this woman—Katie—is checking me out but doesn't have the decency to simply introduce herself and find out if I'm interested? Who do they think they are?"

"Just cool down. She'll make her pitch in her own good time," Kevin assured Anthony. "You should be flattered, not annoyed. A lot of politicians consider Bill Dorset's endorsement one step down from a royal appointment. They fight each other to hire him."

"Good. Let them." Anthony uttered a very rude epithet. "I can't believe this. The last thing I'd take her for is a scalp hunter."

"Would you rather believe that she's a Soviet agent setting you up for a hit?" Kevin teased.

Anthony grimaced. "The thought had crossed my mind. And then I wondered whether she was just one more political groupie with a slightly more interesting approach than the rest of them. After Beth died, it didn't take me very long to figure out that women had gotten more aggressive in the eighteen years since I'd asked one out, but still . . ." He shook his head, looking a little pained. "Nothing at Berkeley could have prepared me for *this*, Kevin. Those ladies out there are barracudas. Or maybe *trophy hunters* is a better description."

Someone knocked on the door and Kevin winked at Anthony, then impersonated the low, miserable moan of a gentleman who had overimbibed and was now paying the price for it. When he was certain that no one was listening, Kevin said to a smiling Anthony, "You don't have to worry about Katie. She isn't interested in your body, only in whether you can win an election. Although," he added cheerfully, "there's no telling how far she'd go to talk you into running. Maybe you'll luck out."

"And maybe she's not interested. Maybe she gets everything she needs from her job."

"She dated an actor for quite a few years," Kevin replied. "Hank couldn't stand the guy and made no secret of it—though as far as I know she isn't seriously involved with anyone right now. But I was really only kidding a minute ago. When it comes to her job, she's a real pro. Politicians she's worked with treat her like one of the boys."

Anthony supposed that California needed a more effective senator than Jack Handlin, but he told himself that it wouldn't be him. Although he had a healthy enough ego to think he'd do a good job, all he wanted at the moment was to see his daughter again and finish his book. Katie Garvey's tactics both amused and annoyed him. He wondered how far she *would* go to make her case. There had been a lamentable absence of female companionship in his life of late, and with that slender body and angelic face of hers, Katie had the potential to be very diverting.

"If she hasn't introduced herself by now, I don't think she intends to," he said to Kevin. "Do me a favor, will you? Hold out a little bait. See that she finds out where I'm staying tonight."

Kevin O'Neal thought for a moment, then said solemnly, "For a man who's performed such a great service to his country, it will be a pleasure. Just give me your room key, Anthony, and have yourself a nice evening."

Chapter 3

KATE STARED OUT THE WINDOW OF HER FATHER'S CAR AT THE storm moving in from the west and thought to herself that she should have been a reporter. The Washington press corps would have sold its collective soul for the information she possessed—St. Croix Hotel, Room 1205—and she hadn't even had to wheedle her father into procuring it for her.

The East Room at the White House had been packed, but she'd somehow managed to keep an eye on Anthony Larimer as she circulated around the room. A reporter from a Los Angeles newspaper happened to mention to her that Larimer was staying at the St. Croix, but he grumbled that Larimer was impossible to reach for an interview because calls weren't put through to his room and the room number was as closely held as a state secret.

Much to Kate's relief, she'd finally gotten her emotions under control. Larimer was a potential client, after all, and thus strictly off limits. She was a thirty-two-year-old woman with a reasonable amount of experience, she reminded herself, not some impressionable adolescent.

As far as she could tell, Larimer had recovered his good humor, now that the news conference was behind him. He talked to a great many people, apparently at ease, and shook hundreds of hands in the process. After watching him for over an hour, she felt far more sanguine about her mission. At one point he disappeared for ten or fifteen minutes, then returned to the room. Soon afterward Kate began to look around for her father, to ask him to find out Larimer's room number for her, but in a stroke of amazing good fortune she'd literally bumped into Kevin O'Neal, who was trying to walk and fish something out of his pocket at the same time. He seemed a trifle unsteady on his feet, probably the result of celebrating his Agency's triumphs with a bit too much zeal.

"Sorry, Katie." She watched him take a hotel key out of his pocket. His index finger only partially covered the second digit of the four-digit number, which was either a two or a three. Probably a two, Kate decided, since many hotels had no thirteenth floor—Room 1205. "Have you seen Anthony Larimer around?" he asked.

Kate pointed to the far end of the room. "Over there. He just got back inside, Kevin."

After Kevin excused himself, Kate followed at a discreet distance. Kevin handed the key to Larimer, slapped him on the back, and then walked away. It didn't surprise Kate to learn that Kevin had taken Anthony's key. He'd probably given it to one of his agents so the room could be checked out for bugs. Although CIA operations within the United States were generally prohibited, the Agency *could* legally take measures against enemy electronic surveillance. The legality of other types of activities was a great deal more obscure. Each president issued a broad executive order on intelligence activities, and in addition there was a set of secret regulations specifically governing the CIA. As a general rule, however, domestic intelligence was the province of the FBI, while foreign intelligence was handled by the CIA.

When Anthony left the reception, Kate promptly requisitioned her father's car for a ride to the St. Croix Hotel. She instinctively glanced around as she entered the lobby, but saw neither armed security guards nor the clean-cut types who wore the label "Secret Service" all over them. Even so, she felt mildly apprehensive as she stepped out of the elevator and walked down the hall to Larimer's room (he wasn't the most easygoing of men) and uncomfortably warm as a result. She slipped off her coat and slung it over her arm.

There was no response to her initial knock, so she knocked again, this time more firmly. It was past five o'clock already; she figured that if Larimer was in his room, she'd suggest dinner, and if not, she'd grab a bite herself and try again later.

He opened the door at once, looking none too pleased that someone had disturbed him. For a moment Kate stared at him, speechless; she hadn't expected him to be practically naked, and it threw her off balance. He was wearing only a loosely belted brown terrycloth robe that ended a good nine inches above his knees to reveal powerful calves and thighs and hung open to display a sizable patch of muscled chest sprinkled with silky dark hair. He was still slightly damp from the shower, his curly hair even more tousled than usual, and he smelled of shampoo and a tangy, masculine shaving lotion. Kate thought to herself that he was even better-looking from two feet away than from across a room. She liked the intensity of his dark eyes and the way that the fine age lines around his mouth and eyes added maturity to his face.

He was checking her out just as thoroughly as she was checking *him* out, and was apparently mollified by what he saw. By the time his gaze had traveled from high-heeled pumps up slender legs to generous breasts and curly hair, the frown was long gone.

"I'm impressed by your initiative," he murmured with a smile. "How did you find out my room number?" Before Kate could come up with a plausible answer, he took her by the arm and led her inside. "It doesn't matter," he said. "Come on in. Give me your coat."

A trifle bewildered, Kate handed it over and watched him close and lock the door. Who did he think she was?

"I noticed you at the reception," he said, taking a couple of steps and tossing the coat on the queen-size bed. He moved very gracefully, she noticed, as though his body would always do precisely what he told it to. For just a moment she wondered whether his masculine grace would carry over into the bedroom, then impatiently dismissed the thought.

"Why didn't you come over to say hello?" he asked, still looking at her with the same smiling warmth. "You should have known I wanted to meet you by the way I smiled at you at the news conference."

It was obviously time for Kate to state her business. "My name is Kate Garvey," she began, wondering if he already knew that. "I wasn't sure *why* you smiled at me. And there were so many people at the White House . . . I wanted to talk to you privately, and—"

"Talk?" he interrupted, cocking an amused eyebrow at her.

"Of course." What did he *think* she wanted? She blushed slightly, hoping that her earlier thoughts hadn't been visible on her face. "You're an impressive man yourself, Dr. Larimer. We . . ."

"Anthony," he interrupted again. He moved a couple of steps closer, making Kate aware that he'd totally misinterpreted her reason for coming to see him. Her pulses sped up from a mixture of chagrin and arousal, causing her to back up a step or two and hold up a protective hand.

"Just a minute, Dr. Larimer. I work for—"

"Anthony."

The warmth of his smile was playing havoc with her equilibrium. "All right," she conceded, "Anthony. I wanted to . . ."

"You're very beautiful, Kate Garvey. If any of the others had looked like you, I wouldn't have been alone when you showed up."

He took another few steps in Kate's direction, giving her no option but to keep backing up. When her spine came into contact with the closed door, she instinctively put up her other hand to ward him off. She was more than a little amused—she couldn't believe what a wolf the man was turning out to be—but at the same time she knew she had to maintain control of the situation.

"Hold it a minute," she said with a smile. "I'm not some kind of Washington groupie." Despite the disclaimer she certainly felt like one. Anthony's closeness had sent the blood rushing to her face, making her feel a little light-headed.

Anthony wrapped a determined finger and thumb around each of her wrists, forcing her hands to her sides, and then moved in even closer until his thighs brushed against Kate's legs. A moment later her wrists came together in the custody of one large masculine hand. He trailed a lazy finger down her cheek with his other hand, murmuring that she was lovely, and then placed his palm just below her throat so that his thumb could explore her jaw. Kate swallowed convulsively, so astonished by this turn of events that it was all she could do to murmur a reproving, "Dr. Larimer!" The man was so sexy that for a few bemused moments she couldn't decide how to cope with him. The feel of his cool, callused fingers against her soft skin—the idea of being his very willing prisoner— appealed to her so much that she really didn't want him to stop. In thirty-two years nothing like this had ever happened to her.

When he bent his head to kiss her, she turned her face so that his lips made contact with her cheek instead of her mouth. The reaction was purely automatic. Kate couldn't imagine that any woman in her right mind would really want to refuse this man. His thumb was absently massaging the side of her neck now, rubbing slowly back and forth just below her chin. Meanwhile his lips were wandering down the opposite side of her face to nuzzle her collarbone. There wasn't a centimeter of space between them, and Kate could feel the desire in his powerful body, a desire she longed to respond to. It was all she could do not to wind her arms around his neck and offer him her lips. She shut her eyes tightly, trying to get control of a reaction that was definitely out of hand by now, firmly reminding herself that getting seduced was not a part of her plan. Larimer would never respect her as a professional if she allowed him to take her to bed like some hot-blooded little groupie.

And in point of fact Kate was only too aware that a hot-blooded groupie was precisely what Larimer had mistaken her for. The thought was so dismaying to a woman of Kate Garvey's intelligence and sophistication that she could have groaned aloud. She gently tried to free her hands, but Anthony wouldn't permit it. At the same time, he tightened his grip on her chin to coax her face around.

"Dr. Larimer, you don't understand . . ." Kate began, but then his mouth brushed her lips and a stab of desire tore through her body, making her shiver. Her heart started pounding so heavily that she could feel the vibrations in her throat. She wanted him to kiss her—very, very much.

Anthony teased her lips, stroking and then withdrawing, exploring her lip line with the tip of his tongue, until Kate felt as if she would explode from frustration. With a low, aroused moan her lips relaxed and parted, seeking his mouth. She was oblivious to his grunt of satisfaction, only aware that she ached for him to press his advantage and deepen the kiss. She'd always called the shots with men, she thought hazily as he continued to play with her mouth, had always set the ground rules and defined the relationship, but now some Don Juan of a professor was driving her absolutely crazy with his seductive, deliberate lovemaking, and she was so turned on that she couldn't utter another protest.

His tongue finally claimed her mouth, slowly probing every soft crevice, rubbing against her own tongue in a hard yet lazy way that left her eager for more. She kissed him back a little wildly, her body arching hungrily against his, her breathing increasingly rapid. His response to her obvious excitement was so torrid that it was like being caught up in a desert vortex. He abruptly released her wrists and grasped her hips, trapping her between the door and his hardened body, kissing her with a savage passion that would accept nothing less than complete surrender. Kate responded to the circular movements of his hips without conscious thought, the world of the senses having conquered all logic and common sense.

And then, just as suddenly as he'd grabbed her, he released her, stiffening up and tearing himself away. He was breathing hard and his eyes were slightly glazed, his arousal so evident that Kate couldn't begin to imagine why he'd stopped. She watched with growing confusion as he slowly mastered his emotions and began to smile. She had no idea how to interpret such a look. It was by turns amused, triumphant, even a little cynical.

Kate looked away, blushing, and tried to regain her composure. The only thing she could think to do was to pretend that none of this had happened. His mistake had probably been a natural one, and she was far too sophisticated to pretend maidenly outrage that an attractive man had made a thoroughly enjoyable pass at her. "Dr. Larimer," she said, managing a smile, "I work for William Dorset and Associates. That's a political consulting firm in Los Angeles. Mr. Dorset—"

"Why should I care who you work for?" he interrupted in a drawling tone. "And I told you, it's Anthony. Now, where were we?" One large hand snaked behind her back to pull her into his arms again, while the other settled just below her breast, brushing the soft underside. Much cooler now, Kate had the wit to realize that Anthony Larimer wanted something more from her than a quick session in bed or he never would have stopped before. But what?

She recalled that peculiar smile of his and asked herself what she really knew about him. Could he be some kind of a sadist when it came to women? Did he want her to fight him off so he could force her to sleep with him? It seemed highly overimaginative, given his eminently respectable background, but just to be on the safe side she put as much authority into her voice as she could muster and demanded frigidly, "Anthony, please let go of me."

"In about half an hour, Katie." He moved closer, pinning her flush against the door again, his lips settling atop her own. Although he was just as gentle and passionate as before, Kate was suddenly a little frightened. She tried to twist away but could hardly even move.

"Anthony!" she said angrily, the name muffled against his lips.

"Katie!" he answered in the same angry tone.

The blasted man was mocking her helplessness. Kate stiffened in outrage, all fright temporarily forgotten. "Damn you," she snapped at him. "Let go of me!"

"Never!" But he released her and backed up, then suddenly grinned at her. "You broke your promise. Don't you think you should pay for that?"

Kate was beginning to wonder if he'd cracked under the strain of the past week. What promise? She wasn't a psychiatrist, so she had no idea how to deal with someone irrational, but feminine instinct told her to try to soothe him.

"I won't break any promises, Anthony," she said gently. "Really. You can trust me."

"Can I?" His wink was nothing short of audacious. And then he asked with little-boy eagerness, "You mean I get to be a senator?"

For a moment Kate simply stared at him, too surprised to respond. Then she felt her face burning with embarrassment and knew that, given her fair complexion, her cheeks must be shocking pink. Anthony Larimer, however, was in absolutely no shape to notice. Her speechlessness had provoked the most humiliating bout of laughter it had ever been Kate's misfortune to endure. At one point he was actually doubled over, clutching his stomach, emitting a mortifying variety of chortles, chuckles, and moans that he made no attempt to control. Kate's sense of humor, usually very lively, totally deserted her. She stood rigidly still, her emotions a tangle of anger, embarrassment, and reluctant admiration. She'd been played for a sucker by a pro and she knew it. She could have kicked herself for falling for Kevin's routine about the key.

She crossed her arms in front of her chest and waited with icy patience until Anthony straightened up, still grinning, and wiped the tears out of his eyes. "Kevin O'Neal helped you set me up, didn't he?"

"Did he?" Anthony parroted back.

"How well do you know him? When did you meet?"

"I've known him since I went to work at the State Department." Anthony waved a hand back and forth to ward off further questions. "No inquisitions, Katie. I've had enough of that over the last few days. I'm tired of denials and 'No comment's."

Kate walked over to a chair next to a small round table and sat down, trying to overcome the feeling that she'd made a total fool of herself. When she got her hands on Kevin O'Neal . . .

Without another word Anthony disappeared into the bathroom, emerging a few minutes later dressed in a navy turtleneck tucked into worn jeans. He was devastating in casual clothing; Kate could already visualize the type of TV spot they would use in his campaign: Larimer in his backyard with his daughter, talking about people's everyday problems and what the government should be doing to help.

There was a second chair on the other side of the table, and Anthony dropped into it and leaned back, apparently at ease. "Don't look so icy," he coaxed. "Nothing happened."

"I hope you enjoyed yourself." Kate was still too stung to unbend. She knew she was acting petulant, but she couldn't seem to help it.

Anthony shook his head, smiling. "How can you say that? You know as well as I do that in five minutes flat I could hardly take my hands off you. Believe me, all I wanted to do was to carry you to bed and make love to you, but I figured you probably would have killed me afterwards, when you found out you'd been set up, so I settled for a little teasing. Frankly, I expected you to be a lot more hard-boiled than you really are. I think the phrase was *persistent, persuasive, and pragmatic.*"

Her feminine ego having been stroked by his admission, Kate asked quickly, "Who told you that? Kevin again?" His source of information had to be someone who knew her through her family, otherwise he wouldn't have picked up the habit of calling her by the nickname Katie.

"No comment. Come on, Katie, stop pouting and admit you had it coming, showing up in Washington and checking me out like I was some kind of expensive horseflesh. Was I supposed to be flattered rather than annoyed?"

Most politicians would have been ecstatic to be singled out by Bill Dorset as prime senatorial material. Kate, reminding herself that Dr. Anthony Larimer wasn't a politician, forced herself to return to her reason for coming to see him in the first place. "It isn't any secret that my boss, Bill Dorset, is close to Governor McClure," she began. "We've been talking about who might be able to give the people of California the kind of representation they deserve. When you got involved in the Odessa—"

"Listen to the way you talk," Anthony interrupted, shaking his head in wonder. "It's amazing—just like one of your commercials. 'George McClure: A Man Worth Following.'"

The slogan was from McClure's second gubernatorial campaign, and Kate thought it was a good one. She and Bill had come up with it. "Those four words tell you a lot about George McClure," she defended. "He's a leader. He has a workable vision for the future of the state of California. People can trust him."

"What they tell you," Anthony retorted, "is that George McClure had a slick media team working for him. As a political scientist I have very real concerns about the role you people play in election campaigns and in America's political life in general. Your work is all image and no substance."

Kate was on comfortable ground now. "That may be true of other consultants, but Dorset runs a high percentage of issue-oriented ads." She elaborated with half a dozen convincing examples from previous campaigns.

Anthony listened attentively, remarking when she was finished, "You *are* persuasive. Also persistent, given the fact that you were still waiting for me when I came out of the bathroom; most people I've met would have been long gone. But how pragmatic are you?"

"My job is to win elections for worthy candidates," Kate told him. "Within the bounds of good taste and morality, I'll do whatever I can to accomplish that."

She didn't understand his subsequent look, except to feel

almost naked when he was through dissecting her. "Tell me something," he said with a smile. "Just how flexible is your definition of morality? Would you sleep with me if that's what it would take to get me to run for the Senate?"

Given how attractive he was, going to bed with him hardly constituted hazardous duty. "Is that a theoretical question?" Kate asked carefully.

"No . . ."

"Comment," she finished for him. She decided to give him her standard answer to politicians' propositions. "I make it a point never to get involved with people I work with." Thus far in her life the rule had been easy to enforce. Working so closely with her clients, she usually saw the worst side of them: temperament, pettiness, self-doubt, egotism. It hadn't given her a high opinion of politicians or of men in general, at least as far as their emotional maturity was concerned. She asked only that she be able to respect them on a professional level.

"Spoken like a true politician," Anthony drawled, "but I didn't say anything about getting involved. I asked if you'd sleep with me—one time. Put me out of my misery. How about it, Katie?"

His tone was so seductive that Kate began to wish he weren't a potential client. "Anthony, try to understand that . . ."

"Dr. Larimer," he corrected teasingly. "It was only Anthony when I was in the middle of seducing you. Answer the question, Miss Garvey. Yes or no."

Kate believed in being honest with her men friends, and she followed the same policy with Anthony Larimer. "If I said yes it wouldn't be because I was willing to sell my body in the service of Dorset and Associates," she told him. "That would make me a prostitute and I'm not. You're a very attractive, magnetic man, Anthony. You'd make a terrific candidate."

"So the answer is yes, but only because I happen to turn you on. I'm flattered."

"I didn't say yes," Kate protested. "We hardly know each other. I don't bed hop, Anthony."

"Persistent, persuasive, pragmatic, and evasive." Anthony stood up. "When you knocked on the door, I was about to phone room service to have dinner sent up. The reason I was going to eat in my room is that the last week has been hellish and I need some time alone." His voice dropped to a sexy murmur. "I'll make an exception if you want to spend the night with me, Katie. I'd like that very much."

Kate shook her head and Anthony immediately gestured toward the door. "In that case . . ."

The dismissal came long before Kate was willing to accept it. "I don't feel you've given me a fair hearing on running for the Senate, Anthony. If I could join you for dinner—"

"I don't owe you a fair hearing or anything else," he interrupted. "Just accept the fact that I'm not interested in politics."

Kate smiled knowingly, then pounced. "If you're not interested in politics, why did you stay in the Peace Corps for four years? Why did you work at the State Department for four years after that? Why do you write books that attempt to influence the foreign policy of the United States, and why did you agree to serve on a faculty committee to protest cuts in the UC budget?"

She shot out question after question, giving him no opportunity to respond. By the time she finished talking, he was looking at her with renewed respect. "Okay, you're right." He sat back down in his chair. "There's no such thing as a political scientist who isn't interested in politics. I'm from a politically involved family that had me handing out leaflets when I was still in grade school. But you want me to consider running for office because a series of somewhat incredible events has made me famous, almost an overnight hero, and it seems to me that there's something fundamentally wrong with that. If I were still an obscure Berkeley professor, you wouldn't be wasting your time with me."

"You weren't exactly obscure," Kate pointed out. "Your

book *did* win a Pulitzer. We prefer to consider your sudden fame as an opportunity to be taken advantage of. The fact is, you would make a good senator. You're an expert on foreign policy with solid practical experience. Ask my father how much we need people like you in Congress and how rewarding it can be. You've lived most of your life in California and you're obviously concerned about what goes on in the state. And as a single parent, you can relate to the problems . . ."

Kate cut herself off when she realized she was losing him. She was smart enough to understand the reason for his impatient look. "Listen, Anthony, I don't mean to sound like a television commercial, but . . ."

"But it's the way you think and the only terms you understand," he said. "We could spend the next hour arguing about who's earned the right to run for public office and still be at opposite poles. In the end it's all irrelevant. I have a fifteen-year-old daughter whom I love very much. You know what it's like to be the child of a senator, except you happened to have a mother around to raise you. Jessica doesn't. I'm not going to sit here and keep pretending that the idea of serving in Congress doesn't appeal to me, because it certainly does. But it's impossible right now. And in six years—hell, in six weeks—nobody will even remember who I am."

The woman in Kate took his argument to heart; the political consultant reflected on his devotion to his daughter and promptly labeled it a campaign asset. "Sometimes parents make sacrifices for their children that their children consider unnecessary. I've never felt that my father wasn't there for me. I'm very close to him, much closer than to my mother. By the time I was Jessica's age, my mother was spending half her time in Connecticut while I stayed in Washington with Dad. Your daughter isn't a baby, Anthony. Talk it over with her."

Anthony walked over to the bed, picked up Kate's coat, and held it out to her. Kate, having done her job to the best of her ability, allowed him to help her on with it. "I'll say this for you," he remarked as he unlocked the door and opened it. "You're one of the most tenacious women I've ever come across. If you were one of my students, I'd probably give you an *A*, just to get you off my back. You must win a lot of elections."

Kate couldn't resist having the last word. "You're right," she said with a smile. "We do. Keep that in mind if you change your mind about running."

Anthony shook his head and smiled back, but didn't bother to answer her.

Chapter 4

KATE TOLD HERSELF THAT THE PROBLEM WITH CONDUCTING A political-strategy session in a crowded capital hangout was that people constantly wandered over to say hello. Although Bill Dorset, Vince Collier, George McClure, and Kate were sitting in a high-backed booth all the way to the rear of the governor's favorite Sacramento restaurant, the local homing pigeons instinctively sensed McClure's presence and zeroed in on his table, either to lobby for a favorite cause or to press the flesh of the powerful. The latest pair of petitioners, an assemblywoman and the consultant to the committee she chaired, delivered an urgent little speech about a criminal justice bill before returning to their Chinese food, satisfied that McClure would support them.

Their appearance had interrupted Kate's summary of her conversation with Anthony Larimer. She'd flown back to California Sunday night after a busy but wonderful weekend with her father, then briefed Bill Dorset on her trip on Monday afternoon. In the meantime Bill had done some quiet investigating of Anthony Larimer's politics, the results of which he passed on to Kate. He also told her that she was accompanying him on a business trip to Sacramento the following morning. For the rest of the day she studied the materials he had handed her, preparing for a few days of intensive lobbying on behalf of one of the firm's corporate clients.

"There isn't too much more to tell," she said as the legislator retreated from the governor's presence. "Larimer pretty much dismissed me, like I was a student who was starting to annoy him. He told me I was tenacious and I told *him* to keep that in mind if he decided to run. He smiled and shook his head as if he couldn't believe that people like me really exist, but he didn't answer me back. I guess he wanted to be alone, just like he'd said earlier. He still has to work through the whole Odessa experience—teaching and writing about foreign policy couldn't have prepared him to find himself in the middle of *making* it."

Kate had left almost nothing out of her recitation, telling herself that she could stand to suffer a little embarrassment in order to paint an accurate picture of Anthony Larimer's personality. Unfortunately, however, her honesty had earned her nothing but merciless teasing.

"He didn't want to be *alone*," George McClure promptly informed Kate. "He wanted to be with *you*." He clucked his tongue reprovingly. "I don't understand why you didn't explore that whole area, Kate. Bill sends you first class to Washington; the least you can do is follow up every possible lead. Wasn't a commitment from Larimer worth an hour or two of your time?"

Men all stuck together, Kate thought irritably. As every ribald interruption brought fresh blushes to her face, her male tormentors would erupt into yet another round of grins and chuckles. All of them knew she'd coolly fended off more than her share of passes in the past, which was why they wallowed in the notion that someone had finally managed to shake her composure so thoroughly.

She waited for their smiles to subside, then retorted, "No way, Governor. After eight years in this business I've been accused of most of the sins in the Bible. I'll keep my amateur status when it comes to men."

"You see?" Vince Collier pounded his fist on the table for emphasis, causing the dishes to rattle. "That's why women will never be equal to men. They refuse to put the same kind of time and devotion into their jobs as men do."

"So *you* sleep with him," Kate shot back, a smile playing over her lips. "I give you three an honest account of what happened in Washington because I think it's important for you to understand Larimer's thinking and appreciate how magnetic he is, and what does it get me? Nothing but grief."

Just then a couple of tourists approached for the governor's autograph; Kate cracked open a fortune cookie while he obliged. The tiny pink slip read, "The road ahead is uncertain, but travel will make it clear."

As soon as the tourists left, Vince Collier abandoned his usual languid pace to reach out and snatch the fortune out of Kate's hand. "Profound," he said, having read it aloud. "This obviously refers to Highway 80."

Kate buried her head in her hands and dropped it to the table in mock defeat. Highway 80 was the road between Sacramento and Berkeley. She'd already chased Larimer to Washington; she wasn't about to expose herself to a second defeat on his home territory. She gave Bill a grateful smile when he took pity on her and suggested that it was time to get serious again.

"I have something to add," he said. "You know that I've been checking Larimer out with my contacts in the university system and elsewhere, but I decided to go one step further. I obtained computer printouts of what mailing lists Larimer is on, who and what he's given money to, and how much. It reinforces our picture of him: fairly liberal on social issues, moderate on the environment and the economy, moderate to conservative on criminal justice and foreign policy. He also does some private consulting, by the way—giving advice to corporations on which countries are safest for foreign investment. Obviously he doesn't agree with you all down the line, George, but you should feel comfortable endorsing him."

Bill looked at Kate, who was sipping a cup of lukewarm Chinese tea and wishing it were either hot or iced. "What's your sense of the situation?" he asked her. "Do you think we can get Larimer on board?"

"You know me." Kate shrugged. "Unless somebody gives me a flat and final no, I don't give up. Being a senator appeals to the man, but two things stand in the way. The first is all that academic agonizing of his over who should run for office. I think we can debate him into deciding that he has as much right as the next guy. The second problem is his daughter. Everything we've heard about him says he's a genuinely devoted father, which means that the final decision might rest with *her*." Sensing an opportunity for some minor revenge, Kate drawled at Vince Collier, "How about it, Vince? His daughter, Jessica, is fifteen. Girls get crushes on older men at that age. Why don't you drive out to Berkeley . . ."

"You got me!" Vince clutched at his stomach as if mortally wounded. "I swear I'll never mention Larimer again, Garvey. Next time I'm out drinking with a bunch of reporters, I'll make it a definite point *not* to mention how Anthony Larimer answered the door in his bathrobe, and almost seduced—"

"Oh, shut up." Laughing, Kate picked up a piece of uneaten fortune cookie and sent it flying across the table in Vince's direction. He ducked, and the cookie bounced harmlessly against the back of the booth and fell onto the seat.

George McClure ignored this bit of horseplay. "What we need to do," he observed blandly, "is keep Larimer in the public eye while we work on those reservations of his. There's a lot of support for awarding him the California Medal of Freedom. Vince can tell you how many letters and phone calls we've gotten. The legislature is working on concurrent resolutions to honor him—the Assembly bill went in this morning, and the Senate resolution will be read later this week. Still, even if they move unusually fast, it will be a month or more before the bills are through committee. What do you think, Vince? Can we speed things up?"

"The Medal of Freedom sounds reasonable. No question that he deserves it. In fact, we'd probably even do it for a

Republican." Vince cast a baleful eye on the plate of fortune cookies, silently castigating them for their deficiencies as a dessert, then pulled a cigar out of his jacket pocket. "At the moment Larimer is still in San Diego with his daughter and his parents. If we don't handle him carefully, he's going to consider the medal a political gambit and tell us exactly what we can do with it. We should wait until both resolutions are introduced, then get a story into the papers about the public clamor for awarding him the Medal of Freedom. At that point—maybe over the weekend, George—you can contact him." He lit his cigar and leaned back to take several satisfied puffs, obviously well pleased with this scenario.

Kate's thoughts jumped one step ahead. Unless she was misreading public opinion, it would be fairly easy to orchestrate a groundswell of grass-roots support for Larimer's candidacy. "Let's assume he agrees to come to Sacramento to receive the medal—the week after next would be perfect. In the meantime we can float a trial balloon. I'd suggest Hal Dunnigan." Dunnigan was the political columnist for a major Los Angeles newspaper, and over the years Dorset and Associates had handed him a number of important stories. "I'm sure he'll be happy to have an exclusive on Larimer's Senate possibilities. Once the column is in print, everyone will pick it up."

"I see your train of thought." Bill gave Kate the kind of approving look that made all the twelve-hour days worthwhile. "By the time Larimer comes to Sacramento to pick up the award, everyone in politics will be talking about his intentions. The press will be all over him. We can almost count on his saying no, which works *for* us, because his public reluctance will take care of charges that he's an opportunist. At that point we can bring in the big guns to change his mind."

"He's too smart not to figure out what we're up to," Kate pointed out. "He's going to be furious, and take my word for it, if he really loses his temper, you don't want to get caught in the explosion."

Bill dismissed Kate's warning with a wave of his hand.

"The bottom line is that he's interested, Kate. And if he's interested, he'll let himself be persuaded. If he could deal with Rvanski, he has to be a lot more pragmatic than you seem to think he is. What we need to do is take advantage of the public's temporary fascination with him and start building support for his candidacy. We'll deal with his anger when we have to."

Bill's strategy was sound enough, except that Kate had come up against Larimer's streak of ethical purity and Bill hadn't. When he found himself the subject of intense media speculation, he was going to rake all of them over red-hot coals. Kate wasn't overjoyed when Bill assigned her the task of leaking the story to Dunnigan, but she accepted his reasoning. As the only one who had actually talked to Larimer, she was the only possible choice. Hal Dunnigan reported facts, not hearsay, and anyone but Kate would be passing on mere hearsay.

Anthony Larimer wasn't the only reason for Kate and Bill's presence in Sacramento. Each of them had a list of appointments that afternoon, their prime concern a trio of bills strongly opposed by their most important corporate client.

Being a lobbyist was a lot like being a lawyer. You represented your client's interests to the best of your ability, regardless of your personal feelings. One of the reasons Kate liked working for Bill Dorset was that he accepted her right to *have* personal feelings. A handful of times over the years he had asked her to represent a point of view she strongly disagreed with. Each time she'd declined, telling him that she doubted her ability to make the client's case as skillfully as the client deserved. Bill Dorset didn't consider her refusals a sign of weakness; on the contrary, just as he himself declined to represent candidates whose views he found objectionable, he would never have asked his staffers to lobby viewpoints they strongly opposed. Luckily, since he chose his clients carefully, those sorts of problems seldom arose.

Over the years Kate had gotten to know the people who really mattered in Sacramento. Sometimes she spoke to the legislators themselves, but more often she talked to their aides, the men and women who valiantly tried to follow the thousands of bills introduced each year. Her approach was a mixture of charming soft soap and no-nonsense hardball—a little political gossip and personal chitchat mixed in with a well-prepared, forceful presentation of her client's position. She made her case with statistics and facts, presenting herself as both a reliable source of information as well as a representative of her client's interests.

She stayed in Sacramento through Wednesday evening, returning home to find several messages on her telephone answering machine, one of them from Jerry Savitch. Jerry was a pediatric surgeon whom she occasionally dated; she'd met him when he operated on her goddaughter after a severe automobile accident. She promptly called him back, accepting a dinner date on Saturday night and suggesting a new Mexican restaurant she'd been wanting to try.

Bill Dorset flew up to the state of Washington to meet with one of the firm's political clients before returning to Los Angeles Thursday night. At ten o'clock Friday morning Kate was summoned into his office for a meeting about Larimer; she arrived to find Sandy Cohen seated on a chair opposite Bill's desk. Since Sandy had been on vacation, Bill was filling him in on recent events. Kate mouthed, "Welcome home" and sat down next to him.

Sandy had been recruited by Bill Dorset four years earlier to serve as the company's resident polling wizard, the previous occupant of the position having decamped to Washington, DC, to set up his own firm. Though somewhat brash and eccentric, Sandy was a genuine treasure. Not only could he tell you who was ahead or behind at any particular moment, he could also deliver accurate and subtle information on the way the public perceived a candidate and why. Once they knew a candidate's strengths and weaknesses, Dorset and Associates designed advertising that played up the former and compensated for the latter. They also taught the candidate how to present his views in the most effective and favorable way possible.

Ideally, Sandy's initial polling took place nine to twelve

months before an election, giving the company a generous amount of time in which to plot out campaign strategy. Polling continued up through the election, so that if public perceptions of the candidate changed, the campaign strategy could be altered and refined.

Sandy had always amused Kate simply because he *looked* so much like her notion of a pollster, happily buried in the bowels of some building with only his data and machines for company. He was one of the only people she knew who could return from two weeks in Hawaii as pale as the day he'd left. Tall and skinny, with reddish-brown hair and a face dotted with freckles, he seemed most at ease when surrounded by a pile of his precious computer printouts. Although he serviced the company's private clients with sophisticated and expensive market research, politics was his first love.

"So that was the situation as of Tuesday," Bill was saying, "and since then Vince has moved faster than I thought he could physically manage. Has either of you glanced at the out-of-town papers?"

Kate had. Stories about the public's support for awarding Larimer the Medal of Freedom had appeared either Wednesday or Thursday in papers all over the state. When she and Sandy respectively nodded and grunted, Bill continued, "I talked to George earlier this morning. He got hold of Larimer in Berkeley last night and persuaded him to accept the medal in Sacramento a week from next Thursday."

"Was it a hard sell?" Kate asked.

"Surprisingly easy. Larimer asked a few questions about who the previous recipients were—it's an impressive list—and then agreed. George was all psyched up to convince him, but it wasn't necessary. Apparently Larimer's daughter saw a story in the San Diego paper and did our spadework for us. He's bringing her along, by the way. She hasn't been to the capitol since the restoration was completed in '82, and George promised to give her a personal tour."

Bill added that there was no indication that Larimer had reconsidered his decision not to run; on the contrary, he'd specifically mentioned that after having taken the current quarter off to write and travel, he looked forward to teaching again. At Berkeley the academic year consisted of three regular quarters and a summer session; the new term would begin in early April and end in June.

"In other words," Kate translated, "I still have to talk to Dunnigan. Should I call his office and set up a lunch date?"

"Let's use a less formal approach," Bill said. "There's a thousand-dollar-a-plate fund raiser for Hendrickson at the Century Plaza Hotel on Saturday night. Hal is sure to cover it. Get one of your rich boyfriends to take you there and talk to him some time during the evening."

Bill Dorset knew perfectly well that Kate had no boyfriends who were both rich enough and political enough to shell out a thousand bucks for dinner with the president. What she *did* have were two or three long-standing family friends who might be able to locate an extra ticket for her.

"It's kind of last-minute, but I'll see what I can do," she agreed. "I hope you realize that I'll have to cancel a date with Jerry Savitch because of this."

"Since when is canceling a date any problem with you?" Bill was totally unimpressed by the magnitude of her sacrifice. "You can go out with Jerry some other night."

"You know me too well," Kate admitted. She looked over at Sandy, who was doodling one of his complicated geometric designs on a company memo pad, oblivious to her bantering conversation with Bill. "You've hardly said a word, Sandy. What do you think about all this?"

He looked up from his design, a frown on his face. "What I think is, I hate working for a candidate who isn't a little hungry for it. The public always senses it. Halfhearted candidates get halfhearted support." He tossed the pad on Bill's desk and sat back in his chair, clearly irritated. "What are you going to do about *that*, Bill?"

Few people would have used such a tone with Bill Dorset, but Sandy's sarcasm rolled right off Bill's back. "The filing deadline isn't until early March," he pointed out. "In the meantime, our friend Jack Handlin hasn't even pulled out of the race yet." His tone turned gently placating. "I understand your concern, Sandy. Bob Woodruff is going to be a tough opponent for anyone who runs, which is all the more reason to give you as much time as possible. Just bear with us, okay?"

Sandy gave a half shrug, indicating that his ruffled feathers had been partially soothed. His track record as a pollster was so impressive that everyone gladly put up with his occasional flashes of ill temper.

"After the award ceremony we'll have a better idea of where we stand," Kate added. "Over the next two weeks the publicity we generate is going to put a certain amount of pressure on Larimer to reconsider. Maybe we can coax a positive decision out of him."

"And maybe he'll tell us to go to hell," Sandy answered.

"That about sums up the alternatives." Bill smiled.

The meeting broke up and Kate returned to her office to think about her next step. Although Dorset and Associates occasionally worked for moderate to liberal Republicans, most of the firm's clients were Democrats. It wasn't only a matter of ideology. Most consulting firms stayed with one political party or the other in order to avoid conflicts of interest or simple awkwardness. Candidates and political parties weren't comfortable with a consultant who produced right-wing commercials for a candidate in one state while designing left-wing commercials for a candidate in a neighboring state. In practice, consistency was the easiest course of action.

Given that fact, Kate knew that her presence at a posh dinner for the Republican president would raise quite a few eyebrows. People would recognize her; she moved in the same circles as many of those who would attend. At least, she thought, Dorset and Associates hadn't contracted to work for any of Hendrickson's opponents. Bill had taken a beating in the previous presidential election at the hands of Eli Hendrickson and wasn't about to look for a rematch.

Kate flipped through her telephone list until she found the office number of one of her father's cronies, a friend of Hank's from his law school days who was now active in

California Republican politics. He was happy to help, saying that he personally had no extra tickets but would try to scare one up for her. Two hours later he called back, amused that the ticket he'd procured would put her at the table of a client in the insurance business. Kate, listening to his teasing description of middle-aged insurance brokers who cheated on their wives, resigned herself to a tedious evening.

Most of her evenings were simply quiet, rather than tedious, these days. More often than not she spent them alone, unwinding from the pressures of her job with the latest best-seller or teaching her blue-point Siamese cat another trick to add to his impressive repertoire. She'd even furnished her house in a way that would relax her, with an uncluttered assortment of antiques and tranquil watercolors on the walls. She wasn't the type for mementoes or knickknacks, and the only family picture she displayed was one of herself and her father, taken when she was thirteen.

Occasionally she went out to dinner or a party with someone new, but the men she'd met since her actor-boyfriend had stormed off to New York in the wake of her refusal to marry him hadn't lasted very long. Sometimes they were threatened by Kate's high-powered career and didn't call back, but more often than not Kate was the one who called a halt. If a man couldn't outthink and outachieve her at least some of the time, she quickly lost interest. She was content to go to plays or movies with women friends or spend a casual evening with a platonic male friend like Jerry.

He wasn't too happy when she called to cancel their date, but he accepted her explanation and suggested that they try again in a few weeks. "I guess I have no right to complain, given how many times I've had to run off to the hospital," he remarked, and Kate answered crisply, "Exactly." In fact, his busy schedule had never annoyed her. She supposed he wanted a closer relationship, but that was *his* problem, not hers.

Kate's career demanded a sophisticated wardrobe, and the dress she chose for Saturday night was both elegant and expensive. Deep blue and heavily beaded, the long-sleeved, wrap-style gown revealed a modest length of leg when she walked or sat down, but very little else.

She had a bit of trouble getting into the ballroom, but fortunately someone she knew saw her talking to the Secret Service agent in charge and came over to help. Her rescuer, Senator Allen Marks of California, had been around Washington long enough to know almost everyone.

He pecked Kate on the cheek, then asked the Secret Serviceman, "What's the problem, Pete?"

"The lady's name isn't on the list, and she has no ticket. Do you know her, Senator?"

"Kate Garvey, meet Pete Harrigan. She's Hank Garvey's daughter, Pete." Allen Marks winked at the agent. "She's a Democrat, but I think we can safely let her in."

As the senator and Kate walked into the room, he asked her why she was there and what had happened to her ticket. She skipped the first question, but explained that her ticket was in the hands of someone already inside, then countered with a question of her own: Was Allen Marks really going to retire in two years?

"Probably. I want to get to know my grandchildren," he said. "Are you looking around for my replacement?"

Kate shook her head. "No. Just—we'll miss you if you do, Allen. Even Dad will miss you."

"And here I thought I'd been a thorn in his side for nearly two decades," the senator laughed, obviously delighted.

The cocktail hour passed quite pleasantly. Kate's reporter quarry Hal Dunnigan hadn't arrived as yet, so she spent her time sipping sparkling water and chatting with acquaintances, including the party's formidable putative senatorial candidate, Bob Woodruff. A ripple of excitement passed through the room when President Hendrickson arrived, and eventually Kate got a turn to shake his hand.

"Scouting the opposition?" he asked.

Kate smiled ingenuously. "Tonight is purely social, Mr. President. If you don't tell my father, neither will I."

"And how about your boss? Is he going to set himself up for another shellacking this November?"

"You'll have to ask *him* that," Kate answered with a smile. "But personally, sir, I wouldn't care to take you on."

Her answer pleased him enormously; he was grinning like the Cheshire cat when he turned to greet the next person in line.

A little while later everyone sat down to dinner. As Kate had expected, her companions were less than scintillating. She minded their shop talk less than their jokes and wondered if the material possessions they kept comparing would have included their mistresses had their wives been absent. If it hadn't been for the fact that the two men Kate worked most closely with were happily married, evenings like this one would have given her a terminally dim view of marriage.

In the middle of the meal she excused herself, heading straight for Hal Dunnigan, who had come in late and was now sitting with a group of well-heeled contributors. She came up behind him and put her hands on his shoulders; he twisted around, startled, and then smiled. "Kate! Are you dating a Republican these days?"

"Not tonight, although I've been known to fraternize with the enemy. May I join you for a few minutes?"

"Of course." Hal made the introductions while one of the other men found a spare chair for her. The conversation was the kind she liked: political, witty, fast-paced. After ripping apart every one of Hendrickson's possible opponents, those present turned to the California Senate race.

"I hear Handlin's not going to run," Hal said, looking at Kate.

"The polls could be better," she admitted, "and all of us agree that Bob will be hard to beat. Personally, I hope he has an opponent who can turn the voters on, really inspire them. Maybe it's time for a nonpolitician—someone like Anthony Larimer."

Hal grinned at her. "Are you handing me a story, Kate?"

She contrived to look as innocent as a babe in arms. "Really, Hal! Just because I mentioned Larimer's name, that doesn't mean Bill plans to work for him."

"Just like it doesn't mean that the governor would support him if he ran?"

"Of course not." Kate paused, then mused aloud, "He'd be a very good senator, though. I'm sure I don't have to list his qualifications."

Hal sighed, pretending resignation. "But you're going to anyway."

Kate managed not to laugh. "My father is always saying that we need more senators with expertise in foreign policy. After all, the Constitution gives the Senate a major role in that area." She gave the assembled fat cats a sweet smile. Those who weren't puzzled by the conversation were listening with amused interest. "Not that I'm criticizing the President," she said. "He's certainly competent, sometimes better than competent. But as a matter of philosophy I think it's dangerous for one branch of government to have too much power in any given area, including foreign policy. We need the kinds of checks and balances that the framers of the Constitution envisioned."

"Thanks for the political-science lecture." Hal rose from his seat, catching Kate's wrist and pulling her up as well. "Excuse us, everyone," he said. "Kate and I are going for a little walk."

They crossed the room, nodding to the Secret Servicemen who were guarding the entrance, and continued out to the privacy of the corridor. "After that speech in there, half of Los Angeles is going to be talking about a Larimer candidacy by tomorrow." Hal leaned against the wall, a skeptical look on his face. "What's the story, Kate?"

"Off the record?" she asked.

"We've done business before. You know you can trust me. Just tell me what I *can* use and what I *can't* use. If I think there's a column in it, I'll run it Monday."

Kate thought for a moment, then answered, "Okay. You can say that someone close to high state Democratic officials has talked to Larimer about running for the Senate. Off the record, me, after the reception in Washington. He told me that the idea of serving in Congress is appealing to him but that family responsibilities would preclude it. He also said that he's not sure that a Berkeley professor who happens to be an overnight hero should run for public office at all. Even so, I think it's a definite possibility. There's been no final decision. I feel he gave me a temporary no"—she smiled—"but not a permanent one."

Hal Dunnigan was too good a reporter to let the matter drop. He pressed Kate for the specifics of her conversation with Larimer, pushing her twice as hard when she gave evasive answers. She was too experienced at this type of game to do more than admit that the "high-level officials" she'd mentioned weren't averse to speculation about a Larimer candidacy. Dunnigan was even clever enough to ask whether the Medal of Freedom was politically motivated, but Kate was able to state firmly and truthfully that the medal would have been awarded regardless of Larimer's political affiliation or personal background.

She opened Monday morning's paper with unusual eagerness. Five minutes later she was smiling into her scrambled eggs. The column was perfect, mentioning the high-level interest in Anthony Larimer, pointing out his qualifications, and noting his reluctance to run for office, which Dunnigan had confirmed in a phone interview with Larimer himself. Dorset and Associates now owed Hal Dunnigan a favor, but in the political-consulting business there were always opportunities for repayment.

Over the next week and a half the story was picked up from San Diego to Susanville. Interviews with local politicians and speculation by prominent public figures kept it alive. It was obvious from the clippings Kate saw that dozens of reporters had tried to interview Larimer, who had resorted to a telephone answering machine as a way to avoid the calls. Those who were enterprising enough to come to Berkeley met with a standard speech from Larimer saying that he looked forward to finishing his latest book and resuming his teaching career. While he was flattered by the public's enthusiasm for his possible candidacy, he didn't feel he could consider running at the present time.

Kate and her colleagues were quick to realize that Larimer's no was something short of unequivocal. They had launched their trial balloon—and not only was it floating, it was soaring.

Chapter 5

WHEN BILL DORSET CAME TO SACRAMENTO ON BUSINESS, HE took a room at a downtown hotel not far from the capitol. But when the reasons behind his visit were purely social, he and his wife were invariably the guests of Claire and George McClure. It was Kate's misfortune that Bill had classified the Larimer award ceremony as social. She arranged to stay at the hotel where she always stayed, which happened to be the same hotel where Anthony Larimer had booked a room. The task of calming him down in the wake of two weeks of intensive publicity thus fell straight into her less-than-eager lap.

On Wednesday night the McClures were giving a private dinner for Larimer at their East Sacramento home. Since Kate didn't have a car, while Larimer would be driving in from Berkeley, she planned to phone his room and cajole a ride to the governor's house. It would give her a chance to assess his mood.

She checked into her hotel around noon and grabbed some lunch before walking over to the capitol for a few hours' work. It was past five when she returned, going straight to the front desk to find out if Larimer had checked in yet.

"About half an hour ago. He asked what time the top-floor restaurant opened, so maybe he's up there now, Miss Garvey. If not, he's in room number 509."

Kate murmured her thanks and started to walk away, then stopped and looked back over her shoulder. "Is his daughter with him?" she asked.

The desk clerk nodded. "He said something about wanting to show her the view from upstairs, but it's fogging up again, isn't it?"

It was. On a clear day the windows of the sixteenth-floor restaurant provided the best view in Sacramento, but to Kate's way of thinking that wasn't much to brag about. The kindest thing she could think to say about California's capital, other than the fact that it *was* the capital, was that it sat midway between the Pacific Ocean and the Sierra Nevada Mountains. She preferred the excitement and intensity of Los Angeles to Sacramento's small-town chauvinism.

Anthony Larimer, dressed in brown slacks, a beige shirt, and a brown V-neck sweater, was sitting at a window table and talking to a middle-aged couple when Kate walked into the restaurant. His hand was wrapped loosely around the stem of a half-full wineglass, but he was making no move to drink. His daughter, dressed in jeans and a long-sleeved blouse, was standing nearby, looking out the window at the Sacramento River and the restored facades of the buildings of Old Town, the original area of the city.

Anthony didn't notice Kate until she was only five feet away from him. He smiled at his companions as they moved away, then looked coldly at Kate, causing a shiver of sensual awareness to snake through her body. She'd forgotten how strongly he could affect her.

She set her briefcase on the floor and thought about extending her hand, but decided that he would probably refuse to take it. "It's nice to see you again, Anthony," she said, trying to seem matter-of-fact. "May I join you?"

His daughter, Jessica, turned around to see who had

greeted her father by his first name. The girl was almost as tall as Kate, even with running shoes on her feet. She had long brown hair that rippled down her back, dark-blue eyes, and a startlingly mature beauty. She started to smile at Kate, then suddenly seemed to become aware of her father's stern expression and plastered the exact same look on her own face that she'd seen on his.

"Of course. Sit down." Anthony made no move to fetch Kate a seat, but stared at her in a way that announced he could do without her company. "Can I order you a drink?" he asked.

"Just a glass of ice water." Kate smiled warmly at Jessica when Anthony introduced them, but there was little response to her breezy, "Your father mentioned you when we met. It must be very exciting for you to come to the capital to watch him receive an award."

The girl nodded almost imperceptibly and sat down, edging her chair a little closer to her father's and taking a sip of her soft drink. Kate, who was beginning to tense up, tried again. "I guess you've been missing a lot of school lately, haven't you?"

Jessica glanced at her father before answering, then said that she was a good student and had no problem making up the work. "You're the one who spoke to my father in Washington, aren't you?" she continued.

Kate wondered if Anthony Larimer discussed the details of his personal life with his daughter. "That's right," she said.

"From the time my daughter was old enough to read, I've encouraged her to follow the newspapers." Anthony took a swallow of wine, as though he needed to fortify himself against Kate Garvey. "Of course, Jessica doesn't have to be able to *read* to know what's going on, does she, Katie? The phone and the doorbell haven't stopped ringing and the local news shows are having a field day. Yesterday Jessica asked me why there was so much talk about my running for the Senate when I told you I wasn't interested. Why don't *you* explain?"

Though shaken by his anger, Kate managed a smile. "Who knows how rumors like that get started, Jessica?" she asked with a shrug. "A lot of people think your dad would make a good senator."

"My father is good at everything." The pronouncement was utterly nonchalant. "And he told me that the story got started because of you and the man you work for. I don't know why you're doing it, but I think you should stop."

Jessica's protective reaction told Kate that she and Anthony were very close—not surprising, since her mother was gone now. When one considered the girl's obvious intelligence, the only possible response to her demand was an apologetic explanation.

"Okay, you're right," she admitted. "But we never wanted you or your dad to be harassed, Jessica. If we've pushed him, it was only because we think he's a very special person—the kind of person who *should* be a senator. Please don't be angry with us for that."

Jessica merely shrugged, but Kate could tell that praising her father had softened her up. Jessica looked at Anthony, holding out her hand. "I'm going down to the room, Dad. Can I have the key?"

He fished it out of his trouser pocket and handed it over. "What are you going to do? Wash your hair for a change?" he teased.

She wrinkled up her nose. "It's gross. It never curls." For a drawn-out moment she studied Kate. "Maybe you're not so bad, if what you say is true. But Dad is really burned. One time he took the paper and threw it into the garbage. And another time . . ." She paused dramatically, then sighed. "You really don't want to know." She flounced off toward the elevator, obviously pleased at how quickly the color had drained from Kate's cheeks.

"Now, Anthony," Kate began in a slightly strangled voice, "you have to understand—"

"I don't have to understand a damn thing," he snapped. "I must say, it's an honor to be talking to a 'source close to top Democratic state officials.' Maybe I should ask for an autograph." He shook his head, giving an unamused bark of laughter. "I really thought you people would stop with the medal. I wouldn't have let Jessica talk me into accepting it if I'd known it was only your opening shot."

Knowing how to retreat and placate were two of Kate's talents, talents that were clearly called for in the present situation. "I promise you, the medal is absolutely legitimate," she said. "As for the rest—we only wanted to prove to you that there's real support out there for your candidacy, Anthony, and to keep your name in front of the public while you think it over. That's just how these things work." Sensing that she'd somehow antagonized him even further, she hurriedly added, "There's nothing sinister about it—it's just politics as usual. We're very sorry if we've angered you, but—"

"You're damn right you have!" Anthony threw a five-dollar bill onto the table and got up. "There's the waitress. Order yourself some ice water." He proceeded to stalk away.

Kate bolted up two seconds later to follow, wondering what more she could possibly say to him. Somehow she had to calm him down. Jessica was gone by now, and both elevators were on their way to the lobby. Kate raised a gentle hand to Anthony's arm, murmuring his name almost pleadingly when he ignored her.

He turned his head, annoyed but also resigned, and she dropped her hand back to her side. "Go ahead and finish the apology," he said wearily.

Although Kate was only a few inches shorter than Anthony in the high-heeled pumps she wore, she was still acutely aware of his physical superiority. A picture flashed into her mind, a memory of their meeting in Washington. Anthony was holding her wrists, his mouth moving against her neck in a way that made her skin burn with desire. She'd never been attracted to men she could push around, and although she didn't particularly enjoy being chewed out, Anthony's stormy reaction only added to his appeal. She conceded him his right to be angry, but she also found herself wondering what it would feel like if all that emotion were to take a more positive, sensuous form.

She jerked back to the present when he muttered her name

impatiently. "Sorry. I was just saying that we want to apologize if we—"

"We?" he repeated sarcastically. "I only see one of you. Who are the others?"

He knew the answer as well as she did. "Bill Dorset, George McClure, Vince Collier. We understand that you're angry, Anthony, but all we did was keep your options open. If . . ."

"Okay, okay. You're brilliant political operators, I'll grant you that. I can be angry about your tactics and still appreciate how well you do your job. Let's drop the subject."

A gray-haired man in a business suit approached the elevator, the woman at his side doing a double-take when she recognized Anthony Larimer. Anthony was staring straight ahead and didn't appear to notice. Just as the elevator arrived the woman whispered something into her companion's ear. After everyone stepped inside, the man moved to Anthony's side and held out his hand. "Dr. Larimer," he said. "It's an honor to meet you."

Anthony shook his hand, his smile a trifle strained. "I hope you decide to run for the Senate," the man continued. "I'm just an ordinary small businessman down from Redding for a few days, but I want to tell you that we could use someone like you out in Washington—someone from *our* half of the state who can get things done."

Anthony's smile warmed a fraction. "How do you know I can get things done?" he asked.

The man shot him a sly grin. "I don't know what you were doing in Odessa, Dr. Larimer, but it wasn't just talking. You helped bust a big spy ring. I'd ask how you did it if I thought you would tell me."

"I suppose I set myself up for that." Anthony shook his head, genuinely amused now. "You're sure you're not a reporter?"

"I own a couple of restaurants up north." The elevator stopped at the eleventh floor and the doors opened up. "This is where we get off. Good luck to you, sir."

"Thanks a lot," Anthony answered.

Kate couldn't resist raising a mischievous eyebrow at Anthony once the doors slid closed. "Grass-roots support," she drawled. "I bet that man usually votes Republican."

When Anthony rolled his eyes in what Kate took for feigned exasperation, she stared into the middle distance as if transfixed and announced dramatically, "Anthony Larimer: A Man Who Gets Things Done." She promptly burst out laughing at his disgruntled smile.

"You're impossible, do you know that?" he demanded. "If you weren't so pretty and you didn't look so innocent, you wouldn't get away with half the stuff you probably pull."

"Can I get away with hitching a ride to the McClures' tonight?" she asked, giving him one of her more ingenuous stares. "I don't have a car with me."

"Only if you promise not to harangue me about the Senate. Don't make the mistake of thinking that just because I'm attracted to you I'll let you charm away my annoyance, Katie. I don't enjoy reading about myself in the paper when I don't expect it, or getting so many calls I have to buy an answering machine, or having my daughter and my niece trailed around Berkeley by reporters. This business in Odessa has messed up my life more than anyone knows, and Dorset and Associates isn't helping matters." The elevator drew to a halt, the doors opening just as Anthony finished talking. "Six-fifteen in the lobby," he said as he got out.

Kate's room was on the tenth floor; as the elevator continued to the lobby and then up again, she replayed Anthony's conversation with the restaurant owner. Once again, she realized, he hadn't ruled out running for the Senate. In fact, he'd acted as wily and noncommittal as a professional politician, promising nothing and pouring on the charm.

She worked out her strategy in the shower, one of her favorite places to think. Anthony was sitting on the fence, which meant that Jessica was one of the keys to his candidacy. Clearly she adored him; not surprisingly, she believed that he would be a wonderful senator. The problem was to convince her that, despite her father's current anger and uncertainty, a career in politics would make him happy. Kate would tactfully point out to her that her own support and reassurance would make his decision an easier one.

She changed into a silk shirtwaist, the predominantly blue print bringing out the blue of her eyes, and read until six-ten. Anthony and Jessica showed up in the lobby almost twenty minutes late. Anthony was dressed in a medium-gray suit with a muted plaid design that made him look like a State Department diplomat, not a Berkeley professor. Jessica was enchanting in a lacy Victorian-style blue and white dress. If her slender, delicate beauty had come from her mother, the late Beth Larimer must have been exquisite.

"I see you managed to get your hair to curl," Kate said. "It looks really good, Jessica." Actually only the ends were curled, into loose corkscrews. The body of her hair fell in thick, gentle waves down her back.

"It took me forever. Dad kept knocking on the bathroom door." Her expression said that although Anthony was a wonderful father, he didn't understand the first thing about fixing one's hair. "I wish I had *your* hair, Miss Garvey. Is it naturally curly?"

Kate nodded. "It was worse when I was a child. The summer humidity in the East made it curl into dozens of tiny ringlets. I hated it then, but I love it now. It's so easy to take care of." Recklessly oblivious to the consequences, she added with a grin. "That's one of the benefits of living in Washington, Anthony—at least from Jessica's point of view."

They were walking outside to the parking garage. "Keep it up and you can *crawl* to the McClures' house," Anthony muttered.

Kate remembered his late-model station wagon from the evening news. Everyone got in front, Jessica sitting between the two adults. "Do you know where to go?" Kate asked.

"I have the address written down." Anthony pulled a slip of paper out of his jacket pocket. "Is it quicker to go through the streets or take the freeway?"

"Once I decided to take the freeway to that area of town and wound up stuck in a traffic accident. Maybe we should stick to the streets."

George McClure lived in a beautiful brick house only fifteen or twenty minutes from the capitol. He'd bought it as a state legislator and remained there after his election to the governorship. Though Anthony wasn't openly hostile as they drove across town, his answers to Kate's questions about the book he was writing and the courses he taught were something less than enthusiastic. After half a dozen one-sentence replies, she gave up and decided to try her luck with Jessica.

"What grade are you in?" she asked. "Ninth?"

"Uh-huh."

Here we go again, Kate thought, but persisted cheerfully. "Is that middle school or high school in Berkeley?"

"High school. It's a parochial school."

"Really?" Kate was relieved that the girl had volunteered anything at all. "I went to a parochial school too, even though my family's not religious. I grew up in Connecticut and in Washington, DC. My father was a congressman at first, and now he's a senator."

"I know. I've seen him on television." Kate didn't miss the admiration in Jessica's voice and thanked the powers-that-be for her father's prominence. "You must have met a lot of famous people when you were growing up," Jessica went on. "What was it like, Miss Garvey?"

"Please, call me Kate. And you're right, I did. My father used to hold some of his meetings at the house—he would even invite people to bring their families for dinner or a Sunday picnic—and since no one ever told me not to, I'd barge right in and listen. That's how I got interested in politics—from listening to some of the brightest, most powerful people in Washington. I'm still interested in politics"— Kate smiled at the girl—"but now I get paid for it. I'm a political consultant. I help get people elected."

"Are you the one who thinks up all those television commercials?"

Kate glanced at Anthony. His mind was apparently on his

driving; there was no sign that answering Jessica's questions would offend him. "Sometimes I work in that area," she said, "but it's not my specialty. Winning elections nowadays has a lot to do with how you look and sound, Jessica. What I do is sit down and talk to the candidate to find out as much as I can about him. My company has a full-time pollster to tell us what people are concerned about and what they think about various issues. His polls help us determine what issues the candidate should focus on. Sometimes, in order to make sure that he's getting his ideas across as well as he can, we'll work on things like how he delivers a speech or even how he dresses. Once I worked for a very qualified woman who was running for lieutenant governor of another state. Her standing in the polls was disappointing, so we held a few focus groups. That's a small group of people who sit and talk about the candidate and the campaign with someone from our office. They answer a series of very general questions while a few of us watch from behind a two-way mirror. What we realized was that people thought our candidate was too glamorous to be serious. We told her to wear more conservative clothes and change her hairstyle to something short and businesslike, and her standing in the polls began to rise. We also worked on her breathy voice and her style of speaking. Eventually she won the election. But to get back to your original question, the TV spots are produced mostly by my boss, Bill Dorset. He'll be there tonight, if you want to ask him any questions."

Jessica made a face. "I'll ask him how come some of them are so vapid."

Kate saw Anthony's lips quirk into a fleeting smile and thought, Like father, like daughter. "I hope none of the ones you think are vapid came from our company," she said aloud.

"There's also the mail we get," Jessica replied. "There's so much of it that Dad doesn't even read it all—he just tosses it into the trash."

Kate could well believe it; Anthony Larimer was on dozens of different lists, a consequence of his generosity toward the

causes he believed in. She explained to Jessica that Dorset
and Associates didn't do direct-mail solicitations, but subcon-
tracted such work to a specialty firm when necessary.

"I love my work," she added. "I could spend hours talking
about it. But maybe you'll get a firsthand look if your father
agrees to run. . . ."

"Katie . . ." Anthony growled.

"Sorry." Kate used her most rueful tone. "I guess I tend to
get carried away."

"No kidding," he muttered.

By the time they reached the governor's house, both sides
of the street were lined with cars. The McClures had issued
invitations to this buffet dinner primarily on the basis of
friendship, but since their friends included important officials
as well as wealthy contributors, the press had turned out in
force. A large group of reporters was milling around on the
sidewalk in front of the house, kept out of the governor's yard
by the wrought-iron fencing that surrounded the property.
Vans from local TV stations were double-parked in front, and
a number of people were standing around with lightweight
cameras perched on their shoulders, looking very bored
indeed.

Anthony mumbled a curse as he braked the car to a halt
about a block short of the house. "Jessica, go ahead with
Kate while I deal with the media. I won't be long."

"Dad's kind of overprotective," Jessica stage whispered as
they got out of the car. Kate smiled at her, feeling the
beginnings of a real rapport. The reporters surged forward as
soon as they recognized Anthony, bombarding him with
questions about his plans. He was giving the usual answers
when someone noticed that Kate and Jessica had almost
escaped the throng, and hurried over to intercept them before
they managed to slip away.

"Do you think your father should run for the Senate?" the
woman asked Jessica.

The girl was the picture of self-possession. "I think my
father should do whatever makes him happy. What do *you*
think?"

The reporter laughed and winked at Kate. "What *I* think about your father isn't for your ears, honey."

"Please excuse us." Kate, who could sympathize with the reporter's sentiments, put her hand at Jessica's waist and coaxed her to move a little faster. "That was a good answer," she said as a security man opened the gate for them. "Is it what you really think?"

Jessica shrugged but didn't reply, and Kate decided not to press her. Anthony was still talking to reporters when Claire McClure opened the door. "I know politicians who would *kill* for the coverage he gets," she murmured to Kate as she let them in. A maid appeared to take their coats and purses, which would be stored in one of the upstairs bedrooms. "My daughter Rachel is off in the den," Claire said to Jessica. "She's seventeen. We have a litter of two-week-old kittens in there—it's at the end of the hall on the right. Do you want to go look?"

Jessica would obviously have liked nothing better, but instead she asked politely, "May I meet the governor first?"

"Of course. The last time I saw him he was talking to some blonde," she teased.

The "blonde" Claire referred to was a state supreme court justice, who had moved away by the time they approached. Anthony finally caught up with everyone just as George McClure was delivering a charming and extravagant compliment on Jessica's beauty. She blushed and thanked him, then went off to the den. The two men cordially shook hands, agreeing that it was a pleasure to see each other under such happy circumstances, as opposed to the time they had sat in a conference room and argued about the budget. Kate excused herself, catching Bill Dorset's eye and meeting him in a quiet corner to report on her progress with Anthony.

"The bottom line," she concluded, "is that even though he's very annoyed about the way we've maneuvered him, he knows we're darn good at what we do. He hasn't shut the door on running and he hasn't told me to get lost."

"So you're going to work on his daughter tonight?" Bill asked.

Kate hesitated before answering; she liked Jessica too much to pressure her. "I thought I'd wait till after dinner," she said. "I managed to warm her up a bit, but I don't want to push her, Bill. She's a nice kid."

He shook his head. "They may leave early, Kate. I want you to talk to her now. You may not have the chance later, and it's important to get her on our side. Talking isn't pushing, you know."

Kate never argued with a direct order from her boss. As she made her way to the den, she decided to state her case as gently and quickly as possible, then leave Jessica alone to sort out her feelings.

The two girls didn't look up when Kate walked into the room; they were sitting cross-legged on the rug next to a large cardboard box, wholly entranced by the four kittens inside. Kate, who had met Rachel McClure on several occasions, reintroduced herself and sat down on the other side of the box, her back to the door. The mother cat, she saw at once, was unusually placid, reacting to the constant touching of her kittens with scarcely more than an occasional glance or yawn. She got up and stretched, disturbing her nursing kittens, and then settled back down to give each of them a bath.

Watching Jessica with the kittens, Kate realized just how much of the little girl she kept hidden behind an adult facade. She picked up a kitten, cuddling it to her face and talking baby talk to it, giggling when it mewed back at her. When its tiny claws got caught in the lace of her dress, she gently disentangled it and gave it back to its mother.

"They're so cute," she said to Rachel. "Can I have one if my dad says okay?"

"The only one that has a home is that one." Rachel pointed to a long-haired black kitten who was trying to cadge some more milk from his mother, who in turn reached over to give him a forceful lick, pushing him away from the nipple. "Pick one out, and if your father agrees, we'll save it for you."

Kate told the girls about her Siamese cat, who could fetch and shake hands, among other things, and about the time she'd helped deliver a litter of kittens for a rather stupid first-time mother. Then she came to the point. "I wanted to talk to you about your father," she said to Jessica. "You know that a lot of people would like to see him run for the Senate. When I spoke to him in Washington, he told me that the idea appeals to him, but that he didn't think he could be both a good father and a good senator. *I* told *him* that you weren't a baby and that he should talk it over with you. I wondered if he had."

Jessica picked up a tortoiseshell kitten and rubbed noses with it. "I don't think I should talk to you about it, Kate."

"What makes you say that?"

"Dad was still sort of annoyed when he got back to the room."

"Annoyed with me?" Kate asked.

"I don't know," the girl mumbled. "I guess so."

Kate could see that she was making Jessica uncomfortable. The girl was using the kitten as a defense, cooing over it and petting it, avoiding eye contact with Kate. Kate, increasingly uncomfortable with what she was doing, decided that perhaps she could simply talk about her own life. Jessica was bright enough to see the similarities in the two situations.

"Let me tell you about myself and my family," she began. "When Dad decided to leave the House and run for the Senate, I was twelve, and he and my mother included me in a conversation about their plans. Since a congressman has to run for office every two years, he spends a lot of time in his district. My father had an apartment in Washington, but my mother and I lived in our house in Connecticut. She's always preferred it to Washington—she likes being married to a senator, but she doesn't care for politics. Anyway, Dad told us that if he ran for the Senate and won, he wanted to buy a house in Washington and have us all live there. He was tired of running back and forth, and since a senator only has to run every six years, he doesn't have to go back home quite so often. I thought of myself as pretty adaptable, but still, I'd never moved before, and I wondered how well I'd adjust to a new home and a new school. In the end we moved and things worked out fine. I can't deny that being a senator is a very demanding job, but my father always had time for me. I got to see more of him in Washington than I had when I lived in Connecticut; in fact, we kept the house up there and my mother used to go back for a week or more every month. By the time I was fifteen or sixteen, she was spending at least half her time there, but Dad and I managed very well on our own. I've never been that close to my mother—she comes from a wealthy, very social family, and we don't seem to have much in common. I suppose I'm a disappointment to her because I haven't given her a rich son-in-law and two-point-one grand-children. Anyway, what I'm trying to say is . . ."

Kate hesitated. Jessica had finally looked up, not at Kate, but at the doorway behind Kate's back. With a sinking feeling she slowly turned around—and promptly confronted the icy eyes of Anthony Larimer. No man had ever looked at her like that—as though he could barely restrain himself from hitting her—and it was all she could do not to tremble. Anger she could cope with, but this white-hot fury was totally outside her experience.

"Go on," he said curtly. "I'm dying to hear the rest of it."

Jessica and Rachel quickly forgot all about the kittens and stared at the two adults in shocked fascination. Kate knew that a straightforward answer wouldn't help matters, but by this point she had nothing to lose by putting her cards on the table.

"I was going to say that it can work," she said softly, looking up at him. "It just has to be what both of you want. Talking something over never hurts, Anthony."

His expression didn't change. Kate stood up, wanting only to change the subject and then disappear. "Jessica is very attached to one of the kittens—the short-haired calico," she said. "I think she wanted to ask about taking it home when it's old enough."

A forced smile nudged its way onto Anthony's face; he approached the box and looked inside. Kate slipped past him, brushing against his shoulder as she left the room. For the rest of the evening her fellow guests would afford her some protection, but later . . . She didn't want to think about later.

Chapter 6

BILL DORSET WAS TALKING WITH A PAIR OF LEGISLATORS WHEN
Kate walked back into the living room. He immediately
excused himself, strode briskly to her side, and hustled her
into the dining room, which was empty except for the
partially set buffet table.

"You look like you've just been run over by a truck," he
said. "I saw Larimer leave the room. What happened in
there?"

"He overheard me talking to his daughter. He must have
noticed I was gone and come in to see what I was up to." Kate
reached up and started to methodically massage her right
temple. She had the beginnings of a throbbing tension
headache. "I doubt we're on speaking terms, Bill. He was
livid, and I suppose I can't blame him. Jessica is only a child.
We shouldn't have involved her. She's crazy about her father
and she wants him to be happy. If she thinks that being a
senator will make him happy . . ."

There was no need to finish the sentence; Bill slipped a
comforting arm around Kate's shoulders and nodded.

"Everything will be okay," he said gently. He didn't sound particularly concerned by what had happened. "At least the issue is out in the open now, where it belongs. Believe me, kids aren't all that fragile. I have two of them myself, so I know."

Kate wanted to think he was right. "Always the optimist," she said. "But you're not the one he's angry with. I think I just lost my ride home."

"I'll run you back myself. Remember, Kate, he's been under a lot of pressure lately. Maybe he's angry about Jessica, but it's probably tied in with a host of other factors. Come back inside, have a glass of wine, and forget it."

Kate couldn't forget it, but at least she could avoid Anthony Larimer in the hope that he would cool down. She made sure that she was at the opposite end of the buffet line from him, and when she noticed him and Jessica heading toward the glassed-in sun porch with their food, she decided to stay in the living room with the Dorsets.

Coffee and pastries were eventually brought around by Rachel McClure and one of her friends. Kate had only picked at her dinner, but she felt calmer by dessert time, and the cream puffs looked irresistible. Then Anthony showed up and her appetite did the opposite. She settled for hot tea.

Anthony and Jessica sat down on the living-room couch with Claire and George McClure; Kate, at a table a few yards away, could eavesdrop on their conversation. The governor was telling Jessica about the restoration of the capitol, explaining that the local mice who'd had their homes disturbed had promptly started to plague the human occupants. When Anthony laughed at one of George's anecdotes, Kate felt a measure of relief. At least his sense of humor was intact.

She was standing in the dining room about an hour later, talking to a college president, when the feel of a heavy hand on her shoulder made her start in surprise. She sensed that it was Anthony even before she turned around, responding to his closeness with a disconcerting mixture of wariness and arousal. Once he had her attention he removed his hand, regarding her with a coldness that would have stopped a mastodon in its tracks.

"Jessica is tired," he said. "I'll get your coat and purse for you."

"Thank you." Kate knew that courtesy had nothing to do with his offer. If he was driving her back to the hotel, it was only because he intended to read her the riot act once they were alone. She silently cautioned herself not to exacerbate the situation by trying to justify her actions.

Not a single word was spoken during the ride home. Kate could cope with temper tantrums far more easily than this unnerving silence, and by the time Anthony parked the car, she was almost ready to beg him to get it over with. But much to her bewilderment he shepherded his daughter into the building and through to the elevator without the slightest indication that he wanted to speak to Kate later.

At the fifth floor Jessica looked at Kate as though she wanted to say good night, but didn't dare, and followed Anthony out of the elevator. A few moments later Kate was clenching her jaw in irritation because a check of her purse had failed to turn up her room key. It was an appropriate end to a miserable evening. She dumped the contents of her bag onto the floor in front of her door, but to no avail. Either she'd left the key in her other purse or else it was sitting somewhere on a dresser or table. It wasn't the first time she'd made that particular goof.

Ready to kick the nearest wall, she dragged herself back to the elevator and down to the main desk to pick up another key. By the time she dropped onto her bed, she felt so emotionally and physically weary that she didn't even bother to look for the missing key. She had a tough hide after so many years in politics, but never before had she encountered the kind of animosity that Anthony Larimer so obviously bore toward her. The fact that she was attracted to him when he was so clearly off limits only added to her strain. She felt guilty about her actions and annoyed with Bill Dorset. Next time *he* could handle some of the dirty work.

Her headache, under control for most of the evening, had returned with a vengeance. Kate took two aspirin and a hot shower, hoping that either one or the other would provide some relief. Afterward, feeling a little better physically but still too keyed up to sleep, she pulled a fashion magazine out of her suitcase and tossed it onto the night table. After slipping on a nightgown of opaque white silk with spaghetti straps and lace-edged cups, she clicked off all the lights except for the one by her bed and crawled between the sheets.

The magazine was breezy reading, but Kate couldn't seem to concentrate on it. She admitted to herself that the problem wasn't her headache: The aspirin had taken care of that. It was that she *liked* Anthony Larimer as a person and had to respect his scruples, even though they made her job much harder. She knew that academia wasn't the ivory tower that many people assumed, but still, Larimer couldn't have come into contact with the kind of political hardball that she and Bill Dorset played as a matter of course. If he had, he wouldn't have been so angry with them. He was a very decent man as well as an attractive one, and Kate was beginning to feel almost corrupt by comparison. She'd violated his privacy, planted stories about him in the press, and tried to manipulate him into making what she'd arrogantly assumed was the right decision. No wonder he despised her.

Eventually she turned off the light and lay in the dark, her eyes closed, yearning for the sleep that so tormentingly eluded her. When she heard her doorknob rattle, she jerked into a sitting position, badly frightened but too groggy to be fully alert, and groped for the light switch. She found it just as the door opened. There was a vicious slam just before she clicked on the lamp.

Anthony Larimer stalked over to her bed, looking so furious that she shrank back against her pillows. He'd removed his jacket and tie and was holding her key between his thumb and forefinger. Kate grabbed the covers and yanked them up to her neck, instinctively shielding her revealing nightgown from his scathing glare. When he dropped the key into her lap she picked it up, clutching at the cold metal as though it could offer her some protection.

"You scared me," she said weakly. And still do, she thought. Anthony's abrupt interruption and boiling anger had alarmed her all over again.

"If you were a man, I'd do a hell of a lot more. What gives you the right to brainwash my daughter?" he demanded. "I just got through talking to her. You've got her convinced that she's the only thing standing between me and the United States Senate—as though that were some cherished ambition I'd spent my whole life chasing after. Couldn't you see that just mentioning the subject would have that effect on her? That she'd wind up confused and guilty and upset? Or didn't you give a damn?"

Kate couldn't quite meet his eyes. She fiddled nervously with the room key, saying hoarsely, "I'm sorry, Anthony. I know we went too far. . . ."

"You went too far." He mimicked the words in disgust, then cursed. "Is that how you see it? A case of well-intentioned excess? Dammit, Katie, look at me!"

She managed to do so, but her defensive flush did nothing to pacify the man towering over her bed. "Sometimes," she said, "you get caught up in things and you don't step back to see the whole picture. I feel awful about Jessica. I'll explain if you want me to. . . ."

"You've *explained* enough already. My God, she's a fifteen-year-old child. How can you use a fifteen-year-old child to get what you want?"

"I didn't think of it that way. I thought the two of you . . ." Kate cut herself off. She had the sudden sensation that Anthony wasn't only angry and upset, he was also extremely disappointed in her. "Look, I'm really sorry, Anthony. I know she's important to you—"

"The most important thing in my life," he interrupted. "That's what being a parent is all about. But someone like you wouldn't understand that."

Though Kate had intended to hold her tongue, she couldn't

allow so harsh a judgment to stand unchallenged. "Okay. I don't know much about being a parent. But I've been a senator's daughter. I was twelve when Dad ran for his first term in the Senate and only a baby when he was first elected to the House. We always talked things over, Anthony, openly and honestly. I never wanted Jessica to think she was standing in your way. I just thought that the two of you needed to communicate."

His face registered cynical doubt. "I don't buy that. You were looking for an ally. The candidate's kid is a problem? Fine. Co-opt her."

Kate couldn't deny that there was a certain amount of truth in the accusation. Anthony ran his fingers through his already unruly hair, the gesture underscoring how tired he looked. Kate placed her room key on the night table, emotionally wrung out but no longer intimidated. She felt that she could talk to him now. She wanted him to know that she and Bill were fundamentally honorable people, that they'd made a serious error in judgment but regretted it.

"Anthony? Will you sit down for just a moment?" she asked.

In lieu of an answer he pulled over a chair and eased himself into it. His eyes, which had never left Kate's face as long as he was yelling at her, slid down to her bare shoulders for several long seconds of study before returning to her face. Desire momentarily flickered in his eyes, then yielded once more to coolness.

Kate was in no shape to cope with sexual tension just then, so she simply dismissed the possibility that it could recur. "I want you to know—I understand that you're an idealist," she began, "that you want to make the world a safer and better place. University politics may get rough at times, but it's child's play compared to some of the stuff I've seen. The difference is, I grew up with it, so I've always accepted it."

Anthony frowned, irritated by Kate's explanation. She had no idea how she'd offended him, so she plunged ahead more urgently. "Believe me, Anthony, we don't pander to the voters' prejudices or play dirty tricks on our opponents or design campaigns that are based on half-truths. Leaking stories and orchestrating grass-roots support—those kinds of tactics may seem unsavory to *you*, but they're just standard operating procedure to *us*. Most of the people we deal with understand . . ."

Kate stopped in mid-sentence when she noticed the half smile on his face. "Look, I'm not trying to be funny," she said, becoming annoyed with him. "It's not easy for someone like me to talk about things like this with someone like you. The Peace Corps, the State Department, Berkeley . . . You said that your involvement in the Odessa crisis had caused problems in your life, but I just know that, even so, you'd do it all over again if you had the choice." She waved a hand for emphasis, unaware that the covers had slipped a fraction to reveal the lace trim on her nightgown. "To be honest, Anthony, the politicians we usually work for are on the cynical side of pragmatic. They know the score. The way we manipulated you—it makes me feel . . . dirty."

Anthony shook his head, laughing softly now, murmuring, "Oh, Katie. What am I going to do with you?"

His reaction both angered and baffled her. "Oh, Katie *what?*" she snapped. "And why should you do anything at all with me? I'm trying to be honest, even though it's painful for me, and you're sitting there and laughing!" She reddened and looked down. "I'm glad you find me so entertaining."

"Not entertaining," he said. "Exasperating, certainly. Condescending in a way that jabs at my ego so much that I permit myself to repeatedly lose my temper with you. But not entertaining. Stop staring at the covers and look at me, Katie."

When she glanced up he was unbuttoning his shirt, the bared flesh reminding her of how graceful and muscular his body was. Her pulse sped up, but only partially due to arousal. Sex was the one area where he'd demonstrated a clear advantage. Although she found him extremely attractive, she couldn't allow him to use her body to soothe his outraged sensibilities. "Anthony . . ."

"Relax." He unbuttoned another button. "I'm not going to

attack you." When the third button was unfastened, he pulled
the shirt to one side to reveal an irregularly shaped patch of
scar tissue just below his left shoulder. "What do you suppose
caused that?"

Kate stared at the strange little mark. "I have no idea."

"A few days ago I wasn't in a position to talk about it. Now
I am. But that doesn't mean *you* will. Agreed?"

"Yes." Kate was totally lost. "But I don't . . ."

"I know. The scar is from a bullet, but I didn't do a very
tidy job of taking out the slug. It happened when I was in the
Peace Corps, but I wasn't *only* in the Peace Corps. I was
meeting a contact one night and I got ambushed. Fortunately
it was too dark for a clear shot and too dark for anyone to
identify me. My contact and I didn't know each other—
sometimes that's the way these things work. He was captured;
his mutilated body was found three days later and I wouldn't
care to speculate on what they did to him in between. In any
event, I couldn't very well go to a doctor, so I took care of it
myself. Beth was in the Peace Corps with me and Jessica was
a toddler. That's when I realized it was time to get out." He
paused. "That much of it will be public knowledge within a
week."

A CIA agent? Kate thought. My God! Was the Agency
planning to admit it? And if so, why? Had the Russians found
out? Shocked by such a matter-of-fact discussion of near-
murder from a man she'd previously assumed to be something
of a white knight, she slowly repeated, "That much of it? You
mean there's *more?*"

"That's all I'm going to talk about."

"That's all . . ." Kate's voice trailed off. What kind of man
was she dealing with? "Are you still . . . ?"

"No." The denial was very firm. "I resigned thirteen years
ago."

Though Kate was tired and a little shaken, she was far too
bright not to look for answers. Had her father not been
chairman of the Senate Intelligence Committee, had the two
of them not been close, she wouldn't even have known where
to begin. As it was, she remembered what Anthony had done

after his service in the Peace Corps and murmured thought-fully, "The State Department?"

"I told you. I resigned thirteen years ago," Anthony stated.

"The State Department," Kate repeated more firmly. What followed was sheer speculation. "You were working for the Agency at the same time as you were serving in the Department, even though most domestic counterintelligence operations are illegal. What were you doing? Keeping tabs on our diplomats? Looking for foreign agents?"

"I was an analyst in the area of Asian affairs. That's all I was." Anthony paused a moment. "My background was very useful in Odessa, Katie. I was walking a tightrope, trying to stall Rvanski in order to give the government time with Borlin. I took that course of action because my training told me to—old habits die hard—but I didn't care for the position I found myself in. In order to be an intelligence officer, you have to place paramount importance on national defense and national security, because otherwise you can't live with some of the things you may be called upon to do. Even though I believed that a great deal was at stake in the Borlin case, I felt responsible for those people in Odessa—for their safety. I hope to heaven I never have to take that kind of responsibility again." He sighed, shaking his head, and then continued in a clipped voice, "After it was over, the Russians started digging. When you know where to look and who to question, it isn't hard to blow an agent's cover. The story will run in *Izvestiya* sometime in the next few days. That's all I'm going to tell you. You want to go ahead and tell Dorset about the Peace Corps, okay. But no one else and nothing else. Just keep in mind that I've seen things you wouldn't want to hear about. So much for idealism and innocence. You should have consulted me before you started playing games—our ends may not be that different. I've been patient with you people, Katie. Let's leave it at that."

There was nothing Kate could say. Larimer wasn't threatening her, merely laying out the facts. When she thought of how they'd tried to maneuver him, she felt downright embar-

rassed. She hugged the covers to her chest, wondering what
would happen if a man with Larimer's background decided
not to be patient. But of course all that was behind him now.
Or was it?

She followed his progress with troubled eyes as he got up
and walked to the door. Her heart was beating heavily, her
primary emotion one of relief. And then he stopped and
turned around, his eyes taking a thorough inventory of her
face and shoulders as he stood there. A quick little shiver ran
through her body.

"You look frightened and vulnerable and very desirable,
lying there that way," he said softly. "It makes me wonder
why in hell I'm leaving." He took his time about walking back
to the foot of the bed. "I'm a professor now, Katie, nothing
more. I wouldn't do anything to hurt you. I'd rather make
love to you."

Katie found the thought appalling. Larimer didn't even
respect her, much less like her. He could only be motivated
by a desire for revenge, or perhaps for conquest. "No
thanks," she said.

He continued around the bed until he drew level with her
waist, then stood looking down at her, legs slightly apart and
arms crossed in front of him. His shirt was still open; between
the raw masculinity of his half-naked chest and the aggressiveness of his stance, Kate was intimidated into silence.
She'd never had a man look at her with such a disconcerting
mixture of passion and determination, and much to her
dismay her body responded with a warm, unbidden ache deep
in its most feminine recesses.

Confused by feelings she didn't want to have, she finally
managed to threaten, "If you touch me, I'll scream!" The
statement sounded hopelessly melodramatic, even to Kate
herself. Anthony reacted by grinning at her.

"You won't scream, because if you do, it will wind up in the
papers. You wouldn't want to support an accused rapist for
the Senate, would you?" He was teasing rather than mocking,
making Kate understand that using force was the furthest

thing from his mind. Even so, when he sat down on the edge of the bed, she started to wriggle away, mildly alarmed.

He bent over, his large hands coming to rest on either side of her shoulders. As they stared into each other's eyes, he drawled, "Why so terrified? I'm not touching you."

Now he *was* mocking her, and she was furious with him for it. "You're trying to intimidate me," she accused, her face flushed with anger. "You're bigger and stronger than I am and you want to make sure I know it. It's nothing but a power play, but I'm *not* terrified!"

"I'm trying to seduce you, not intimidate you," he corrected. "But you're not being very cooperative." He brushed his finger down her cheek, the caress feather-light, and then trailed his hand along her jaw and neck and down to her shoulder, pushing aside one delicate strap of her nightgown. The ache in her body spread upward, suffusing her breasts and making them swell. "Are you always so difficult?" he asked with a smile.

Kate's emotions were in an agonized tangle by now. She couldn't control Anthony Larimer the way she'd controlled every other man in her life, and like it or not that fact seemed to excite her almost as much as his silky touch did. At the same time she resented the way he was treating her, like a slightly thick-brained, obstreperous female who had to be shown what she wanted. It took her a moment to realize that, from his point of view, that was exactly how she'd treated *him.*

He slowly pushed aside the other strap of her nightgown, then ran his fingers from her bare shoulder along her collarbone and over to the opposite shoulder. If she released the protective covers, the slightest little tug would send the gown falling to her waist, exposing her breasts to his intense brown eyes, his hands, his lips. Kate stared at his mouth, thinking that she should stop him, but making no attempt to do so.

"When I first saw you," he murmured, "I didn't think you were beautiful. I hereby revise my opinion. You're *very* beautiful. Let me make love to you."

The seductive words were all but mesmerizing when growled by someone whom Kate found so terribly attractive —in fact, all but irresistible. She felt increasingly breathless as he continued to explore her body, his fingers sliding under the lace of her nightgown to brush the bare skin along the tops of her breasts. Although she longed to offer more, her common sense refused to let her.

"Let go of the covers, Katie," he coaxed. "I want to see the rest of you."

She shook her head, denying what her body craved. "Please stop it, Anthony. I don't sleep around, especially with men who don't even *like* me."

He smiled at her with genuine warmth and tucked a finger under her chin to lift it up. "Women are unfathomable," he said. "How can you think I don't like you? You're beautiful, intelligent, and sexy as hell, and you make me laugh even when I'm annoyed with you. If I didn't like you, I wouldn't put up with your tactics. I also wouldn't be here."

Before Kate could manage to object, Anthony started to toy with her mouth, nibbling gently at her lower lip, lifting his head a fraction, and teasing first one corner of her mouth and then the other with light, tantalizing kisses. The effect on Kate was nothing short of devastating. The sensual ache had filled her entire body by now, becoming a burning hunger too powerful for her to deny. Without volition she responded to the kiss, giving Anthony passionate little nips of her own that made him catch his breath and groan her name. Her eyes fluttered shut and her clenched fists relaxed, the sheet dropping to her waist. Moments later her hands snaked up around Anthony's neck and began to play with his already tousled hair. She loved the thick, crisp feel of it.

He deepened the kiss, slowly probing her mouth as though each sweet recess had to be explored and conquered before he could bear to move on to the next. Kate arched against him, pliant with desire, rubbing her breasts against his chest like a kitten asking to be stroked. She had never felt this way with a man; she actually wanted Anthony to take control, to arouse her until she was mindless with need for him, to prolong their lovemaking until one or both of them either surrendered or exploded.

The kiss went on and on, Anthony's mouth just rough enough for Kate to find the caress enticingly exciting. Anthony was the one who finally eased away, firmly grasping Kate's hands and placing them at her sides. Without a word he slid her nightgown down to her hips, his eyes darkening with appreciation at the sight of her generous breasts and full, erect nipples.

"You're exquisite," he murmured.

Kate, flushing at the passion in his gaze, stared at the front of his shirt for several uncertain moments before her hand followed her eyes to the fourth button. She slid it through the buttonhole, then repeated the maneuver on its twin to the south. The other buttons were hidden below his waist. Her hand brushed over the dark, silky hair on his chest, slowly working its way lower, but hesitated when it reached his belt.

"Don't stop," he said hoarsely. He looped a lock of her hair around his fingers and gently tugged, then turned his attention to her soft, slightly dewy skin. When he cupped a breast in his palm and rubbed his thumb slowly back and forth across the nipple, a spasm of fiery pleasure shot through Kate's body. As their lips met in an impatient kiss, she fumbled with his belt buckle, barely able to concentrate on what she was doing.

Never in her life had she been teased so skillfully. One moment his hand was light and playful against the soft underside of her breast, and the next it was rough and demanding with the nipple, catching the hard little nub between thumb and forefinger and massaging it just firmly enough to cause a sharp, intoxicating sensation. Kate realized that he was telling her, "I'm the boss here. No matter how much I want you, I'll set the pace and call the shots," but she murmured no protest, made no effort to withdraw. Choosing to submit was a new and dazzling pleasure for her.

His shirt was fully unbuttoned and pushed aside now. Kate

wanted to arouse him, but even more than that she wanted to please him as he was pleasing her. Once her fingers gained their objective, they danced to their own teasing rhythm, accelerating the pace and intensity of their caresses.

Anthony gave an incoherent moan into her mouth, as though caught in the throes of the most delightful kind of agony. Hard fingers bit into her shoulders, pulling her against his body, the hair on his chest soft yet prickly against her sensitive breasts. For a few long moments he kissed her as though he could no longer control himself, but then he pulled away and stood up.

His clothes wound up in a heap on the floor; a moment later he was sliding under the covers to join her. Kate moved over to the other side of the bed and lay back against the pillows, but when she began to remove her nightgown, Anthony caught her hands and stopped her.

"Leave it for now," he said, pulling her onto her side.

Their bodies melted together along every torrid inch. Kate wound her arms around Anthony's neck as he moved against her, his hands on her hips controlling and slowing her response. The sheer fabric of her nightgown was a tantalizing barrier to total intimacy, but Kate could feel his fiery maleness straining against her flesh, close, but not close enough. As he probed her mouth and turned her body to flame, she realized that she was too aroused to wait even another minute. With an urgent little moan she began to hurry him again, only to be promptly punished for her sins when he set her firmly away from his body and forced her to be still. Only their mouths were still clinging, but his kiss was so dominating that he might just as well have pinned her underneath him and taken her like some sultan's besotted concubine.

He slipped his thumbs beneath her nightgown and gently tugged, pulling it from her hips to her thighs and, with Kate's cooperation, entirely off. One warm palm explored the gentle curve of her stomach, then brushed down her hip and parted her legs. When it slid higher and began to stroke her with delicate, fleeting motions, she thought she would faint with longing. "Anthony, please," she finally whispered.

"Please what?" Kate opened her eyes to find Anthony smiling much too complacently.

Something inside her abruptly rebelled. It didn't matter that he could offer her mindless ecstasy, or that his erotic brand of lovemaking excited her in a way that she'd never before experienced. She wouldn't be controlled this way any longer—turned into a passive, powerless female. She pulled away and turned around, showing him her back.

"Katie?" He cuddled up behind her and pushed aside a few stray curls to nuzzle her neck. The feel of his warm lips brought a renewed flush to her face.

Ignoring the demanding body snuggled so intimately behind her own, Kate shrugged away. "I've changed my mind," she said. "I don't want you to touch me anymore. Just go away."

Anthony stiffened for just a moment before nipping at her earlobe and murmuring contritely, "I'm sorry, honey." His fingers brushed a still-taut nipple and then gently fondled her breast. Mollified by his apology, Kate began to wonder whether he would accept her continued refusal to make love. The idea that he wouldn't was suddenly very exciting.

She supposed that Anthony's hand could pick up the wild tempo of her heart, which made a mockery of her whispered "I mean it, Anthony."

She had no time to react to his subsequent laughter or amused "We'll see about that." Within seconds she was flat on her back, her hands pinned over her head, her body trapped beneath his. "You were saying?" he drawled wickedly.

"You're not all that irresistible," Kate retorted, starting to struggle. Anthony didn't fight back; he simply prevented her from escaping. Determined to pay him back, Kate made her body go limp, waited for Anthony to relax his guard, and then wriggled in a way that caused him to jerk away defensively without actually hurting him. She couldn't help giggling when he muttered something about her being a "blasted wildcat," and when she renewed her struggles, they were even less convincing than before. Both of them knew that she didn't want him to leave.

"You want to play games?" he asked. "Okay, lady, you're on. But things may get a little rough."

He was as good as his word, holding her captive while he mounted a triple assault on her senses. His mouth was merciless with her lips, coaxing and promising but not satisfying, while his free hand toyed with an eager nipple. The torment inflicted by his powerful body had Kate arching against him and moving seductively, but to no avail. He teased her until she longed for his possession, parting her thighs to briefly and repeatedly invade her femininity, but persisting in withholding the ultimate pleasure.

Finally, accepting the fact that he could hold out longer than she could, she surrendered. "You win," she murmured against his lips.

He released her hands and rolled onto his back. "That's a relief," he said, sounding slightly winded. "You sure know how to test a man's self-control, Katie. I'm running on fumes." His voice dropped to a husky growl. "I'm in agony, honey. Let me make love to you."

He was asking instead of demanding, and the last little wisp of Kate's ambivalence fled. She snuggled closer and kissed him on the shoulder. "I'm not going to let you stop and refuel," she teased.

Anthony pulled her on top of him, smiling tenderly at her. When they kissed, Kate was filled with an incredible sense of emotional peace. And when he took her, the feeling of his slow, compelling movements filling her body blocked out everything but her own mounting desire. Their lovemaking quickly flared out of control, their mouths wild with hunger, their bodies impatient for release. Kate was only half aware of the little guttural noises coming from her throat. She dug her nails into Anthony's back, hardly able to bear the insistent stroking of his hand working in tandem with the driving need of his body. She stiffened, arched against him, was pushed over the edge. For endless seconds she was totally immersed in the intensity of the pleasure that wracked her body. Then Anthony moaned aloud, a feverish "Katie—honey . . ." and she eased back down to earth, making love to him with a mixture of tenderness and roughness that swept away even the fumes of his self-control.

Chapter 7

ANTHONY WAS SLEEPING PEACEFULLY WHEN SHE CAME INTO THE room, so beautiful and healthy, her long, dark hair streaming down her back, her hand extended in a mute summons. He murmured her name, "Beth," and jerked awake with a start, his heart pounding heavily. The sudden movement failed to disturb Kate, who was curled up on her side a few inches away from him. A little shaken, he plumped up his pillow and lay back against it, trying to settle down.

Naturally he thought of Beth often; he had only to look at Jessica to be reminded of her. But the rage and self-pity were gone now, and the dream came very seldom. After three years of staving off death and three more years of learning to accept it, Anthony was more than ready for a new relationship. His marriage to Beth, an unusually happy one, had been intensely close during their final few years together. He wanted that same closeness in his life again.

He stroked his fingers along Kate's bare arm, feeling a mixture of tenderness and hopelessness. She was sleeping soundly and didn't stir. He hadn't barged into her room with the intention of taking her to bed. Quite the opposite: He'd been coldly angry, all desire for her frozen. Not only had he been furious about her conversation with Jessica, he had been fed up with being treated like a rather dense Good Samaritan whose head, if not his entire body, was up in the clouds somewhere. He was sick of being cajoled and manipulated and flattered. Every time Kate had annoyed him, she had also managed to charm or amuse her way out of it, and Anthony was irritated by his own susceptibility.

If they'd wound up in bed together, it wasn't because of the nightgown, although the revealing lace and silk had certainly aroused him. It wasn't even the sincerity of her explanation or the look in her eyes, so shaken and vulnerable. He'd stayed in the room because he'd wanted total victory. Conquering her in bed would help make up for every implicit put-down, every disregarded wish.

He hadn't expected it to be so sweetly exciting, to bring him such incredible physical satisfaction. He'd had his share of women since Beth, but not one of them had pleased him the way Katie had. The desire for conquest had slowly given way to a desire to give as well as take. He was tempted to wake her up and make love to her again, but he didn't want to leave Jessica alone any longer. With genuine reluctance he slid out of bed and put on his clothes.

Jessica was fast asleep when he let himself into the room. She'd thrown back the covers to her waist, and looked more like a little girl, in her flannel pajamas, than a maturing young woman. Anthony sat down on the edge of her bed and bent to kiss her forehead. She shifted onto her side and murmured something unintelligible. Anthony knew that she was growing up much too fast for his liking; he hated the idea that in three and a half years she'd go off to college.

After sleeping for an hour in Kate's room, he wasn't tired, so he changed into pajamas and a bathrobe and sat down in an armchair, propping his feet on its twin. He'd met a lot of women—attractive, successful women—but they were so caught up with their own problems and careers that marrying any of them was out of the question. Even women his own

age were hungry for "self-fulfillment," and someone like
Kate Garvey, though only seven years his junior, lived in a
world different from that of the women he remembered from
college. She had nothing in common with Beth, whose
dearest ambition had been to take care of her family and
serve her community. Totally trustworthy, warm and open,
generous and caring—what did Kate know about such qualities? Anthony admired her intelligence and perceptiveness
and had tasted the sweet softness beneath that hard-boiled
exterior of hers, but he suspected that work rather than a man
would always come first for her.

He would never remarry over Jessica's objections, but
then, Jessica was always urging him to settle down again.
Anthony hoped that any woman he chose would be at least
a friend to his daughter, possibly even a confidante. He
couldn't picture Kate in that role. If she'd reached the age of
thirty-two without marrying, she obviously had no use for
commitments. He wondered how many lovers she'd had.
Probably more than he wanted to know about.

He stretched and rubbed his eyes. If there was one thing
he'd finally gotten through his head, it was the necessity for
compromise in his personal life. It wasn't easy to find another
woman like Beth. In the meantime, he considered Kate
Garvey an interesting companion and an exciting lover. The
lady didn't have to be marriage material for him to continue
seeing her. Maybe he'd run for the Senate. If he did, he and
Kate would be working together closely. The thought was
highly agreeable.

Anthony awoke to the sound of a running shower. He
glanced over at Jessica's bed, which was empty. For a child
who'd once whined and moaned about taking a bath, she'd
developed an amazing affinity for water in recent years.
Sharing a bathroom with her was beginning to try his
patience. She'd probably spend the next hour in there,
fooling around with her hair. Although Anthony's salary as a
professor allowed them to live quite comfortably, he wasn't a
wealthy man. He was concerned about affording a private

college for Jessica, should she choose to attend one, and since he had no intention of asking his well-heeled mother-in-law to help foot the bill, he never wasted money on unnecessary luxuries. Unfortunately, he now realized that separate rooms constituted a necessity rather than a luxury when one's traveling companion monopolized the bathroom and demonstrated appalling taste in her choice of music. And, he thought, he'd be able to get rid of the pajamas.

He shot a moody look at the telephone. Although the prospect was less than appealing, he knew he needed to call Kevin O'Neal. The two of them would have more than enough time to talk before Jessica finally emerged from the bathroom.

Anthony dialed Kevin's office, trading several minutes' worth of gossip with him before he came to the point.

"Listen, Kevin," he said. "Kate Garvey made some pretty accurate guesses about the State Department. I was telling her about the Peace Corps, and—"

"Why?"

Anthony had expected the curt question, but that didn't make it any less awkward for him to answer. "Because she got under my skin, treating me like a naive kid who was shocked by her big-league tactics." He hesitated, embarrassed and uneasy. "Look, do I really have to go into my psychological motivations? It happened and I'm sorry. I figured the Peace Corps stuff will be public knowledge anyway in a few days. And she was only guessing about the Department. Naturally I denied it."

"It's nice to hear that you haven't taken total leave of your senses," Kevin drawled. "But if you had to show off like some boastful little boy, Anthony, at least you chose Katie to impress. If you told her not to talk, she won't. You *did* tell her . . . ?"

"Of course I did," Anthony answered irritably. "Am I supposed to go stand in the corner for opening my mouth?"

"You managed to keep it shut for seventeen years," Kevin pointed out.

"I also managed to avoid Katie for seventeen years."

"Okay, Anthony. We've been friends too long for me to stay on your back about this. You know the rules as well as I do, and if you broke them . . ." Anthony could picture Kevin's characteristic shrug. "What are you going to do about the Senate?" he went on.

The change of subject was only too welcome. "I don't know yet. When I make up my mind I'll give you a call."

"Right. And, Anthony, when the Peace Corps story breaks, do you think you can limit yourself to following the party line?"

Kevin was now amused. An amused Kevin O'Neal was almost as aggravating as an annoyed Kevin O'Neal. Anthony replied that he would do his best, then hung up and glared at the bathroom door. He waited another five minutes, then knocked.

"Jessica?" he called out. "I need to get in there."

She poked her head out, a curling iron in her right hand. "I'll be done soon, Dad."

"You can finish your hair in a couple of minutes. Come on. Now. Out!"

She rolled her eyes, labeling him wholly unreasonable, but strolled out of the bathroom. A minute later Anthony shot a longing look at the shower, but knew it was hopeless. His daughter's hair had a higher priority than his own cleanliness.

After he was finished he phoned for breakfast and a newspaper, then sat down to wait. When the food arrived twenty minutes later, Jessica was still in the bathroom. Anthony unfolded the paper to find a front-page picture of himself, Jessica, and Kate arriving at the McClures'. The accompanying story focused on the previous night's dinner and that day's ceremony.

The bathroom door opened just as he finished reading the article. Jessica looked so enchanting that he instantly forgave her. Her long hair was held back from her face with matching tortoiseshell clips, and the touch of lipstick and blusher she wore brought out her fine-boned beauty. In her wine-colored corduroy suit she looked as mature as some of his students. One of these days some sex-crazy college kid was going to

spot her around town and mistake her for a fellow student.
Anthony could picture his innocent daughter in the back seat
of this juvenile delinquent's Chevy, in imminent danger of
seduction. The thought terrified him.

"Beautiful, as usual," he said. "Hungry?"

"As usual." She sat down on the other side of the table and
plucked the cover off one of the platters on the tray. "Umm.
Pancakes. How come you got room service?"

"I'm going to be stared at all day today. I don't need to put
up with it over breakfast."

After they divvied up the food, Jessica noticed the front
page of the paper. "Another story?" she asked. "What did
they write about you this time?"

Anthony handed it to her. "Here. Read it yourself."

She did so, tossing it onto the table when she was finished.
The way she was looking at him, so thoughtful yet gentle,
reminded him of Beth. "You didn't go for a walk last night,
did you? You went to talk to Kate."

Anthony shrugged, a little embarrassed. "You're right."

"It's okay. I *am* fifteen, Daddy." Jessica pretended to study
her food for several moments, then visibly plunged ahead. "I
think you should run for the Senate, if that's what you want.
Last night you cross-examined me about every word Kate
said and then pretended you were too tired to talk about it,
but both of us know you weren't. You *always* have some
reason why we can't talk about it. I know you were angry at
Kate for even speaking to me, but she's right: I'm not a little
girl, and if I'm the only thing that's stopping you . . ."

"You're not the only thing that's stopping me. I don't even
like that phrase. I love you and I want what's best for you.
You've been through a lot in fifteen years, and I'm not going
to add to it."

Jessica laid down her fork. Her face was wearing the kind
of determined look that Anthony hated to deal with. "For
twelve years of my life," she announced, "I had two of the
most wonderful parents a person could have. Now I have a
father who arranges his schedule to give me more time and
attention than most kids get from their mothers, even if their

mothers don't work. And I have a cousin who—who—well, you know how great Kris is." Jessica's voice was a little husky by now. "I'd be almost sixteen by the time you took office. I think it's time for you to do what *you* want."

Anthony didn't say so, but Jessica was all he had left of Beth. It wasn't easy to let go. "There are plenty of people who can represent California in the Senate," he said, "but I only have one daughter."

"Suppose I was already in college? What would you do about it then?"

Anthony shot her a disgruntled look and stabbed a hapless piece of omelet with his fork. He felt a mixture of pride and irritation that she could back him into a corner this way. It was fruitless to insist that, since she *wasn't* in college, there was no point discussing it. It took a lot to make Jessica dig in her heels, but once she did, she inevitably wore him down.

"I'm not sure," he muttered. "I'd probably go for it." He took another bite of his omelet, then watched his daughter attack her stack of pancakes. For someone so slender she had an impressive appetite. "It's a very complicated situation, Jessica. I've always felt that celebrities shouldn't run for political office."

"You're an expert on foreign policy. It's not as though you're just some actor or something."

"That's true. And I probably wouldn't run if I thought I could continue to write the kind of book I want to write. . . ." He paused, wondering how an innocent fifteen-year-old could possibly understand his dilemma. "The problem is, after this business in Odessa, a lot of people who used to talk to me—Communist leaders, for example—aren't going to talk to me anymore." He sipped his coffee, hoping she wouldn't ask why. He would have to explain his background when the story hit the US papers, but he wasn't looking forward to it. "That means that I won't be able to do the kind of inside look at their thinking that I've done in the past."

Jessica nodded her understanding. "You mean the Russians are burned because they figured out you used to be a spy. Well, you aren't anymore, are you? Won't they get over it?"

Anthony almost choked on his coffee. He sputtered, grabbed a napkin, and then started to cough. How could Jessica know about such things? Had she overheard one of his conversations with Kevin? She was so matter-of-fact about it.

She gave an exaggerated sigh at his fit of coughing. "Oh, honestly, Daddy. It isn't as though it's a secret. It's about time we talked about it."

Anthony gulped some water and fought down the urge to protest. At least she was sparing him that dreaded explanation. "I mean, I realize that everyone in the family played this game that we didn't know," she went on, "but Kris told me years ago. I guess I was ten. So I asked Mom if you were like James Bond, and she said no. She made it sound very boring. And she told me not to talk about it, but I already knew *that*. She said that even *she* wasn't supposed to talk about it and that the two of you pretended she didn't know, even though both of you knew she did."

Everyone in the family? Anthony thought, a trifle dazed. He was related to a bunch of poker players. They'd never dropped the slightest hint. "The answer to your question is no," he finally managed. "I'm not—that is, I don't, uh, spy on anyone anymore. And Mom was right. Most of the time it was very routine. I kept my eyes and ears open and reported what was going on in the different countries where we were stationed. Sometimes other people arranged meetings for me with people who had information to sell, and that's how I got the scar on my chest—from being shot at when I was supposed to meet someone. But that was the only really dangerous thing that happened." The statement shaded the truth to a substantial degree, but Anthony wasn't about to list all the near-misses.

"Well, I never really *thought* it was a hunting accident," Jessica sniffed. She demolished the last piece of pancake on her plate and pushed it away. A calculating smile lit up her face. "Do you think fifteen is too young to campaign?" she asked.

* * *

Kate opened her eyes, remembered the night before, and quickly twisted around to look at the other side of the bed. When she found it empty she checked the floor to her right. Anthony's clothing was gone. Her brain worked a little slowly first thing in the morning, so it took a moment for her to recall that Anthony had a teen-age daughter whose existence no doubt explained his absence. It never occurred to her that the night before might have been a one-night stand.

She shoved a second pillow behind her and sat up in bed to think. Making love with Anthony Larimer had been sensational. She'd never experienced anything like it, either mentally or physically. And that was precisely what troubled her.

She could probably forgive herself for tumbling into bed with a man she barely knew, even though she'd never acted that way in her life before. She was only human, and the sheer animal attraction of the man had swept away her usual common sense. It was over and done with and she'd have to accept it. What she couldn't accept was her submissive response to his aggressiveness. In the cold light of morning she recognized that his husky "Let me make love to you" had only been good manners. From the moment he'd announced that he wanted her, she'd been his for the taking.

The fact was, Anthony Larimer threatened her peace of mind. She had the feeling that getting involved with him would cause her to question the way she thought and everything she'd worked so hard to achieve, and she didn't need that kind of confusion in her life. He was a complicated, demanding man, hardly the type to put up with canceled dates or condescending dismissals. Kate had learned that the hard way.

There was an alternative, a casual affair, but Kate didn't believe in casual affairs. Even if she did, it would be a mistake to sleep with a client. She planned to be one of Anthony's most important advisors, should he run. He was a strong-willed man who would be hard enough to control even without a personal relationship to complicate matters, but if she started sleeping with him, he'd be impossible. She'd been around men all her life and she understood the way they thought. Wives and fiancées were respected, while casual girl friends were the unwitting targets of off-color jokes and sardonic put-downs. She wouldn't allow herself to be placed in the second category, either by Anthony or by her colleagues, who would surely learn of their relationship.

That left only one problem for Kate: how to handle the physical hunger that Anthony so easily aroused in her. Having scratched the itch, she hoped it would go away. If it didn't, she would have to remember all her reasons for ignoring it.

She had some paperwork to catch up on after the previous day's meetings, so she phoned for eggs and coffee and took a shower while she waited for the food to arrive. As she ate she read through legislative testimony and a stack of amended bills, making notes of the information she would need to effectively represent their client's point of view.

When the phone rang, she was sure it was Anthony. She refused to admit to any disappointment when Bill Dorset's voice came over the line. He offered her a ride in his rental car to the Larimer presentation, remarking that it was too bad the weather hadn't cooperated with plans to hold the reception outside. Kate's curtains were closed; she hadn't even noticed the rain. They agreed to lunch together at noon and then walk across the street to the capitol for the reception.

Kate finished checking out of the hotel just as Bill walked into the lobby. She waved him over and pointed to her suitcase. "Can I leave this in your trunk?" she asked. "Or aren't you and Emily leaving today?"

"Unless something comes up, we're going on the same flight as you are." He picked up the suitcase for her. "Don't you want your raincoat?"

Kate was wearing a medium-weight wool suit. "It isn't raining anymore. I packed it away so I wouldn't have to carry it around. It barely fits over my suit jacket."

Their conversation remained innocuous as they drove to the capitol and parked the car. The restaurant Bill had chosen was a local political hangout filled with people they knew;

they had to decline a couple of invitations before settling themselves at a quiet table in the corner.

"So," Bill said, once the waitress had poured their coffee, "what happened after you left last night?"

Kate had expected the question. "Anthony swiped my key from my purse—I assumed I'd left it in the room—and showed up half an hour later, out for blood." Kate summarized the conversation, leaving out any reference to Anthony's job at the State Department. She had no proof of her speculations, and he'd told her to limit her explanations to the Peace Corps.

"It sounds like we're in almost the same place," Bill said. "He might have hinted a bit, but he didn't say yes and he didn't say no. Give me an opening chord and I'll sing it for you."

The waitress was approaching with a basket of bread and an order pad, so Kate picked up her menu and ran down the list of sandwiches. Only when the woman had left did Bill pick up the thread of his comments. "Let me get this straight, Kate. Larimer scared the wits out of you with all that stuff about the CIA, warned you not to pass it on except to me, and told you you'd better watch your step in the future. And then he left. Period."

When Kate nodded, her face slightly flushed, Bill cocked a skeptical eyebrow at her. "Or didn't leave," he drawled, "as the case may be. Your private life is your own concern, Kate, but I don't want to see you hurt, either professionally or personally. If you remember, I told you something about Larimer didn't add up."

"I guess I got a certain image of him into my head and couldn't let go of it," she admitted. "But he played the role of the well-intentioned academic to the hilt. I'm beginning to wonder who the real Anthony Larimer really is."

"If he runs, it will be your job to find out," Bill reminded her. "I don't want any surprises in mid-campaign."

It was standard practice to talk to the candidate at length, searching for skeletons in the personal and family closets. If Kate's suspicions were correct in Larimer's case, the skeleton was a dandy, but the chances of discovery were mercifully small. Once in a while stories of similar activities hit the papers, but names of individual agents were almost never mentioned.

Recalling Anthony's firm denials, Kate said glumly, "Larimer's the kind who'll say as much as he feels like and not one word more."

The statement provoked the kind of smile that Kate could have cheerfully done without. "I'll be damned," Bill said. "You've met your match and you actually admit it. I never thought it would happen."

Kate didn't think of Anthony in quite those terms, but even if Bill were right, she wasn't about to comment. She asked about a bill that was scheduled for committee the following week, and they spent the rest of lunch analyzing which legislators were in their camp and which needed further attention. Afterward they dashed across the street through a foggy mist and entered the capitol through one of the side doors leading into the newer, unrestored part of the building.

Inside the governor's office one of the receptionists, Doris Hernandez, was talking to a tall, balding man dressed in a plaid sports coat, brown shirt and tie, and herringbone pants. He was carrying a plastic department-store shopping bag from which he withdrew several hundred sheets of paper held together by two crisscrossed rubber bands.

"Is the governor in his office?" he asked.

Doris said that he was but that he couldn't see anyone without an appointment. The man in the sports coat promptly asked to make an appointment.

"It would help if you told me what you wanted to speak to him about," Doris said politely.

"My study." The man held up the dog-eared pages, giving them a little shake for emphasis. "I can tell the governor how to get rid of half the government departments and still do the same job. They could repeal the income tax. I've been working on my reorganization plan for three years now, but no one believes it will do what I say. That's because they haven't studied it."

Kate had witnessed many such encounters over the years. "The governor likes to have a letter first," Doris answered. "If you would write to him with a brief summary of your ideas, I'll see if someone can discuss them with you."

"They're very complicated," the man said unhappily. "That's the trouble."

Doris gave him an encouraging smile. "Just do the best you can." He nodded and carefully packed his study back into his shopping bag.

Several other people were sitting or milling around the room, one of them an elderly gentleman who was holding a sign protesting a tax increase passed ten years before. He was a capital regular, mad as a hatter but perfectly harmless. There was also a woman dressed in a pink leotard and blue-and-red leg warmers who was sitting on the couch next to a conservatively dressed man, both of them reading magazines. As Kate and Bill approached Doris's desk, the dancer suddenly jumped up, executed a pirouette in the center of the room, and then sat down again. No one paid any attention.

"Having a nice day?" Bill asked Doris with a perfectly straight face.

"Maybe it's the Larimer reception. Either that or the full moon. The governor is in Vince's office with Dr. Larimer and his daughter. Do you want to go inside?"

A secretary emerged from the inner quadrangle of offices to summon the man next to the dancer for his appointment. He darted a wary look at the dancer as he crossed in front of her, obviously relieved to escape her company.

"I think we'll go ahead and sit down," Bill answered. "Is the presentation being held in the Senate chamber?"

Doris said it was. "You can watch from the upstairs gallery," she added. "Your names are on the guest list—just give them to the sergeant at arms. Mrs. Dorset is seated downstairs with Mrs. McClure, by the way."

"Some people just have pull." Bill smiled. As they turned to leave the office, the tax protester approached the reception desk and asked to speak to "McClure."

"The governor has a very busy schedule today," Doris explained, "so he won't be able to see you. But I'll certainly tell him you stopped by, Mr. Douglas."

Apparently satisfied, he wandered away. Meanwhile, the dancer was doing several pliés near the couch. The governor's receptionists, Kate thought, had the temperaments of saints. Democracy demanded free access to public officials, but some of the fruits and nuts who wandered into the capitol—or into her father's Washington office—were darn near certifiable. They came seeking five or ten minutes with a George McClure or a Hank Garvey, confident that this would solve either society's problems or their own. The great majority were harmless, and the rest of them, God willing, would be dealt with by the security men. Even so, Kate sometimes worried about her father's safety.

"From the ridiculous to the sublime," Kate said as she and Bill reached the restored building. More than two thousand craftspeople had worked on the five-year, $68 million project, undertaken to return the original building to its turn-of-the-century elegance and ensure everyone's safety in the event of an earthquake. The rotunda dome, painted in a series of intricate pastel designs and trimmed with carved plaster and gold-leaf detailing, was the most stunning feature of a glorious effort. The interiors of modern buildings couldn't begin to match its majesty and artistry.

The Assembly half of the building, done in shades of green, and the Senate side, done in red, had a grandeur largely absent in the men and women who sat at the antique desks in each chamber or met in the beautifully restored committee rooms. Yet the original denizens of this capitol had been no better and probably far worse than the current ones, and for all the pettiness and arrogance and egotism that were exhibited daily in this building, there were also conscientiousness, good intentions, and genuine concern. The California legislature, though not perfect, was one of the best in the country.

Kate and Bill stood in the third-floor corridor and talked shop with a couple of capital correspondents before going into the gallery. The ceremony was scheduled for one-thirty but began ten minutes late. There was polite applause as Anthony Larimer and George McClure walked down the chamber aisle, accompanied by legislative leaders from both houses. The governor read the official proclamation and then offered his congratulations. Kate had never known him to be so concise.

The two men shook hands several times for photographers and posed as though exchanging the small gold medal. Then Anthony approached the microphone and thanked the people of California for what he termed "a singular honor."

"In accepting this award," he continued, "I feel privileged to join a group of outstanding California citizens, a group composed of men and women who, in many different ways, have contributed to the security of our nation and the well-being of our society. I can't think of any work more vital than the struggle for a free society." He paused, then added softly, "I'm honored and I'm grateful. Thank you."

There was a split second of silence followed by enthusiastic applause. Kate ascribed the warm response to two factors: Larimer's quiet sincerity and his brevity. During one of these events a few years back, a scientist being honored for his work in developing a much-needed vaccine had droned on for forty-five minutes, using his acceptance speech as a forum for his opinions on everything from the arms race to the funding of medical research. Anthony Larimer had known enough to keep it short.

The reception that followed was held in the rotunda, underneath that wonderful dome. In keeping with the frugal spirit of the McClure administration, no public money had been spent on the affair. The champagne had been donated by a California vintner and the food underwritten by a major corporation. So many people filled the rotunda and surrounding hallways that the guests had to elbow their way from place to place. Kate managed to find herself a glass of champagne and slowly nursed it as she exchanged polite small talk with anyone she recognized. As time passed, the crowd thinned, people going back to work or leaving early for the day.

Eventually she maneuvered close enough to watch the

guest of honor. Although he shook hand after hand, his smile never wavered and he never ran out of appropriate comments. Jessica stood next to him, and every now and then one would turn to the other with a whispered word or two. For a moment Kate envied them their closeness. The bond between father and daughter was apparently so strong that any adult woman in Anthony's life would be hard pressed to compete. All the more reason, Kate thought, to steer clear of him.

She walked to the end of the line, inadvertently catching his eye. The warmth of his smile went straight through her body. Her answering smile was forced. She didn't want to respond that way. When she reached his side, he took her hand and looked at her in a way that virtually asked her how soon he could take her to bed again.

Kate withdrew her hand. "Congratulations, Dr. Larimer," she said politely, pretending that the night before had never happened.

His smile disappeared. "Thank you, Miss Garvey," he mimicked. "I saw your boss a while back. We're meeting in my hotel room in about an hour. Please be there."

Kate wasn't about to take orders from him. "I thought I might cram in a few more appointments this afternoon—that is, if anyone is around to talk to. If Bill wants me to come, though, of course I will."

She could see that he was displeased with her. "*I* want you to come," he said.

Her back went up even higher. She couldn't stand there and argue with him in front of his daughter and assorted politicians, so she gave him one of her more wide-eyed looks and asked, "Am I working for *you* now?"

"That's what we're going to talk about." Before Kate could answer him back, he turned to the next well-wisher, a Northern California legislator whom he greeted by name. Kate, granting him the victory in this particular skirmish, said hello to Jessica and moved away.

As a political consultant her job was to provide expert, forceful advice whenever she felt it was warranted. Since Anthony Larimer wasn't exactly a pushover, she had the feeling that they would clash early on and often. A series of images flashed through her mind: a difference of opinion, an argument, Anthony carrying her off to bed. In her fantasy he was imposing his will on her, both physically and professionally, and she was submitting without a murmur. When pigs have wings . . . she thought irritably.

Chapter 8

"I ASKED THE THREE OF YOU TO COME HERE BECAUSE I THINK WE need to talk about the kind of campaign we're going to run—speaking theoretically, of course." Anthony stopped pacing the room and glanced around at the four people listening to him.

Vince Collier, an unlit cigar in his left hand, was sitting at the table near the window. His jacket was unbuttoned and his tie loosened, his right arm sprawled casually along the tabletop, his fingers toying with a glass ashtray.

Bill Dorset was seated on the other side of the table from Vince. Though attentive to Anthony's comments, he radiated the polished confidence of a man accustomed to being in charge.

Kate was sitting on the end of Anthony's bed. She'd found it warm in the room—perhaps because she was on edge—so she'd removed her suit jacket and hung it in the closet. Her eyes flickered between Vince and Bill as she listened to Anthony talk. The two men, she realized, had discussed Anthony Larimer at length, but they really didn't know him.

As for Jessica, she was lying propped up on her bed, thumbing through a teen magazine and sipping a can of soda. Although she was acting as though the discussion didn't concern her, there was no question that she was a factor to be reckoned with. She influenced her father much more heavily than the average fifteen-year-old.

Anthony walked over to Jessica's side and took a sip of her soda. Then he sat down on the edge of the bed, facing Vince and Bill. "If I have an unpopular viewpoint on an important issue," he said, "I'm not going to hide the fact. That doesn't mean I'm going to mention it in every speech, but if someone asks me about it, I'll answer honestly. Allen Marks could be a model for every politician in this country. If the issue is important enough, he has the guts to fight for what he believes, even when what he believes will cost him votes. I plan to do the same."

Allen Marks, the senior senator from California, was also in the middle of his fourth term. He hadn't been so forthright in his first campaign. Kate could discuss that with Anthony later, but now she concentrated on the list of particulars he was reeling off to Bill.

"I expect to maintain full control over the campaign. Nothing goes on radio or TV without my specific approval. Nothing gets leaked to the press without my knowledge. No one makes promises on my behalf for the sake of a fat check or an important endorsement unless I okay it first. And no one sends out direct-mail pieces until I approve of what's inside. Understood?"

Bill crossed one leg over the other, a bland expression on his face. "You're the candidate, Anthony. Dorset and Associates never violates the express wishes of the candidate. I have to point out, however, that you'll have a very heavy schedule, particularly in the months before the general election. You can't expect to supervise every detail of the campaign."

"I don't." Kate noticed that Anthony was making no attempt to be charming or even particularly pleasant. "Just the important ones." He turned his attention to Vince Collier. "When it comes to running statewide California campaigns, Vince, nobody does it better than you. I'd like to spend the rest of February exploring how much support—hard *financial* support—I really have. I'll make a decision in early March. If I decide to run, I'd like to be able to count on eight months of your time and experience."

Vince fiddled with the ashtray, then pushed it away. He lit his cigar and puffed a few times. Anthony showed no impatience with his silence. "I'll have to talk to George," he finally said.

The governor wouldn't be eager to give up his top aide, even for eight months. Vince Collier could juggle ten different items in his sleep. His campaigns for George McClure had been characterized by smooth scheduling, effective use of volunteers, and superb advance work. When McClure showed up to address a gathering, the bodies were in place and the media were out in force. The candidate was almost always on time, and his supporters were positioned in the audience to ask the questions he wanted to answer.

She guessed that George McClure would forego Vince's services as chief of staff in hopes of obtaining a second Washington ally as effective as Allen Marks. Anthony Larimer, if elected, would wield far more influence than the usual freshman senator. In an era when public dollars were scarce, the state's representatives in Washington had to work very hard to obtain the public-works projects, military installations, federal grants, and government contracts so vital to the state's economy. Allen Marks was a Republican and he and McClure sometimes disagreed, but he'd done his job. Jack Handlin hadn't.

Kate was lost in thought, vaguely aware that Anthony was pushing Vince for a commitment, when she heard her name rapped out. Her head jerked up, her eyes colliding with Anthony's cool gaze. "Are you with us, Katie?" he asked.

His sarcasm provoked her. Did he think that taking her to bed gave him the right to use that tone with her? She stared icily back at him and stiffly apologized that her thoughts had been elsewhere. Then she added irritably, "I had a late night last night. I'm a little tired."

The moment she closed her mouth she could have kicked herself for opening it. Anthony abandoned his stony expression in favor of a complacent smile. "In that case, I forgive you," he drawled.

Kate straightened, trying to look professional instead of embarrassed. Anthony Larimer had a way of putting her at a disadvantage, something no man had ever accomplished before. She wasn't pleased when Bill Dorset covered his mouth and coughed, hiding a smile.

Satisfied that he now had everyone's attention, Anthony continued, "As I understand your role in the company, Katie, you're the image maker. You make sure that the candidate comes across as well as possible. I'm willing to go along with you to a certain extent, but don't tell me to call myself 'Tony' so I'll seem like one of the guys, or give interviews about my personal life so reporters can titillate their readers."

"How about a haircut?" Kate suggested.

Vince Collier burst out laughing. "Not a bad idea, but it's the radicals who need the shortest hair. Anthony's books have given him a moderate image—so far."

"Since he teaches at Berkeley, it wouldn't hurt him to come across as conservative in his personal life." Kate addressed her explanation to Anthony. "The voters in California are sophisticated; they don't expect a candidate to have a family life straight out of a Norman Rockwell painting. They only want to know that he's a decent, honest person. It's been our experience that Bob Woodruff runs a clean, issue-oriented campaign, but he's no more a saint than the rest of us. If the positions you take or the way you behave give him an opening to picture you as a wild-eyed 'Berserkeley' radical, he's going to take advantage of it."

"Which brings us to the issues." Anthony's tone was somewhere between ironic and sarcastic. He stood up again, remarking as he walked to the center of the room, "I notice that nobody has bothered to ask my viewpoints on the great issues of the day. Are any of you even interested in that?"

Bill Dorset glanced at Kate, then smiled. "Come on,

Anthony. You know better than that. Naturally we checked you out."

"Really."

Kate knew that look. If the explanation didn't suit him, Anthony would deliver a scathing tongue-lashing. During her eight years with Bill she'd seen candidates whine, rant, cry, and smash inanimate objects against the walls, but she had the feeling that Anthony's cold-blooded anger could top anything in her experience. It seemed politic to soothe him.

"There was nothing underhanded about it," she said. "We talked to someone who served with you on the ad hoc budget committee that met with the governor last year, and also to a few of your colleagues at Berkeley and elsewhere. You do private consulting for a few corporations, so we checked with their top officers. It was very low-key." When Anthony nodded calmly, she directed a questioning look at Bill. His shrug was as clear as a verbal command: "Go ahead and tell him the rest of it, Kate. If we're going to work with the man, we have to be honest with him."

Her face was a little flushed as she continued, "We checked public records on campaign contributions and, uh, we asked all of our direct-mail contacts to run your name through their computers. That told us what lists you were on and who you'd given money to."

Anthony was clearly displeased. "And you don't think that checking up on me that way was a violation of my privacy?"

Kate didn't know what to answer. Some of the lists were either public knowledge or available to buy, but not all of them. The use of computerized records *did* involve serious questions of ethics and privacy, and the fact that their intentions were good might not justify their actions.

It was left to Bill to shake his head knowingly. "Larimer, I'd lay odds that you've been involved in stuff that would make us look like a bunch of Sunday-school teachers. If you don't want to do business with us, fine. But spare us the self-righteous lectures."

There was an awkward silence. Bill waited calmly while

Vince puffed on his cigar, looking puzzled. Kate stared at Anthony, whose face told her exactly nothing. All of a sudden Bill swung his head to look at Jessica, his cheeks turning pink. The girl was apparently absorbed in her magazine, but even so, Bill's composure visibly faltered, a rare occurrence indeed. "I think . . . we'll be in touch, Anthony." He stood up, checking his watch. "We have a plane to catch in a little over an hour. Kate?"

Just as Kate got up, Anthony crossed in front of her, holding out his hand to Bill. There was no trace of his earlier annoyance; on the contrary, he seemed amused. "We'll talk again in a few weeks," he said to Bill. "And by the way, don't worry about my daughter. She isn't easily shocked." Father and daughter exchanged the kind of secret smile that an outsider could never interpret.

Anthony shook hands with Bill and then with Vince, who had lumbered to his feet with his usual show of reluctance. Kate stood and waited her turn, only to have Anthony walk right past her to Jessica's side.

"Come on, lazybones," he said, pulling her up. "Get your nose out of that magazine. Mr. Dorset and Mr. Collier are going to take you downstairs for a hot-fudge sundae. I have some business to discuss with Kate."

Jessica wrinkled her nose. "A hot-fudge sundae? I'll get fat."

"As a house," Anthony agreed. He held out a five-dollar bill, but Bill Dorset waved it away.

"It will be my pleasure," he said. "I always enjoy getting to know a candidate's family. Twenty minutes," he added to Kate. "Emily's meeting us at the airport; she'll kill me if I miss the plane."

Kate waited near the table while Anthony ushered everyone out of the room. She didn't believe that "business" had anything to do with why he wanted to see her. After he closed the door he leaned back against it, smiling in a way that she was hard pressed to resist.

"A haircut, huh?" He crooked his index finger at her. "Okay, Delilah. Come over here and we'll talk about it."

Remember what you decided this morning, Kate said to herself. No affair. No involvement. "You wanted to speak to me?" she asked aloud.

"What I had in mind was more along the lines of nonverbal communication. I have fantasies of pulling you down on the carpet . . ." He stopped and smiled. "I think I'd better leave it at that. Let's just say that the fantasy was very graphic and very agreeable. For both of us, Katie."

A woman would have had to be deaf not to have responded to that seductive growl of his. Unfortunately for Kate her hearing was excellent. Her body was reminding her of how this man could make her feel, while memories of their lovemaking crowded out sensible thoughts from her mind. "Last night just—happened," she said quickly. "That doesn't mean I want to repeat it. If that's the only reason . . ."

Her words trailed off as Anthony crossed the room. It was pure instinct to back away, but the edge of the table put an end to her retreat. "If the mountain won't come to Muhammad . . ." Anthony said, wrapping a firm hand around each upper arm.

A reminiscent ache invaded Kate's body, mocking the morning's cool logic. When Anthony's lips brushed against her neck, she had to force herself to turn away from him. "Anthony, please," she murmured. "I don't want to."

He ignored her protest, just as he had before. His lips were undermining her will to resist, trailing insistent kisses along her neck and jaw and then nuzzling their way to her mouth. When she put her hands against his chest to hold him away from her, his lips mounted a sudden attack, dropping teasing kisses against every part of her mouth.

Kate stiffened, aching to respond, but only too aware that she shouldn't. Her body had reached a fever pitch of arousal so quickly that desire for Anthony became like a raging wind blowing away everything in its path. At first she couldn't understand how it could have happened so abruptly, and then she simply didn't care. Coaxing turned to conquest as his mouth hardened, parting her lips with an urgent hunger that seemed to match her own. Within seconds she was returning his probing kiss, not just with her mouth, but with her entire body. Anthony's hand was firm against the small of her back, drawing her body close to his in a way that proved he wanted her very much, too much to stop. The pounding of his heart reinforced the message, and the thought of being taken with a quick, savage passion made Kate's blood run hot with excitement.

As they clung and kissed, she permitted him to do as he pleased, moaning his name when he pulled up her blouse to caress her breasts, making no objection when he reached for the button on the waistband of her skirt and slid it through the buttonhole with practiced ease. Moments later the zipper was down and the skirt was on the floor.

Kate didn't want him to stop—not when his hand was so sensuously teasing against the most vulnerable part of her body. She was aware of how little time they would have, but much too aroused to mind. Anthony reached back to unhook her bra and then cupped an exposed breast, toying with the hardened nipple, sending a sharp spasm of desire ripping through Kate's body. The sensation made her weak in the knees and eager to please.

When Anthony started to roll down her slip and panty hose, a hazy mental picture filtered into Kate's mind. She was stripped naked, imprisoned between the edge of the table and Anthony's fully clothed body, used for his pleasure and then dismissed. The image was both exciting and disturbing. Anthony was too skilled a lover to overlook his partner's satisfaction, and Kate knew that he would tease and caress her until her pleasure equaled his own. Then why, she wondered, was a small part of her still holding back?

Her head began to clear as Anthony slid her panty hose down over her hips and began to stroke her thighs. Like some overheated little tramp, she was disregarding a decision that was surely right for her in favor of ten minutes of seedy passion. As sure as she was standing there and allowing it to happen, she would berate herself when it was over.

Torn between desire and self-reproach, it was all Kate could do to remove Anthony's hand before he succeeded in arousing her into mindless cooperation. She twisted her head away from his mouth and buried her face against his shoulder, trying to catch her breath.

Anthony's hand was stilled beneath her own, then slipped away and reached for her chin. "What's the matter, Katie?" His eyes were sober and a little anxious. "Did I rush you? Hurt you?"

She shook her head. "No. It isn't that." She pulled up her panty hose and slip and took a few steps to one side. She could tell that Anthony was releasing her only with the greatest reluctance.

When she reached down for her skirt, he stopped her, pulling her up again and holding her slightly away from him. "Wait a minute. What are you getting dressed for?"

He sounded irritated and Kate couldn't blame him. She never should have let things go so far. "I'm leaving," she said. "I don't want to sleep with you. Please let me go, Anthony."

He did so, looking more baffled than annoyed now. "But why? Last night—I don't understand, Katie."

Kate answered only after her skirt was in place and her bra refastened. She noticed the coolness seeping into Anthony's eyes as she tucked in her blouse but refused to let it sway her. "I don't want a relationship with you," she said. "I told you before, last night just happened and I know I can't change that. I'm sorry, but just because I'm attracted to you, that doesn't mean . . ."

"*Attracted* to me?" he repeated in disbelief. "Whenever the two of us get together, you explode like a damned tinderbox and so do I. You don't know *what* you want. I'm not going to listen to you!" Before Kate could grasp Anthony's intentions, he had picked her up and was stalking to the bed with her. He tossed her on top of the covers before she had the wit to struggle; by the time she bolted up, he was already unbuttoning his shirt.

"Don't you dare treat me like a stupid female who doesn't know her own mind," she sputtered. "I said no and I meant it."

When she tried to get off the bed, he pushed her down with

his hand—not roughly, but very firmly. "I heard you. But I've been thinking about you all day. First you taunt me with that 'Dr. Larimer' stuff and then you respond in a way that drives me half crazy and *now* you want to change your mind. If you think I can keep my hands off you, you've got a lot to learn." He flung off his shirt and started on his belt.

Kate didn't even try to escape. None of this seemed real. She could only stare up at Anthony, almost as appalled by her earlier lack of control as by his incredible display of aggressiveness. One moment she couldn't believe that any man would treat her like this, and the next she felt that she deserved it. Without any warning she burst into tears.

She was immediately furious with herself. Tears were for weaklings and she never used them. She wanted to talk but couldn't seem to stop crying.

Anthony ran his hand through his hair, looking rankled. "Tears. The ultimate female weapon." With a defeated sigh he rebuckled his belt and reached for his shirt. "Beth used to do that too," he said. "I never won a single argument with her."

Kate scrambled off the bed and grabbed her purse before he could change his mind. "I'll get my jacket and go," she mumbled.

"Wait a minute." Anthony's hand closed around her wrist before she'd taken two steps toward the closet. Kate regarded him warily. "Okay, okay, I'm sorry, Katie," he said. "Just don't look at me that way. Go into the bathroom and—I don't know, wash your face or fix your hair, whatever it is you women do when you're on the verge of hysterics."

He managed a rueful smile. "Then come on out and we'll talk. I won't touch you. Believe me, my actions were way out of character. You have a strange effect on me."

Kate nodded and escaped to the bathroom. Her hand was shaking as she brushed out her hair. Never in her life had she had such an experience. Until last night her self-control had been as perfect as her control over the men in her life. She'd rarely even argued with her lovers, but when she did, it was always verbal, and she never lost. No man had ever tried to use physical superiority to bend her to his will.

Anthony hadn't persisted, of course, but it humiliated her to realize that her tears, rather than her logic, had stopped him. She took another thirty seconds to fix her makeup, wondering if he was really that aggressive only with her and not with other women.

He was sitting by the table when she walked out, staring into space. When his eyes focused on her face, he cocked his head at the chair nearby. Kate sat down, feeling unaccountably guilty for refusing him. Anthony looked at her, waiting for her to speak, so she cleared her throat and started to explain.

"I just want you to know that I enjoyed last night—very much. I realize that a part of me wanted the same thing again today." The admission was made partly for the sake of honesty, partly out of an awareness of the fragility of the male ego. "But I know it would never work out, Anthony. In my business you can't combine professional advice with a love affair. The personal relationship would get in the way of objectivity and good judgment, but even more important, my professional reputation would wind up in shreds. As a woman in a mostly male field I'm always on trial. Fooling around with a client is the quickest way to get myself labeled a joke. I won't do it."

Anthony looked skeptical. "Come off it, Katie. This isn't 1950. No one cares who you sleep with these days."

"Maybe not in Berkeley," Kate answered. "But the rest of the world isn't Berkeley. You know as well as I do what happens when a man has an affair with a woman in his office. Everyone says that *he's* just having some fun, but *she's* accused of sleeping her way to the top. If she happens to be the boss, they say that she's a foolish older woman who's being taken for a ride. There are a lot of male chauvinists in politics, and I'm not giving them any ammunition."

"You're making assumptions instead of looking at facts." Anthony leaned forward, both arms on the table. "The fact is that I'm probably going to run for the Senate. We'll be working together closely. We enjoy each other's company and we're so physically attracted to each other that trying to be impersonal would be a form of mutual torture. But nobody has to know about what we do in private."

Anthony was of course talking about a convenient affair, not a relationship with any long-term implications. "Why, Anthony," Kate said sarcastically. "What a charming proposal!"

"Are you looking for a proposal?" he shot back.

"Just because I've never been married, that doesn't mean I've ruled it out. I just haven't found the right person."

"Am I the right person?"

Kate looked into her lap, giving him high marks for his ability to twist the conversation and throw her off balance. Evasions and half-truths weren't her style, and she didn't resort to them now. "The thought of getting involved with you frightens me," she admitted. "I'm not sure why—I feel as though I'd lose my identity somehow. But I won't have a casual affair with you. I don't believe in them, but even if I did, people will find out. Don't tell me they wouldn't—they *always* do."

It was a long time before Anthony answered. Kate sat and watched him, wondering what was going through his head. She envied him his ability to concentrate in such a situation; Jessica would return any time now, and yet he was calmly sitting there and analyzing the alternatives.

"All right," he finally agreed. "I accept your point of view. I'd have to be selfish and unreasonable not to—either that or besotted by love. And I'm not any of those things." Kate didn't know whether to be relieved by his capitulation or disappointed by his bluntness. "It's going to be incredibly tough, though." He gave her a lazy smile. "Even now, I feel like throwing you on the bed. We'll have to avoid bedrooms."

That smile was almost her undoing. "If you're going to try to charm me into sleeping with you . . ."

"I'll be obnoxious and obstreperous." He looked so wounded that Kate almost believed her remark had cut him to the quick. "I'll irritate you so much that making love will be the last thing on your mind. Once the election is over and I'm on my way to Washington, you'll start dreading the next campaign, even though it's six years away." He paused. "Will that solve the problem?" he asked hopefully.

Kate couldn't help but smile. "Save the blarney for the voters," she retorted.

They got up at the same time, Anthony fetching Kate's suit jacket and helping her into it. His hands didn't linger on her shoulders; he stepped back at once. "Come on," he said. "I'll walk you down to the coffee shop."

Bill Dorset was sipping his coffee while Jessica spooned up the last few dollops of her ice cream. Vince, Bill told them, had returned to the capitol for a meeting. He pushed away his cup as Anthony slid into the booth beside his daughter. "Did you get everything settled?" he asked as he stood up.

Kate said yes, but Anthony shook his head. "Let's just say that the meeting was candid and fruitful and that we've negotiated a temporary cease-fire. Final resolution will depend on further developments."

"You're running for the Senate, Anthony, not lobbying for a diplomatic appointment." Bill winked at Jessica and held out his arm for Kate.

Temporary cease-fire? she thought. Final resolution? She looked at Anthony in confusion and decided that he was only teasing her. Then she took Bill's arm and walked out of the restaurant with him.

Chapter 9

THE WASHINGTON *POST* WAS THE FIRST AMERICAN NEWSPAPER
to report the Soviet allegation that Anthony Larimer had
been an intelligence officer while serving with the Peace
Corps in Asia. The article in the *Post* followed the article in
Izvestiya by mere hours. Anthony had known it was coming
because Kevin O'Neal had called the day before with details.
Anthony had agreed that the Agency should issue a formal
statement before he himself commented.

Kevin believed that denying the story would only lose him
hard-won credibility on Capitol Hill. His statement read
simply, "During his four years with the Peace Corps in Asia,
Anthony Larimer was also a highly valued member of the
American intelligence effort. He resigned shortly before
returning to the United States, citing a concern for the safety
of his family. The Agency accepted his resignation with the
greatest regret."

The press immediately laid siege to Anthony's phone and
doorbell. Kevin had no objection to a general description of
the incident that had triggered Anthony's "resignation," but

took the position that any further details about his service in Asia would compromise national security. As for Anthony's role in the Odessa crisis, although it had been unofficial and highly irregular and Anthony could probably say whatever he wished, he played the game as though he were still a member of the team. He talked about the ambush that had nearly cost him his life, but answered every other question with some polite version of "No comment."

Anthony had discussed running for the Senate with his family, then waited for the Peace Corps story to break before going any further. There was no question in his mind that his background would cost him liberal support in the primary, but he hoped to gain conservative support by November. All in all, the furor died down surprisingly quickly. There was a token campus demonstration, but Anthony was gratified to hear that even his more radical former students didn't take part in it. The political climate in the state was apparently such that the great majority of people no longer considered intelligence work anything more than a necessary fact of national security.

Talking to people about their willingness to commit money to his campaign was the most difficult thing Anthony had ever willingly done. The only saving grace was that so many of them anticipated the reason for his call. About a third of the time he'd get no further than "I'm exploring the possibility of running for the Senate," when the person on the other end would answer, "You can count on me to help." It made it a little easier to ask, "How *much* can I count on you for?"

Every night at dinner Jessica and his niece Kristin would smile archly and ask how the day's "begging" had gone. Kris even offered to organize the Berkeley campus; some of her friends, she reminded Anthony, came from very wealthy families. Anthony knew he was a serious candidate when he agreed to let her do it.

"What about Grandma?" Jessica asked at the end of the first week. "Have you talked to her yet?"

"Grandma" was Anthony's mother-in-law, Alice Shipley. Like her late husband, she was an old-line New Englander, wealthy, influential, and conservative. The Shipleys had resisted their only child's decision to attend Stanford University (where she later met Anthony Larimer) and had forcefully opposed their marriage. They had had nothing against Anthony except for the fact that his parents were in the grocery business, happened to be of the wrong religion, and hadn't sent him to prep school. When Anthony and Beth signed up for the Peace Corps and took off for Asia, the Shipleys' temper tantrum had rocked both coasts.

Jessica's birth and Anthony's four years in the State Department had placated them somewhat. They'd disapproved of his decision to become a teacher, but winning the Pulitzer had scored him a few compensatory points. His current relationship with his mother-in-law was politely correct; when Alice Shipley came to visit, she hugged her only grandchild fiercely and then shook her son-in-law's hand.

"No," he answered Jessica, "I haven't. It isn't as though she lives in California, honey."

Jessica gave him one of her exasperated looks, silently reminding him that she knew perfectly well that her father and grandmother weren't the best of friends. "She doesn't have to live in California to send you money," she pointed out.

"Maybe I'll call her," Anthony said, knowing he wouldn't. "But the most she can give is a thousand dollars. According to the Federal Election Campaign Act, that's the maximum amount an individual can contribute to a specific election campaign."

Now Kris chimed in. "That's per election, Jessica. A thousand dollars for the primary and a thousand dollars for the general. But she must have a lot of rich relatives who can give the same. Then there's the whole area of political action committees." She proceeded to explain that a political action committee was a committee set up by a corporation, trade union, or other organization for the purpose of giving money to political parties or campaigns. "It seems to me," she continued airily, "that Mrs. Shipley must know a lot of business people whose companies might contribute the five thousand dollars per election maximum if she twisted their arms."

What did I ever do, Anthony asked himself in pained silence, to deserve a political science major for a niece?

"Is that true?" Jessica asked.

Anthony mumbled that it was. "But let's just drop the subject, okay? Your grandmother is a fine woman and she loves you very much, but I don't think she'd appreciate my asking her for favors."

"Okay." Anthony didn't trust Jessica's quick surrender, but before he could question her, she was rattling on to Kris about some boy she liked who might ask her to the junior prom.

As matters turned out, he should have listened to his instincts. The following evening he received a scolding call from Alice Shipley, saying that she'd talked to Jessica earlier that day and that Anthony was utterly impossible not to have phoned himself. Of course she would help; she was terribly impressed with what she called Anthony's "experiences" and thought he would make a fine senator. She was thrilled that her darling granddaughter would be only eighty minutes away by plane if he won.

Only a stiff-necked idiot would have turned down the promise of a hundred grand, and Anthony wasn't an idiot. He stayed annoyed with Jessica for approximately fifteen minutes and then hugged her. The next morning, a Friday, he called Bill Dorset in Los Angeles and arranged a meeting for Monday.

Anthony had been much too busy lately to dwell on Kate Garvey, but the prospect of seeing her again kept her on his mind all weekend. He remembered how good it had felt to subdue her struggles, to direct her sensuous movements, to feel her teasing caresses and lose himself in her firm, soft body. She gave herself with such passion that the memory of it made him ache, and he knew that, once he saw her again, the ache would grow still hotter. He already regretted his

promise to keep their relationship on a professional basis and
doubted he'd be able to keep it.

The first thing Kate noticed when Anthony Larimer walked
into Bill's office was that he'd gotten a haircut. The second
thing was that seeing him again was hitting her with all the
force of a hundred-pound bag of cement dropped from a
two-story crane. Two and a half weeks of ten-to-twelve-hour
days had left her with little time or energy to think about him,
but her body didn't have to think; it merely reacted.

"I feel like a cross between a prostitute and a used-car
salesman," Anthony began, sounding unusually subdued.
Kate could hardly blame him; two and a half weeks of fending
off the press and hustling for money would have taken the
sparkle out of Pollyanna. Even seasoned politicians loathed
fund raising. Since there was no limit to the amount a
candidate could spend on himself, an independently wealthy
man like Bob Woodruff had a great advantage. Anthony,
unfortunately, was in no position to finance his own campaign.

He ran down a list of the people he'd spoken to: family,
friends, colleagues, corporate contacts. "Taken all together, I
might be able to come up with $75,000. My mother-in-law—
her husband was one of the Massachusetts Shipleys—is
willing to help, and she could probably raise in the neighbor-
hood of $200,000. But with statewide campaigns costing $5
million or even more, $275,000 doesn't seem like very much."

"It's a reasonable start," Bill reassured him. "Raising
money is part of what you pay us for. Two years ago, Kate put
together a rock concert for George McClure that raised over
$100,000. An effective direct-mail campaign can net hundreds
of thousands of dollars, too, particularly when the candidate
has nationwide name recognition. No candidate in his right
mind ever stops worrying about money, Anthony, but I'm
less worried about you than about a lot of other people.
Frankly, your unsavory past"—Bill smiled at him—"is going
to help in that area by pulling in some conservative support."

Sandy Cohen unfolded the newspaper he was holding and

tossed it onto the coffee table, back page upward. "Have all of you seen this morning's California Poll?" he asked. The California Poll, an independent survey of voter preferences and public opinion, was known for its accuracy. "Anthony hasn't even announced yet, but he's running first with thirty-four percent of the vote. Handlin gets seventeen percent. We've got another twenty-four percent spread among four possible candidates, and the rest undecided. Once Handlin is out of the race . . ."

"Is he dropping out?" Anthony asked.

"George is going to appoint him director of the Commission on Foreign Trade," Bill explained. "He knows he can't beat Woodruff, so he's looking for something else to do. Sandy?"

"I was going to say that most of Handlin's support will probably go to Anthony. I'm not worried about the primary. Nobody with a statewide reputation wants to run against Bob. They're waiting another two years on the theory that Allen Marks might surprise all of us and retire, the way he keeps threatening to." He turned his attention to Anthony. "What you need to do before the primary is build solid support among Democratic voters. Establish the kind of momentum that will carry through to November. Thirty-four percent of the people polled say they would vote for you if the election were held today, but they don't know much about you and could easily change their minds. As soon as we sign a contract, I'd like to go ahead and do a fairly lengthy poll, perhaps forty to fifty questions, two thousand respondents interviewed house to house. I want a solid reading of the state's mood and detailed information on what people want out of a senator—and what they think they'll get out of *you*. That kind of survey is expensive—between $50,000 and $100,000—but when we're dealing with a candidate who's basically an unknown quantity, I don't think we can design an effective campaign without it."

Anthony remarked that although the price tag seemed high he would consider it, and then asked Bill Dorset to explain the company's fee structure. In addition to a $50,000 consulting fee and reimbursement for all incurred expenses, Bill told him, the company charged a fifteen-percent commission on any work or commodity purchased for the campaign through the company: media production work, television time, printing, computer work, and so on. The total amount typically comprised about twenty to twenty-five percent of the campaign budget, with most of the rest of the money going to purchase television time.

"I know that sounds like a lot of money," Bill added, "but the fact that *we're* doing your campaign is going to bring in enough contributions to cover our initial fee. We'll make sure that every dollar you spend is spent effectively—that your media spots and direct mail reach the right audience, for example. All of us in this room do political campaigns because we love them, Anthony. My company makes much more money from its private clients. Believe me, we'll work our tails off for you if you give us that opportunity."

"I'm impressed." To Kate, Anthony sounded almost the opposite. "Maybe I should forget foreign policy, forget the Senate, and do a book on you and your colleagues." He softened the ironic statement with a half smile.

Kate caught Sandy's black look out of the corner of her eye. She could see that he was revving up for a lecture on how a candidate's commitment and enthusiasm, or lack of same, could win or lose an election. "If you have some time, I think we should talk a little," she quickly suggested to Anthony. "I'd like to find out—"

"The question," Sandy interrupted firmly, "is whether the man wants to run for the Senate at all."

Anthony stared at Sandy, clearly aggravated with him. "I think I have a real contribution to make, particularly in the area of foreign policy. My problem is the things I have to do to get elected. All that money . . ." He shook his head, suddenly a bit deflated. "There's something almost obscene about spending millions of dollars just to select one rather ordinary man or woman to represent this state in Washington."

More academic agonizing, Kate thought wearily. In her

eight years with Bill she'd heard candidates moan and groan about everything under the sun, which explained why Bill had become such an expert in soothing away their complaints.

"You're a political scientist, Anthony," he said now, "so I'm sure I don't have to lecture you on the political facts of life. I've been in this business for almost fourteen years, and every year the trend is more pronounced. Voters don't want to come out to rallies and candidates' nights. They want the information to come to *them*—through TV and radio advertising and interviews, newspaper stories, direct mail, whatever. In a state as large and populous as California, that costs a bundle. Unfortunately."

"Yes." Anthony stood up, looking at Kate. "Are we going to use your office?"

"It's right down the hall." She hesitated, then asked, "You *are* going to run?"

"All the way to November," he answered. Kate got up and smoothed her skirt, waiting as Anthony shook hands with Bill and Sandy, saying he would see them before he left. His hand dropped to the back of Kate's waist as they walked out of the room together, but the gesture was courteous, not romantic. Even so, his closeness induced a sensual current that flowed through every nerve of Kate's body.

Her office had a round oak table at the far end, with brocade-covered armchairs all around. She'd come across the table in an antique shop and bought the chairs at a specialty store. She'd also selected her own carpeting, bookshelves, desk, and chair. The fancy office had come along with her position as one of Bill Dorset's top aides.

Anthony declined a second cup of coffee and sat down across from Kate. "I wouldn't have expected this type of office from you," he said. "You seem streamlined and modern. Steel and glass and a futuristic desk."

"Don't forget that I'm from the East." Kate ran her fingers over the top of the golden oak table. "This is a twentieth-century piece. Compared to the furniture I grew up with, it *is* modern."

"I think you just dodged my observation."

"I'm the one who's supposed to ask the questions," Kate reminded him. "Let's start with your family. Tell me about your parents."

She wasn't discouraged by the wariness in Anthony's eyes. She'd come across her share of taciturn candidates, but they always wound up telling her the stories of their lives. When she suggested to Anthony that he loosen his tie and take off his jacket, he unbuttoned the latter and left the former alone. Kate kicked off her shoes and tucked a leg up underneath her; then she rested both arms on the table and leaned toward him. "It would really help if we knew a little more about you," she coaxed gently. "It's a conversation, Anthony, not an inquisition. You don't need to feel uncomfortable about it."

His eyes made a quick survey of her face. "Don't go all feminine and soft on me, Katie, because if you do, I'm going to lock the door and find out if the carpet is as soft to lie on as it is to walk on."

Her face heating up, Kate straightened and put her shoes back on. "I was trying to be empathetic, not seductive. Why don't you make this easy instead of difficult?"

"Right." He reached into his pocket and ultimately fished out a paper clip, twisting and bending it as he spoke. "My parents own a chain of four grocery stores in Southern California. My father, Howard, is a second-generation Californian who's always been politically active. My mother, Theresa, is the daughter of Italian immigrants who came to California when she was a child and opened the original grocery store in the chain. I have one brother, Douglas, who's forty-two. He designs computer components for a company in Palo Alto. My sister-in-law, Anne, is a math teacher. I have a nephew, Adam, who's a high school senior, and a niece, Kristin, who's a junior at Berkeley and lives with me and Jessica. I had a happy, normal childhood, graduated second in my high school class behind Mary Claire Jenkins, and played varsity soccer and baseball. I also played tennis and swam. Is that good enough?"

Kate smiled. "What positions?"

"Forward and shortstop. My best stroke was butterfly and my backhand is stronger than my forehand."

Anthony wasn't exactly loquacious, but at least he was talking. "What was your college major?" Kate asked.

"History."

"Why?"

"I found it interesting."

Kate took her time about asking the next question. Sometimes an awkward silence could loosen up someone's tongue. She should have known that the tactic would fail with Anthony Larimer. She watched him continue to mangle the paper clip, feeling rather sorry for him. He was hating every minute of this.

"How did you happen to go to work for the CIA?" she asked.

"I was recruited out of college." He tossed the paper clip onto the table. "Look, Katie, I'm not going to analyze my motives for you. I wanted to serve my country. I was idealistic and a little too romantic at twenty-two."

"And the State Department?"

Anthony didn't even hesitate. "It was a way to put my expertise to use, but the job wasn't so demanding that I didn't have time to study for my doctorate."

Kate knew that was all she would get out of him on the topic. She decided to spend a Saturday or two going through copies of the Los Angeles *Times* that dated to the years when Anthony was at the Department. Maybe she would hit on something.

She continued with her questions, aware that she was about to tread on very sensitive territory. "Tell me about Beth," she suggested softly.

Her pulse rate sped up at the way he straightened his body and stared at her, his expression somewhere between annoyed and furious. "That's none of your business," he snapped.

Kate paid no attention to him, at least outwardly. Inwardly, she could cheerfully have dived under the table. She seemed to have a rare talent for antagonizing this man, both in the line of duty and under more personal circumstances. "When I first saw Jessica," she said, "I thought to myself that if she looked anything like Beth, Beth must have been very beautiful."

"She was. Beautiful and gentle and generous."

Something in his tone prompted her to ask, "Unlike the women you've met since then?"

"You could say that."

Kate ran nervous fingers under her bangs, pushing them to one side. Her forehead was slightly damp. "Beth's illness must have been very difficult for you," she said, wishing she didn't have to go on. "No one would blame you if . . ." She hesitated, searching for a tactful turn of phrase where none existed. "If you looked for comfort or temporary escape . . ."

"You really have a hell of a nerve!" Kate almost jumped out of her seat at the curt explosiveness of his tone. His features were taut, angry. She had a sudden impulse to stretch out a hand, to caress away that look, but of course she didn't.

"I'm sorry to have to ask," she said, "but if there's anything—messy—about your personal life, it's better if you tell us about it now, rather than leave us to find out when someone opens his mouth—or *her* mouth—to the press."

"So if I'd slept with half the Berkeley faculty while Beth was sick, you'd quietly spread the word about how much tension I was under in case it came out. Is that it?" He was glaring at her, waiting for her answer.

"Something like that," she agreed.

After a nerve-wracking silence he finally sighed and agreed. "Okay. I suppose you've got to do your job." He picked up the paper clip again, staring at the table. "I met Beth when I was eighteen and dated and married her over her family's objections—my background wasn't patrician enough for them. Until ten months after her death there was never anyone else." His tone was husky and a little pained now. "We lived on two levels those last few years. On one level, life went on the way it always had, and on the other we were trying to prepare ourselves for what we hoped wouldn't happen. I could never admit to myself that it really *would* happen until the last few months, and by then she was in so much pain . . ."

His voice trailed off. Kate silently finished the sentence: She was in so much pain that I began to hope it would end for her. She couldn't imagine how it would feel, to love someone as much as he'd loved Beth and then lose her.

When he began to speak again, a poignant smile was playing over his face. "I was thirty-six years old and felt like a teen-ager. Beth was the only woman I'd had any kind of relationship with . . . any intimate relationship. But it didn't take me very long to figure out that things had changed in eighteen years. Within a month women were asking me to dinner, parties, lectures, concerts. I don't dislike it, but I've never gotten used to it. Most of them are willing to jump into bed on an evening's acquaintance, and I've never gotten used to *that* either. I like to get to know a woman first. You and Bill don't have to worry about my personal life, Katie. My friends tell me I'm almost straitlaced."

Kate's primary reaction to this speech was astonishment. The picture Anthony was painting bore absolutely no resemblance to her own experience of him.

Perhaps he saw the confusion in her eyes, because his smile broadened as he admitted, "You've been the only exception, Katie. Part of it was the way you treated me—like a stubborn, naive child who had to be humored or soothed. I don't like being pushed around, and seducing a woman is a time-honored way of gaining the initiative." His voice dropped to a husky growl as his eyes flickered to Kate's breasts. "But it's more than that. The way I felt when we made love—I didn't know that could happen anymore. I haven't been able to think of anything else since I got off the plane. I could spend the night in Los Angeles if you want me to."

Kate looked away, flushing. As much as she ached to have Anthony stay with her, she'd made the right decision and she intended to stick to it. "You were supposed to be obnoxious," she said. "Remember?"

"It goes against my natural instincts," he teased. "I could be charming, which works fairly well, or I could steamroll your objections, which works even better. It's exciting when you resist and twice as exciting when you give in. A man could get addicted to it."

The desire in Anthony's voice was turning Kate's backbone to jelly. She wanted to protest that he wasn't playing fair, but couldn't really fault him for asking. It wasn't as though he was touching her. Annoyed by her inability to dismiss him from her mind as easily as she'd dismissed every other man, she jumped up and walked to the window. Anthony sat and watched her, not so much hungrily as thoughtfully.

"Why don't you let someone else handle my campaign?" he suggested.

Kate didn't even have to think before refusing. "California politics is my primary interest. Bill is already committed to two campaigns—a governorship in Washington and a Senate race in Montana. We've accepted one other job—a congressional campaign in Northern California that I'll be in charge of, but that will be all. I'm the best person at Dorset to work with you, and we couldn't in good conscience send you to a competitor who can't do the kind of job for you that we will. Let's leave things where they were a few weeks ago, Anthony."

When he stood up and walked to the center of the room, Kate tensed. But all he did was glance at his watch and ask, "Why don't you take me to lunch?"

Kate quickly agreed, telling herself that being in a public restaurant would lessen the intimacy between them. As she crossed to the closet to fetch her coat, Anthony caught her wrist and turned her into his arms. For just a moment Kate couldn't hide the desire in her eyes, but she quickly pulled away. Seconds later he was at her side, helping her into the coat. She could feel the warmth of his breath ruffling her hair, and when he gave a sharp nip to her earlobe, a mimicking stab of arousal pierced her intimately.

"You're totally unscrupulous," she murmured.

"It must be my early training." He ran his hands up her

arms to her shoulders, gently coaxing her to turn around. When she resisted, he abruptly intensified the pressure, catching her off guard. She lost her balance and tumbled into his arms.

The next moment an insistent hand was twined through her hair, pulling her face up to his. Kate was torn by conflicting emotions as she gazed into his eyes. When a man who set your blood on fire silently announced that he wanted you, every feminine instinct cried out for surrender. At the same time, she'd spent her entire life in a world where logic overruled emotion. "We were on our way to lunch," she reminded him.

He mumbled something about having the first course in her office and captured her mouth. Kate's common sense started to switch off the moment his lips parted her own. As his tongue searched her mouth, her fists drifted up to his shoulders, at first lightly pushing, then clenching, and finally clutching at the fabric of his suit. He took her face between his hands and kissed her with a burning passion she was hard pressed to resist, but before anything else could happen, he was pulling away, still holding her face, but putting a few inches between their bodies. Kate's arms dropped to her sides.

"You can't have it both ways," he announced gently. "If you weren't attracted to me, it would be different—I would leave you alone. But you send me messages with your body and your eyes that I'd have to be a saint to ignore. You have to accept the fact that if we work together, we're going to become lovers, Katie."

Kate couldn't deny the truth of his complaint. She reached up and grasped his wrists, pulling his hands away from her face. "Then we'll meet in public places," she insisted stubbornly. "I'm not going to jeopardize my professional reputation for the sake of a temporary affair." The very word *affair* brought her the rest of the way back to reality. "And that's all it would be, wouldn't it? An affair."

Anthony smiled at her. "Haven't we had this conversation before?"

"Not exactly." Kate took a few steps backward. "We were

talking about *me* that day, not you. I was honest with you about *my* feelings, but you didn't say a word about yours. I heard the way you sounded when you talked about Beth. I'm nothing like her, am I? And that's what you're looking for, someone like Beth."

Kate had never seen a man sober so quickly. One moment he looked wickedly teasing, the next cool and withdrawn. "That's right," he said, "but I didn't know anyone cared about commitment or giving these days. I've learned to settle for what's available."

"And you think that's fair to *me?*" Kate asked.

"Maybe not," Anthony admitted. He opened the door and walked out, and Kate followed. She didn't care for the notion that a man would merely "settle" for her, but maybe *that* wasn't entirely fair. After all, she couldn't pretend that she was ready for the kind of give and take required for a successful marriage between two professionals. Unlike Saint Beth, she was accustomed to suiting her own convenience.

There was a gem of an Italian restaurant on the next block, and since Anthony's mother was Italian, Kate decided to take him there. The street was crowded with office workers on their lunch hours who glanced up at the sky every now and then and hoped that the rain would hold off until they reached their destinations. People were waiting in line for tables at the restaurant, but the owner motioned Kate over immediately and whisked a "Reserved" sign away from a booth. The reason for this special treatment was simple: Two years ago Dorset and Associates had managed a successful local campaign for the owner's son. Prompt service was their reward for taking on such a minor job.

After they had ordered, Anthony crossed his arms on the table and leaned forward a little, watching Kate drink her wine. The only words the two had exchanged since leaving the office had concerned the merits of various menu items. "I've told you something about myself, but I know almost nothing about *you,*" he said. "How did you wind up working for Bill?"

When Kate was asked that question by a client, she usually

offered only a brief explanation. Her job was to ask the questions, not answer them. She was far more open with Anthony, and not just because she wanted to gain his trust. She couldn't very well say, "I'm a nice person, Anthony, even though I'm different from Beth," so she did the next best thing. She tried to explain herself.

"It never occurred to me that I *wouldn't* wind up in politics," she began. "From the time we moved to Washington, I lived in a house that was filled with important people talking about important issues. I just always gravitated to my father's company, and that meant that I spent a lot of time with those same people. My mother isn't the maternal type—I think she had a child mostly because Dad wanted one. I've always gone to *him* with my problems, even when I lived in Connecticut and had to wait for him to come home. By the time I was fourteen or so I'd started to take part in the discussions instead of just listening. My father encouraged it, and if someone new to his circle made a comment about Katie belonging with the women, he'd give the man a look that made him want to slink right out the door."

When the waitress arrived with the antipasto, Kate took her time about filling her plate, using the food as a cover to organize her thoughts. "Go on," Anthony prompted.

She looked across at him, wishing he would turn his attention to his food. His gaze, which combined sensual awareness with a demand for honesty, made her uncomfortable. "I can't remember a time when I *wasn't* involved in a political campaign," she said. "In the beginning it was only stuffing envelopes or making photocopies, but by the time Dad ran for reelection to the Senate, I had major responsibilities. I started at Radcliffe a semester late so I could work on the campaign. I was only eighteen, but I handled the scheduling for all his appearances, traveled around the state with him to make sure everything went smoothly, and even talked to the press at times. More often than not I stood in for my mother at the kinds of meetings where wives usually showed up. My mother enjoys being a senator's wife and she plays the role very well when my father asks her to charm money out of contributors' pockets or arrange fancy dinner parties, but she doesn't enjoy politics at all. Election campaigns bore her. The ins and outs of getting a piece of legislation through Congress bore her. Her whole identity is tied up in being Mrs. Hank Garvey, in sitting on charity committees or going around with New York big shots or helping Dad with the kinds of things I mentioned."

"Your parents' marriage doesn't impress you very much, does it?" Anthony said.

Kate supposed that was obvious. "I guess they're happy enough," she said. "I've heard people say that Dad is too involved in public service to be a good husband, but it didn't stop him from being a good father. The things I told Jessica are true, Anthony. At sixteen I was almost on my own, at least as far as maternal guidance went. Sometimes I wonder if Dad wouldn't have been happier with a woman who took an interest in his career—in what he was trying to accomplish, not in the trappings that go along with power. But it doesn't seem to bother either him or my mother." She hesitated, then admitted softly, "From the time I was in my teens I knew I couldn't live the way she does—taking my identity from my husband or father. I'm not saying that she doesn't contribute a lot to the community, because she does. But if she weren't Mrs. Hank Garvey and the daughter of Clayton White, they wouldn't ask her to chair a different charity every year. It even bothers me that people are always introducing me as Hank Garvey's daughter, but it also opens a lot of doors, so I'd have to be a hypocrite to complain."

Anthony studied the antipasto and speared a piece of cheese, but not before Kate noticed a flicker of disapproval cross his face. Beth Larimer, she decided, must have been the kind of woman who was *thrilled* to take her identity from her husband.

After disposing of a piece of salami and some olives, Anthony asked Kate what she had done after finishing college. "I worked as an aide to Senator Andersen of Massachusetts," she answered. "When he ran for reelection two years later, I was the assistant campaign manager. I realized that I enjoyed the campaign much more than the routine office work I'd been doing in Washington—handling constituents' problems, answering mail, that kind of thing. Bill Dorset was making quite a name for himself out here, and I heard through the grapevine that he was looking for good people. So here I am."

"And every campaign is as exciting as the last?"

"Every campaign is different. If you're asking whether I ever get tired of it all, the answer is yes." Kate had never before been so honest with a client; each of them wanted to think that his own campaign was uniquely interesting. "A Senate campaign in my home state between two strong candidates will be *very* exciting and challenging. An election in, say, a less populous western state is less fun, but I like to think I work just as hard. Like everything else, a lot of the time it's just a job, but I can't think of anything else I'd rather be doing."

Anthony set his empty plate to one side and picked up his wineglass. Kate tried to interpret his thoughtful expression, finally asking, "Are you still having doubts?"

He looked at her, puzzled. "What makes you think that?"

"You look pensive, almost brooding."

He shook his head. "No, it's not that. I'm comfortable with my decision. Actually, I was wondering about you. Why haven't you ever married? Because of your parents' marriage?"

It wasn't a question that Kate could easily answer. "Maybe. I don't know. I dated an actor for three years, but I just couldn't see myself spending the rest of my life with him." Kate hesitated, a smile tugging at her lips. "To be honest, Anthony, Dad hated him. He said Jeremy was an intellectual lightweight, but he wasn't, really. He just lived in a different world, a world I enjoyed for quite a while as a kind of escape but eventually got tired of. Maybe the truth is that I like what I'm doing and I've never met anyone worth compromising for." Surprising herself a little, she admitted, "I've been told I don't give men a chance. As soon as they get too close, I start backing up."

The statement seemed to delight him. "Ah, now we're getting closer to the truth," he announced with a smile. "All that business about your professional reputation was rationalization. You once told me that you felt threatened by the idea of getting involved with me, but it isn't just *me*. It's anyone. Should I be more persistent?"

A slow flush crept up Kate's neck. "I don't believe we've ever talked about *involvement*, Anthony. We've already established that I'm not a fit replacement for Beth. I'd appreciate it if you'd drop the subject and deal with me on a professional basis."

"It *is* getting repetitious," he drawled. He could probably tell that Kate was itching to throw down her napkin and stalk away. "Okay." He held up a hand in surrender. "I'll just have to tell myself that sooner or later you'll come to your senses and admit that you can't keep your hands off me."

If Kate had taken him seriously, she would have spilled her wine in his lap. She chose to believe that he simply enjoyed needling her. "Why don't we talk about your campaign organization?" she suggested.

For the rest of lunch that was precisely what they did.

Chapter 10

TEN DAYS LATER ANTHONY LARIMER OFFICIALLY ANNOUNCED what had been rumored for over a month and widely known for the past week: He was a candidate for the Democratic nomination for United States senator from California. The incumbent senator, Jack Handlin, had dropped out of the race a few days before. When he left office at the end of the year, the governor would promptly reward him for his cooperation with the directorship of the Commission on Foreign Trade. The only other serious opponent, a state senator from San Diego, had also pulled out of the contest. *His* reward would be a larger suite of offices and an important committee chairmanship when the newly elected legislature convened the following January.

Statewide officials seldom endorsed candidates in contested primary elections, but Anthony Larimer was able to point to statements of support from half a dozen prominent party leaders. Veteran political reporters watched this show of party unity in amusement, aware that the infighting would resume in its own good time. When a party smelled defeat, its leaders had more incentive to cooperate. Nobody gave the Democrats much of a chance of winning the presidency. Eli Hendrickson was much too popular. And with Hendrickson and his surrogates running around the country, exhorting the country to vote in a Republican Congress, the election was looking more and more like a sweep.

Over the years, announcing one's candidacy for statewide office in California had evolved into an air-age ritual. The idea was to hit as many major cities as possible in a single day. Anthony, flanked by his parents and his daughter, delivered the day's first speech at seven-thirty A.M. at a breakfast for San Diego business leaders. Kate Garvey and Vince Collier sat at one of the tables, taking notes, something they would continue to do for the rest of the day.

Afterward, Anthony and his entourage boarded a chartered plane to Fresno, the largest city in California's agricultural heartland. Anthony was introduced to a waiting lunchtime crowd by his uncle, a local farmer. The third stop, in late afternoon, was a San Francisco hotel where a party hosted by Douglas and Anne Larimer was already in full swing. By the time they hit Los Angeles for an evening rally, everyone was mildly slaphappy, including the reporters who were covering this grand-slam extravaganza.

That such a day could be arranged at all on such short notice was a tribute to both Vince Collier and Kate Garvey. In Fresno, Vince admitted to Kate that he felt as though his ear were still glued to the phone. He'd started calling key people from George McClure's gubernatorial campaigns just after talking to Anthony in Sacramento. By the time Anthony actually decided to run, most of the old McClure network was already in place. People didn't just show up at breakfasts and lunches and fund raisers; they had to be asked and begged and dragged there. In rustling up the bodies, Kate had found that Anthony Larimer was enough of a celebrity that people were curious to get a closer look at him. The television news made it seem as though he'd played to packed houses all over the state, and that was what mattered.

Both Anthony and Vince were spending the night as guests

of Emily and Bill Dorset. At a little past midnight the three men were joined by Kate for an evaluation session in the den.

As everyone trooped into the room that had been the site of so many strategy sessions in the past, Bill remarked to Anthony, "You certainly have your family behind you. I heard a reporter talking about the Larimer Mafia."

In fact, Anthony's father, Howard, was the campaign coordinator for the San Diego area, and his sister-in-law, Anne, was the finance chairman. His mother's brother, Giulio Cellini, the Fresno farmer, was chairing a local campaign committee, and his niece, Kristin, had decided to take time off from school to work on getting the college vote. During the course of the day Kate had made it a point to talk to the various members of Anthony's family, finding that they seemed to know what they were doing, which wasn't always true of volunteers.

Vince dropped himself into his favorite chair and took out a cigar. "It's when the bunch of you start chattering away in Italian that I have a problem," he said. "Maybe I should get myself a translator."

"You and my father." Anthony followed Kate over to the bar and helped himself to some brandy, then walked over to the couch with her. "My mother also has a brother and two sisters in the East. When the family gets together, my father hides out near the TV. My mother spoke Italian to me and my brother when we were kids—she wanted us to learn it—but my father never picked it up."

Bill Dorset removed his jacket and loosened his tie, sitting down in his usual armchair and stretching his legs out in front of him. When Bill became this casual, things were serious indeed. He looked first at Vince, then at Kate. "So how did it go today?"

Bill had only joined their party in Los Angeles and thus had missed the first three speeches. "I have some suggestions for improvements we can make," Kate said. She'd seen Anthony twice during the past ten days, always in the company of other people. He'd been working very hard but hadn't looked this tired. Of course, seventeen hours of speech making and handshaking and smiling would take its toll on anyone.

Her comment about "improvements" caused him to tense up. Kate found herself wanting to massage the back of his neck, to soothe away the fatigue. "You did fine," she added quietly. "This isn't the time to go into . . ."

He frowned at her. "No, go ahead."

She reached for her purse, taking out a small notebook filled with fragmented impressions hastily scribbled down. She didn't really need to look through the pages, but did so anyway. "Good points first," she said. "You spoke a lot about what you feel you can contribute, primarily in the area of foreign policy. You're an expert and you sound like one. You gave a lot of details, and people were impressed. But I think you should give more attention to domestic issues—that's what hits people in the pocketbook. And never lose sight of the fact that people want to be inspired. They want a vision of the future laid out for them."

Kate was always honest with her clients, but that didn't rule out tact. She waited for the right moment and chose her words carefully. What she'd momentarily forgotten was Vince Collier's propensity for dispensing with the niceties when he deemed it necessary. "Katie is trying to tell you that you blew it," he said bluntly. He took a puff on his cigar, more for dramatic effect than anything else, and Kate felt like taking the blasted thing and shoving it down his throat. Anthony sipped his brandy, his eyes moving from Vince to Kate and back to Vince again.

"You're a magnetic guy," Vince continued. "Every group you spoke to was ready to love you. Even the people who were dragged there by their friends wanted to respond. And you stood up there and lectured them like some damn professor. Sure, you impressed them, but you didn't win their hearts. They wanted to clap and cheer, but all you got out of them was respectful applause. That's enough to win you the primary, but you'll never beat Bob Woodruff with it."

"If you were looking for a demagogue, you should have gotten yourself a different candidate." Anthony's apparent calmness was belied by the tightness of his tone. "I'm not going to stand up there and mouth a lot of buzzwords that mean nothing just for the sake of turning on a crowd. I thought I'd made that clear in Sacramento."

"Did I say anything about buzzwords?" Vince's incredulous tone suggested that he should have known better than to become involved with a professor. "You have to appeal to people's emotions as well as their brains. For the hero of Odessa, that should be a piece of cake, but—"

"Don't lecture me, Vince," Anthony interrupted. He set his brandy snifter on the table so gently that Kate was sure he longed to do the exact opposite. "I'm a political scientist. I know about winning elections. But I played by someone else's rules for too many years of my life to keep doing it now. For four years I put national security over every other consideration, and it isn't always easy to live with memories of men who considered themselves patriots dying because I—" He cut himself off abruptly, sighing irritably. "I'm tired and I'm saying too much. All you have to know is that some of the things that are done in the name of necessity turn my stomach."

Kate could see that the conversation was accomplishing nothing. The candidate was touchy and tired and miles from being receptive to criticism. As far as she could see, CIA stealth had nothing to do with running for the Senate. She glanced at Bill, the expert in smoothing over such situations, but his attention was on the Scotch in his glass, which he was twirling rather absentmindedly. She had to prompt him by softly calling his name.

He finished off the drink and cradled the empty glass in both hands. "I was just thinking," he said to Anthony, "that it's hard for me to work with someone I don't understand. You can tell us almost nothing about your experiences in Asia, but obviously they affected you deeply. You don't like manipulation and deception, and you want to run a clean, honest campaign. We're with you, Anthony, but you're going to have to help us out by bending a little. I hope we can manage to find a common ground."

The final sentence was tacked on for Vince's benefit, a not-so-subtle reminder that they were dealing with a man who was both intelligent and strong willed. He could be led but not pushed.

"We made tapes of your speeches today." Vince took a final puff on his cigar and stubbed it out. "Will you sit down with us and watch them? You have a speech tomorrow afternoon at the businessmen's roundtable, but your morning is free."

When Anthony silently agreed, Kate placed a gentle hand on his arm. Her gesture was meant only to reassure and encourage, but one look at Anthony told her he'd misinterpreted it.

She hastily removed her hand, saying, "It isn't that you were *bad* today, Anthony. It's that we know you have the potential to be electrifying. I remember the way the audience reacted when you told off that reporter at your Washington news conference after the Odessa crisis. We were on the edge of our seats. You were angry then, but if you could put the same emotion into inspiring people, you could have the voters eating out of your hands." Before he could make the obvious objection, she quickly added, "I'm not suggesting all style and no substance. Just . . . a reasonable compromise."

Bill Dorset spoke for everyone when he said it was time to go to sleep. Kate knew she would never make it to the office on time tomorrow. "I'll see you all in the morning," she said.

"I've got to catch an early flight to Sacramento," Vince told her. "I checked in with George at dinner, and he has a few items that can't wait. It's going to take a few more weeks to wind things up before I can join the campaign full-time."

Kate got up, opening her purse and taking out several books of raffle tickets. A little cheerful begging might lighten everyone's mood. "In that case, you can write me a check for twenty-five dollars," she said with a cheeky grin. "That's six tickets, Vince."

Vince pulled out his checkbook, looking resigned. "Let's see. This is March, so it must be Pacific Children's Hospital."

"Just be grateful you don't live in LA," Bill drawled. "She hit me up for two sponsor's tickets at a hundred bucks a throw, and the worst part of it is that Emily insists on going." His expression turned reproachful as he complained to Kate, "She'll sit in that fashion show tomorrow night, and I guarantee you, she'll fall in love with the three most expensive outfits. You have any idea how much this is going to cost me?"

"Deduct it from my salary," Kate teased. She was about to slip the raffle books back into her purse when Anthony snatched one out of her hand. "You're raffling off designer dresses?" he asked, reading a ticket. "What's this all about?"

"One of Kate's charities," Bill explained. "She helps them with their major fund raiser every year. This year she lined up what Emily claims are five of the top West Coast designers to put on a fashion show while the rest of us choke on rubber chicken."

"It's sliced filet of beef and it's going to be delicious," Kate retorted, then explained to Anthony, "If you win something you don't want, you can take a credit toward something else instead. Some of the designers do sportswear that even Jessica could wear. Five dollars each or six for twenty-five dollars, and it's tax deductible." When Anthony hesitated, she added, "It's a very good cause. The people at Pacific Children's do wonderful work. They saved the life of my goddaughter when she was hit by a car. That's how I got involved." She took Vince's check and handed him the stubs to fill out.

"After the surgery Kate came bursting into my office with some nonsense about spending a morning a week with the patients," Bill told Anthony. "I pointed out to her that even if she could spare the time, which she can't, she would do a lot more good for the hospital if she raised some money for them. I never would have opened my mouth if I'd known what it would cost me."

Kate smiled at Anthony. "How about it? Buy the book of tickets and you can come to dinner on the house. I buy a table every year and I still have an empty seat or two. We're supported by some very fat cats. You can do some campaigning."

"I'll have to think about the dinner. It would mean changing my plane reservations." He wrote out a check, muttering that he was half terrified by now of Kate's persistence.

"I'll walk you to the car," he said as he exchanged the check for a book of tickets.

His hands lingered a moment as he helped Kate on with her coat, but there was nothing romantic about the question he asked her as they walked outside. "Bill said the hospital was *one* of your charities. What are the others?"

It was still quite warm out, about 65°. All of the outside lights were off, and the night felt close and dark despite the clouded half-moon. Kate had left her car in front of the garage, which opened off the far side of the house. She knew that Anthony was going to make a pass at her once they reached it; she just wasn't sure how she would respond.

"There's only one other," she told him as they made their way down the flagstone walk that crossed the wide front lawn. "It's called the Women's Legal Foundation. They have nine attorneys, three of them men, and represent women who can't afford a lawyer to fight cases that have to do with sexual harassment on the job, kidnapping of a child by a noncustodial parent, mental or physical abuse by a lover or husband, and other issues that most people call 'feminist' but I call human. Their major fund raiser is in early September, and since I'm always busiest in the two months before an election, it works out very well. Most of my work on the fund raisers is finished by mid-February and mid-August."

They were about six feet from the car when Anthony put his arm around Kate's shoulders. She had the same reaction that she always did: She felt as though the outside temperature had risen a good ten degrees. "I had you pegged as a hard-boiled career type with a vulnerable streak you wanted to eliminate," he said. "All day long I've been watching you watch *me* and I decided I was right. When you weren't writing in that damn notebook of yours or whispering to Vince, you were looking at me like my third-grade teacher used to. She was the one who always rapped me across the knuckles when I did something wrong."

They had reached the car and were facing the door on the driver's side. Kate was beginning to wish that Bill Dorset's expensive Beverly Hills property was a little less extensive and secluded. With its generous lawns and tall trees to screen out the neighbors, it made her forget that she was in the middle of a major city. "Maybe I should have warned you how serious I am when I work," she said. "I know I should smile and look encouraging, but half the time I forget."

When she reached for the door handle, Anthony turned her around, trapping her between her car and his body. A single step forward by either of them and their bodies would touch. "You were forgiven the moment you glared at Vince tonight," he said. "You've been so cool the last few times we've met that I figured the physical thing was over for you, but now I realize that you care about me as something more than just a candidate. I like that, Katie."

The statement caught Kate off guard. "I just thought it was the wrong time . . ." she began, and then stopped. She never bothered to worry about her clients. Naturally she wanted them relaxed, well rested, and enthusiastic, but only because they performed better that way.

"You're right," she admitted, looking into his eyes. His expression, so solemn and penetrating, went straight to her heart. "You're special, Anthony. I have personal feelings for you and I'm not doing a very good job of keeping them out of the campaign. I'm sorry about that."

"Don't be sorry." Anthony slipped his arm around her shoulders again. "I want to come home with you tonight," he murmured, bending his mouth to nuzzle her neck. His face was a little scratchy, but his lips were so warm and soft that Kate barely noticed.

Having acknowledged to herself and to Anthony that her

emotions were involved, Kate knew that it would be almost impossible to refuse him. "Maybe after the election." She considered that a major concession. "You know how I feel."

His mouth wandered to her lips, brushing gently back and forth before retreating. "I know what you keep saying. What you feel is something else again. Why can't you stop being so rational and let your emotions tell you what to do?"

Her emotions told her to cooperate. She felt tenderness and passion and bewilderment, all at once. Anthony was driving her crazy, teasing her lips with butterfly-soft caresses and demanding nips, so how could he expect her to answer him? She raised her hands and pushed against his chest, not because she really wanted him to stop, but because she considered her own reaction unprofessional and somehow weak.

He quickly forced her hands down, pinning them behind her back. Kate didn't even bother to struggle. "You're always doing that," she complained huskily.

"Why should I let you fight me? Besides, you love it." When Anthony started to unbutton her blouse, Kate took a sharp, surprised breath.

She couldn't pretend he was wrong: He seemed to know exactly how to arouse her. If she continued to resist him, he would probably pin her against the car and make love to her until she was quiescent in his arms. A strong enough objection would stop him, but both of them knew she wouldn't make it.

His fingers were much too sensuous against her skin, unbuttoning her blouse with teasing slowness before dealing with the front closing of her bra. For a man who had once claimed only a modest amount of experience with women, he certainly seemed to know what he was doing. He pushed aside the silk of her blouse and the lace of her bra, then ran gentle fingers back and forth over her breasts. Kate shivered, unsure whether the cool night air or Anthony's warm hands had caused the sensation. She was dying to touch him back, but when she tried to free one of her hands, he tightened his grip on her wrists.

"What are you planning to do with it?" he growled.

"Touch you," she whispered back.

Her intention obviously met with his approval. With a groaned "Katie . . ." he released her, his hands spanning her waist to pick her up and swing her onto the hood of the car. Kate wound up clutching his shoulders for balance.

She held him even tighter once she realized why he'd set her on the car. "You have the kind of breasts that soldiers pin up pictures of," he teased softly, stroking a vulnerable nipple with his thumb. "I think I'm fixated."

His tongue followed his thumb, circling and probing in a way that made Kate moan his name. When he started to suck on the nipple, her whole body began to throb. She closed her eyes and threw her head back wantonly, her fingers twining through Anthony's hair to keep him close. When his mouth temporarily retreated and the night air met her moist breast, she shivered, but he was soon arousing her even more deftly than before. His teeth were gentle at first, and then, as he felt her excitement mount, just a little rougher.

Kate moved still closer to him, wrapping her legs around his hips. Her hands were becoming restless now, leaving his hair to explore the planes of his face. "You need a shave," she murmured.

He took the comment as a challenge, abandoning his preoccupation with her breasts to hoarsely announce, "You'll have to stop me if you mind." When he started to toy with her lips she gave a moan of frustration and slid off the car, her arms going up around his neck. His body hardened with desire as he held her against him and murmured how badly he wanted her.

The way he kissed her drove the point home. His tongue was almost savage in her mouth, conquering rather than persuading. A button from his suit jacket was pressing into her bare breast, but she scarcely noticed it. She was utterly languid now, clinging to him submissively, following his lead as he swayed against her. She remembered only too well that those same seductive movements felt even more exciting when both of them were naked, when his graceful body

coaxed her and teased her and made her feel empty without
him. She made a passionate sound somewhere between a
moan and a whimper, and Anthony pulled his lips away from
her mouth to bury them in the soft curls that lay against her
neck.

"It drives me crazy when you make those little noises," he
said, sounding almost pained. "Do you have a blanket in the
car?"

"A blanket?" Kate was so aroused that it took her a
moment to figure out what he meant, and by then Anthony
was playing with her lips again, keeping her excitement at
fever pitch.

"I—I do," she said, "but we can't—I mean, not *here*,
Anthony." A flush rose up her neck; although the idea was
certainly erotic, she couldn't bring herself to say yes.

"Where is it? The trunk?"

"Yes, but . . ."

"But nothing. What happened to your purse?"

"I dropped it on the ground. But we can't—you can't make
love to me on—on the ground outside my boss's house."

Anthony was paying absolutely no attention to her, a habit
of his that was beginning to grow on her. He picked up the
purse and rummaged through it until he found her keys, then
walked around to the trunk and unlocked it. A moment later
he was carrying the blanket over. "Be grateful I even
bothered with this," he said arrogantly, catching hold of her
wrist. "Come on."

Kate stood right where she was. She wanted to be coaxed,
not ordered around. "No. You can spend the night, but . . ."

"I told you, 'but' nothing. If I go inside to get my suitcase,
you'll change your mind by the time I come out. I know you
too well. It would be an announcement that you're sleeping
with me and you'd never allow that. You have two choices,
Miss Garvey. You can either walk over to those trees with me
or you can get carried."

Kate shook her head firmly and pulled her wrist away. "I
said no," she whispered vehemently. "Suppose someone
comes . . . ?"

"If the two of us are out here together, the last thing anyone will do is come look for us. And even if they did, they wouldn't see us way over in the trees. It's too far and too dark." Anthony pulled Kate into his arms and kissed her lightly on the mouth. "C'mon, Katie," he coaxed. "Don't be a prude. You know you want to. And you wouldn't want me to lie awake all night suffering, would you?"

When he used that teasing tone and played with her lips that way, she found him impossible to resist. He deepened the kiss, probing her mouth and then withdrawing, expertly rekindling her hunger for him until he was satisfied with the intensity of her response. By the time he was through with her he could have taken her right there in the car. And this time when he pulled away he didn't bother with requests, simply picked her up and tossed her over his shoulder, walking off toward the stand of trees with her.

Kate wriggled fiercely, trying not to giggle, but all she managed to accomplish was to earn a threatening little slap on her bottom that stung and aroused at the same time. "Behave yourself," he said.

He stopped just inside the stand of trees and set Kate down, still holding her arm. "If those businessmen from San Diego could see you now," she pouted, "they'd never believe it. Where did the ever-so-factual Dr. Larimer go?"

"The same place as the ever-so-proper Miss Garvey. If I let you go to spread the blanket, are you going to take off?"

"Maybe," Kate said, knowing that she wouldn't.

"If you do, I'll catch up with you, throw you down on the ground, and make love to you on the spot. You might have noticed how damp the grass is. You wouldn't want to ruin your suit, now, would you?"

Even in the dim moonlight Kate could see the smug self-confidence on his face. She was finding this whole episode deliciously barbaric by now. No man in her life had dared to try this kind of caveman tactic, but then, no one but Anthony could have gotten away with it. A slow smile spread over her face. "You're right," she said. "I wouldn't."

She slipped her hand away and took the blanket from him,

shaking it out and spreading it between a couple of trees. Then she started a seductive striptease. First she peeled off her jacket, then her unbuttoned blouse and bra. When Anthony reached out to stroke her breasts, the warmth of his hand shot straight to her loins. He was still caressing her as she unzipped her skirt and slowly stepped out of it, then repeated the process with her slip. She kissed him lightly on the mouth and backed away, telling him to be patient.

"You've got to be kidding," he groaned. "If you don't hurry up I'm going to rip the rest of your clothes off."

Smiling, Kate kicked off her shoes and removed her panty hose. She and Anthony stared at each other for several long moments before she divested herself of her bikini panties, then stood there, totally and gloriously naked. Anthony, she noticed, was breathing rather rapidly by now.

When he reached for her again, she pushed him away. "Oh, no," she said. "If I'm going to freeze my backside off, so are you. Come on. Take off your clothes."

He laughed softly. "You're insane, you know that?"

"You started it. Come on."

He was a lot less stylish and much more impatient than Kate as he struggled out of his clothing. Instead of putting everything into a neat pile, as Kate had, he threw each item to the ground. Just as he finished, Kate sprawled down on the blanket, stretching out with feline grace, trying not to shiver. "I'm probably going to catch pneumonia, thanks to you," she grumbled.

When he dropped down beside her and covered her body with his own, the chill started to leave her bones. "No, you won't," he promised. "I guarantee it, honey."

Kate's arms went around his waist and then ran down the sides of his muscled thighs, lightly exploring. They teased each other's lips, only gradually giving in to the need to kiss. Kate wasn't at all deceived by how lazily Anthony's fingers traced patterns on her skin; his movements might have been deliberate, but he was trembling with need for her. As his body pressed her into the soft earth beneath the blanket, she forgot about being cold and melted against him. Her legs parted invitingly to allow his possession, but he seemed to derive much more pleasure from making both of them wait.

His mouth roughened with hunger as he held himself back, his fingers grasping her hips to still them. After a number of achingly intimate forays that left her trembling, just as he was, he invaded her body with a quick but gentle passion that left her eager to surrender. She clung to him, her mind focused only on her own pleasure now. He was trying to drive her crazy, she was sure of it. She arched her body high to meet each thrust, silently begging for release, wondering if he had any idea what it did to her when he stroked her inner thighs that way.

Earlier, by the car, she hadn't been aware of the noises escaping from deep in her throat. Now she was, because it was so hard to stifle them. Her hands roamed over his body, ultimately working their way underneath to his stomach and then lower, to touch him intimately and insistently until he lost control. She heard his grunt of surrender just before his lovemaking went from sensuous to wild. For the last several seconds the two of them held on to each other as though each were afraid that the other would disappear. The pleasure Kate felt at the end was so intense that it bordered on an assault. She was barely able to respond to Anthony's final convulsive movements.

For almost a full minute they lay wrapped in each other's arms, unable to say or do anything. Finally Anthony dropped a kiss on Kate's nose and rolled off her. "I'm freezing my tail off," he said. "Next time we do this, *you* go on top."

Now that it was over, Kate's doubts were beginning to return. They couldn't go on this way, she thought. People would notice. What was she supposed to do? Anthony seemed to sense her feelings, saying as he helped her up, "If anyone asks, I'll say we went for a walk—to talk. Okay?"

"Okay." Kate didn't want to think about how rumpled his clothing would look. A glance at the house told her that everyone had gone to bed. It was dark except for a single light in one of the bedrooms.

As they silently dressed and started for the car, Kate

admitted to herself that she'd wanted Anthony to make love to her from the moment they'd coolly shaken hands that morning. There was no point in refusing to accept the situation. She'd never been the type of woman who allowed herself to be seduced and then denied all responsibility for it, so where did that leave her? Only a fool or a hypocrite could pretend to herself that this wouldn't happen again. If people talked, she supposed she'd have to grit her teeth and ignore them.

When they reached the car, Anthony told her he would see her in the morning. "And you don't have to worry that I'll make anything obvious. I have a lot of practice in deception, remember?" He helped her inside and shut the door, then walked around to the other side of the car and let himself in.

"I'll take you to the dinner tomorrow night," he said, tossing the blanket onto the back seat. "Promise me you won't give me a hard time about spending the night."

He was assuming much more than Kate was willing to give. "I already have a date—" she began.

"Break it," he interrupted.

The command pricked at Kate's temper. "I'm not going to do that. You may sleep with me, but you don't *own* me, Anthony."

"Who is he?"

"His name is Jerry Savitch. He's a pediatric surgeon at the hospital. He was one of the doctors who operated on my goddaughter."

"Okay. You can go with him." Despite the concession, Anthony sounded nettled. "And when does this date of yours end? Midnight? Nine in the morning?"

"Would you listen to yourself?" Kate demanded. "You wanted a no-strings affair, and I guess you've got one, because I don't seem to have very much success in getting myself to say no to you. But don't expect me to stop seeing my other friends or to change my plans every time you snap your fingers."

"Right!" Anthony started to get out, then changed his

mind. "Your 'friend' Jerry Savitch—is he your lover or isn't he?"

"That's none of your business."

"I don't give a damn what you think is my business. Is he or isn't he?"

Kate was just angry enough to taunt back, "What were you doing in the State Department, Anthony?"

"I was an expert in Asian affairs," he said stonily.

Kate had spent ten long hours in the library the previous weekend, checking every entry from the newspaper's index that even mentioned the State Department. One particular article had aroused her curiosity, but she hadn't planned on mentioning it tonight. Now she did, partly because she was tired of being stonewalled, but mostly just to change the subject away from her personal life.

"I've been rereading the newspaper lately," she began. "Eight months after you went to work at the State Department, the assistant secretary for Asian affairs was killed in a boating accident. In the middle of winter, Anthony. No one could explain what he was doing in a small boat near an uninhabited island in the middle of Chesapeake Bay. The official explanation mentioned tension caused by personal problems. The article also said he was a close friend of the secretary of state. Less than two months later the secretary resigned. I thought that was very interesting."

"Was it?" Anthony sounded furious.

"Yes. Do you want to know about Jerry? How many times he's made love—"

"Dammit, just shut up!" For a moment Kate was afraid she'd pushed him too hard. He looked like an explosion about to happen. But after a rather terrifying few moments of silence he ran his hand through his hair and told her, "Kevin had reason to think there was a mole working in the Asian-affairs section." The words came out through clenched teeth. "Do you know what that means?"

"Of course I do. An enemy agent."

"Right. So he slipped me into a sensitive position and told

me to find out what I could. The secretary wasn't informed—
Kevin didn't trust him. I'm sure you know enough to realize
that my activities were . . . rather irregular."

Flat-out illegal, Kate thought. The Agency wasn't allowed
to infiltrate another government department. Perhaps if the
president and the secretary of state had given their approval,
an exception would have been made, but according to the
rules, the FBI and not Anthony Larimer should have carried
out the investigation.

"It took time to chase down the leads," Anthony went on,
"but once I did—the 'accident' you read about resulted from
an Agency-controlled operation. By the time we were ready
to move, Kevin had brought in the FBI and met with the
President, so we kept on the right side of the law. The
assistant secretary was the Soviet agent. He thought he was
meeting someone on that island to buy information on a new
American missile system, but somehow he realized that one
of the men in the other boat was an FBI agent and he crashed
his own boat and killed himself rather than get arrested. We
had enough information by then to trace his network of
informants and clean it out. The President waited a few
months, then asked the secretary of state to resign. I stuck
around for three more years, keeping an eye on the place for
Kevin. That, of course, was also irregular." Anthony paused,
then snapped, "I've answered *your* blasted questions. Now
you answer mine."

Kate was so wrapped up in Anthony's explanation that it
took her a moment to remember what he was talking about.
"He isn't," she finally answered. "We don't see each other
very often—maybe once or twice a month."

"You were in bed with me the second time we met,"
Anthony reminded her.

"What is this, an inquisition?" Kate's face was flushed with
a mixture of embarrassment and irritation. "I told you the
truth. What more do you want from me?"

"I don't know. I don't even know what I'm doing."
Anthony sighed and rubbed his eyes. "I'm so damn tired.

This day must have started at least a month ago. I must be crazy."

Before Kate had a chance to say a word, he was out of the car and on his way back to the house. She watched him slowly walk away, hunched over with fatigue and what she took for self-reproach.

Chapter 11

KATE AND SANDY COHEN WERE WAITING IN THE COMPANY'S screening room when Bill Dorset and Anthony Larimer walked into the office the next morning. It was just past nine; Kate had been on edge since arriving at work half an hour before. What was she supposed to expect from a man who made passionate love to her one moment and lost his temper with her the next?

His friendly "Good morning," which encompassed both herself and Sandy, was followed by an acerbic comment about being thrown to the lions. Vintage Anthony Larimer, Kate thought, starting to relax.

For the next ninety minutes the candidate was subjected to the unpleasant, even brutal experience of watching taped excerpts of himself speaking. Almost every office seeker cringed a little at such sessions. People hated everything from the sound of their voice to the way their hair looked to the gestures they made.

"Maybe I should go back to teaching," Anthony muttered as Kate clicked on the lights.

Everyone got up and stretched, Bill clapping Anthony on the shoulder. "Let's go down to the conference room and get ourselves some coffee"—he smiled—"or a stiff drink, as the case may be."

Bill's secretary brought in the coffee and cake just as they sat down. "The thing you have to remember," Bill said to Anthony as he poured him a cup of coffee, "is that your style is appropriate to what you're used to doing—teaching. You were factual, thoughtful, interesting. You know how to throw in an anecdote here and there to break up a lecture. You're a more skillful speaker than many people we've worked with, but the best politicians put more passion into what they say. Some do it by waving their arms and exhorting the crowd, and others manage to rivet the audience to their seats with a soft-spoken intensity that no one can ignore, but the end result is the same. Votes. Over the next few weeks Kate will work with you on modifying your style so that it comes out less dry. She's very good at it. I once saw her take a candidate who generated about as much excitement as a bump on a log and bring him to the point where people actually stayed awake. Since you obviously understand the problem, there's no reason to sit here and pound the point home."

Though Anthony grunted his agreement, Kate could see that he was still trying to recover. When people who were used to excelling in everything were faced with evidence of their own shortcomings, their reactions ranged from embarrassment to disbelief. At least, Kate thought, Anthony wasn't sitting there like one recent candidate and insisting that it must have been an off day.

"I think we agree on style," Sandy said. As usual, he was doodling on a memo pad, and Kate craned her neck for a better view of the latest masterpiece—a futuristic-looking spaceship.

"My kids dragged me to that new science fiction movie last weekend," he admitted sheepishly. "I kind of liked it."

"Be grateful it wasn't a two-hour tearjerker," Anthony told him with a smile. "Jessica insisted that *Forgotten Love* was

the best movie ever made and nagged me into going. It was all
I could do to keep my popcorn down."

This brief exchange lessened the tension in the room.
Sandy reached for a piece of coffee cake and continued, "I
started to say that we need to look at content as well as style.
Two things hit me hardest. First of all, Anthony spent too
much time on foreign policy, but I understand from Kate that
you covered that last night. And second, he has to learn to
soften his opinions." Sandy took a bite of cake and sat back in
his chair. "Take that question on water policy that someone
asked in San Francisco. You gave a five-minute lecture
explaining the conflict, Anthony, and then you came down
smack on the side of big agriculture. You must have known
that you'd alienate Northern California environmentalists
with an answer like that."

"The question was about a specific project, a project I
happen to support," Anthony pointed out. "What was I
supposed to do? Lie about it?"

Kate wasn't about to let Sandy answer; he'd irritated
Anthony already. "Of course not," she said. "You were
supposed to explain your position and then point to another
project or issue in the same general area where you take an
environmentalist stance. You're supposed to let people know
that you're flexible and that you'll listen to what they have to
say."

"But if that same question had been asked in Fresno,"
Anthony retorted, "you'd be delighted with my response—as
long as it didn't wind up quoted outside of the farm belt, that
is."

By now Bill Dorset was the only calm person in the room.
"I've known some candidates who've gotten away with saying
different things to different groups, but you couldn't do that
even if you wanted to. Not in the general election against Bob
Woodruff. He'll throw every inconsistency straight in your
face. If you're both honest and outspoken, you'll wind up
alienating everybody in the electorate sooner or later. After
last night we understand that you're uncomfortable with
evasions, but . . ."

"I know, I know." Anthony took a sip of his coffee. "I've seen the tapes, Bill. I *do* understand what you're saying. I'll try to find a middle ground between academic honesty and political expediency."

"You're spending $65,000 to have us conduct a benchmark poll on voter attitudes," Sandy reminded him rather curtly. "I'll have the data in a month or so. But if you're not going to make any use of it, there's no point in my—"

"Back off, Sandy." No one disputed Bill Dorset when he used that clipped tone. He added more gently, "Anthony, I know we've thrown a lot at you this morning, and we'll give you some time to think about it. You have a speech at twelve-thirty; why don't you spend some time going through it with Kate?"

As Kate and Anthony left the conference room, Sandy started to argue with Bill. "Don't pay too much attention to Sandy," Kate said. "He's famous for being abrasive, but he can also be terrific. We put up with the former because his work is uncanny in its accuracy."

"He reminds me of a kid who used to get punched out at least once a week when I was in high school," Anthony muttered. "But not, you'll be relieved to hear, by me."

They spent the next hour reviewing the speech Anthony had written for an influential local business group. Since Anthony had done consulting work for major corporations, advising them on which countries provided the most promising investment climates, the speech would be easy for him to give. He planned to focus on how the policies of the federal government affected the international business climate, making suggestions for changes. Kate had him add a few of his experiences as a consultant and delete some unnecessary facts and figures, leaving room for comments on domestic economic policy. They were running short of time and she wanted to work on delivery, so she drove him to his meeting and listened to him run through the speech en route.

"It sounds good," she said as they pulled up in front of the hotel. "I wish I could stay, but I have an appointment to go to. Would you tape it for me?"

When he agreed she handed him her mini–cassette record-
er. He hadn't said a word about coming to the fund raiser that
night, and she wondered if he'd changed his mind. All
morning she'd attributed his impersonal behavior to the fact
that they were in the office, but now she wasn't so sure. In all
the time they'd been alone, there hadn't been so much as a
smile or an admiring look, and his attitude was beginning to
hurt.

"Will I see you later?" she asked.

"I don't know if I'll be able to make it." He started to get
out of the car.

Kate wasn't going to spend the rest of the afternoon
wondering. "Did something happen between last night and
this morning?" she asked. "Are you still angry because I
leaned on you about the State Department?"

He checked his watch, visibly impatient. "It isn't that.
Look, I don't have time to talk about it now. I'll call you."

Since it was almost twelve-thirty, Kate had no choice but to
let him go. Obviously things had changed, and she was
stunned to discover how upset that made her. She didn't
understand how Anthony could have displayed violent jeal-
ousy only last night and then give her the brush-off today.
Had he lost interest because she'd finally given him the
no-strings affair he wanted?

As she dressed for dinner that evening, her glance kept
straying to the telephone. Anthony hadn't called yet; she
didn't even know if he was still in Los Angeles. She chose the
kind of dress that attracted attention because her ego virtually demanded it. The gown was a shimmering abstract print in
shades of red, violet, and gold, with full sleeves and skirt, a
deep V neck, and a wide fabric sash.

The fund raiser was being held at the private country club
where the hospital's chief of staff played golf. Kate arrived
forty minutes early with a detailed checklist in her evening
bag. She and her committee members moved around some
tables, complained about the taste of one of the pâtés, and
relocated the band when the singer pointed out that a third of
the room couldn't see her, but everything else was fine.

Kate was checking on last-minute preparations for the fashion show when a friend came in to tell her that Jerry had arrived. She slipped out to say hello and would have promptly disappeared had he not taken her arm to stop her. "I've never seen you so keyed up," he said. "Have a drink and relax. Thank the people for their generous donations. It's what you do best."

He was right. She'd been hiding herself away after taking an hour to dress, and all because she hadn't wanted to know whether Anthony had showed up. Disgusted with herself, she walked over to the bar with Jerry and ordered a glass of wine.

Twenty minutes later the Dorsets arrived, along with Anthony and their daughter and son-in-law. They promptly walked over to Kate and Jerry to say hello, and for the first time in her life, Kate was glad that a man had his arm around her shoulder. Unfortunately, Anthony didn't seem to notice, much less care.

He took a book of raffle tickets out of his pocket. "I forgot to give these to you before. Am I too late?"

"We can toss them into the barrel," Kate said as she took them. "Jerry, this is Bill and Emily's daughter, Carrie, and her husband, Jim Lightner. And Anthony Larimer. Anthony, Jerry Savitch."

"Are you here to do a little campaigning?" Jerry asked.

"I'm here because Kate asked me to come," Anthony said with a smile. "That was just after she cajoled me into buying a book of raffle tickets."

Jerry shot a questioning glance at Kate but didn't say anything. Both of them knew that she never involved clients in her private life. Jerry's unspoken demand—What makes Larimer different?—hung in the air so tangibly that Kate felt a little sick to her stomach. "We were having a few problems with the fashion show," she said hurriedly. "I'd better go check on things."

As she walked away she tried to figure out why she felt such a strong need to escape. There was an old song that ascribed the kind of reaction she was having to love rather than illness, but she couldn't cope with that idea. She felt enough internal turmoil without pinning the label *love* on her emotions and making herself totally miserable. She wasn't about to change her life for the man; even compromise was difficult. Whatever she felt had to be something else, because she hadn't even known him long enough to fall in love with him.

By the time she assured herself that the right models were matched with the right outfits, Kate had calmed down enough to join Jerry and several of his colleagues in the lounge. Eventually she began to work the room, aware that Anthony was doing the same thing. With Bill at his side to make the introductions, he was shaking hands with all the right people, smiling and talking and hopefully avoiding anything controversial.

Kate had almost managed to forget his presence by the time dinner was served. People were having a wonderful time, the band was spectacular, and with the exception of the banished pâté, the food was excellent. Unfortunately, as soon as Anthony sat down across from her and started to charm one of her friends, she felt as though she'd eaten a pint of the rancid spread.

The fashion show, a sassy extravaganza complete with colored strobe lights and a jazz accompaniment, was a smash. Kate realized that the designers would easily recoup the cost of their donations in orders and decided that if she ever did this again she'd ask for a small percentage of the profits.

She tried to keep her thoughts off Anthony, but it wasn't possible. He seemed to be enjoying himself, and judging from the number of people who mentioned him to Kate, he'd made a lot of friends tonight. If he could only learn to talk out of both sides of his mouth, he'd be a shoo-in.

As for Kate, she danced with more men than she could count, charmed anyone who got within a yard of her, and coaxed thousands of extra dollars out of people's wallets. She wanted to believe that Anthony was ignoring her out of a desire to keep their relationship private, but that didn't explain his earlier behavior. Finally, fed up with wondering, she appropriated her friend's chair and sat down next to him.

"Did you bring along the tape?" she asked.

"The—oh, the tape. I gave it to Bill."

"Could we grab a few moments alone? I'd like to hear how it went." And if you tell me you already spoke to Bill about it, she thought, I'm going to kick you.

Someone a few seats away laughed and asked Kate, "Don't you ever forget your job, even for one night?"

"Not if I want to win," Kate told him.

Anthony looked like a trapped animal. When Kate stood up, he reluctantly did the same; they walked into the now empty cocktail lounge and sat down at a table in a darkened corner.

"I thought the speech went very well," he said. "Of course, after you listen to it you'll probably tell me that—"

"Anthony," Kate interrupted in exasperation, "I didn't drag you out of the room to talk *business*. You must know that."

There was a paper coaster on the table, which he promptly started to shred. "You must have been a terrific spy," Kate said. "Every time you get uncomfortable, you attack the nearest inanimate object."

He stared at the partially dismembered coaster as if surprised to learn he'd even touched it. "Actually, it's just with women," he said. "Particularly with you."

Kate was smart enough to see the handwriting on the wall. It hurt like hell, but she couldn't let Anthony see that. He was going to cause them enough trouble as a candidate without her giving him a guilt complex into the bargain. "If you didn't want to see me anymore, all you had to do was say so," she said gently. "You don't have to explain, although after last night . . ." She shrugged to cover the tightness in her voice. This was turning out to be tougher than she'd imagined.

"I had the wrong impression of you. I thought you were harder, that you'd had plenty of men, that you didn't care about anything but yourself and your job and maybe your father. I figured . . ." He paused, staring at the pile of paper strips in front of him. After a moment he picked one up and began to rip it into even smaller sections. "I figured that you'd be the perfect casual affair. Sexy, smart, great in bed—but last night I realized how wrong I was. It just took till this morning for it to sink in, that's all."

Kate was totally lost. "I'd be a *rotten* casual affair?" she asked.

His lips quirked upward, then settled back into an uneasy frown. "I couldn't *have* a casual affair with you. You're not what I thought." He stopped fiddling with the paper and looked across at her. "You care about people. You go out and raise money for them. I finally got it through my head that the list of my predecessors is hardly legion. I know you've been trying to tell me that all along, but I got a certain impression from the way we met and for a long time I couldn't see beyond it."

"I don't understand." Kate knew that if she had any sense she would drop the subject, but she couldn't make herself do it. "Usually when a man says things like that to a woman, it's because he wants to keep seeing her, not dump her."

"Don't use words like that. It's just—it's already gone too far, Katie. I realized that when I started telling you things I shouldn't have, things that I've never told anyone else. I'm trying to explain that if we got involved, it wouldn't lead anywhere. I don't want that kind of pain for either of us."

By now Kate was seething with frustration. "But *why?* Just because I've never married, that doesn't mean I wouldn't consider it." A blinding revelation hit her. "It's *you,* isn't it? What's the problem, Anthony? Some kind of morbid fidelity to your wife?"

Her sarcastic question hit a very raw nerve. When Anthony's jaw tightened, Kate instinctively drew back a bit.

"When I find the right woman I'll get remarried," he said stiffly. "I want someone who puts me first, the same way I'd put her first. Someone who isn't so wrapped up in her career that a man can't compete. Someone who looks up to me instead of telling me everything I do wrong." As Anthony continued to talk, his anger boiled to the surface. "Someone I can trust, dammit! Someone who wants a family. I can't see you pushing a stroller, Katie. You're just not right for me."

"Not right for you?" Between Anthony's male chauvinism

and his arrant arrogance, Kate was angry enough to throw something at him. "What you're saying is that I'm not *good* enough for you," she said in a soft, fierce voice. "That you might even be tempted to marry me, and we both know what a disaster *that* would be! If you're looking for some meek little housewife who worships the ground you walk on, Anthony, why don't you import a child bride from Asia? Better yet, if all you wanted was a bunch of babies, why didn't you have them with your precious Beth?"

"Don't you think we tried?" he growled back. "She had two miscarriages with a stillbirth in between." All the fury suddenly seemed to drain out of him. "It took a heavy toll on her body. I always wondered whether that made her more susceptible . . ." His voice choked up; he couldn't go on.

"Oh, God." Anthony's feelings toward his dead wife were more than Kate could handle. Love, guilt, adoration . . . what living woman could compete with that? She forced herself to think about salvaging their ability to work together because everything else was too painful. "All right," she said, managing a smile. "Maybe I'm not your idea of wife material, but there's only one political consultant in the whole blasted state who's any better than I am, and he's already working for you. Let's just concentrate on getting you elected, okay?"

Surprise and then gratitude chased each other across his face. "Okay," he agreed. As they got up, he added, "And, Katie . . . I just want you to know—I realize I didn't handle this very well. You're a terrific lady, but . . ." His jaw clenched and he looked down. "I'm not proud of the way I've behaved. And—I appreciate the way you're responding."

Kate didn't want to discuss it anymore. All the talking in the world wouldn't change his attitude. "Forget it," she said. "I'll do my job and you do yours."

"Right. I'm sorry." He stared at her for a moment, then shoved his hands into his pockets and walked away. Kate followed a few seconds later. She felt as though she'd been socked in the stomach by a very unexpected curveball, but she'd be damned if she'd let anyone see it.

Chapter 12

"WE'RE OUT OF TIME." ANTHONY NOTICED SMILES ON THE FACES of several of his seminar students and realized that he sounded like a broken record. "I know it's the third time I've said that, but we've really got to break this up. In the first place, I'm hungry, and in the second place . . ." He hesitated, gave a mental shrug and grinned. "In the second place, Kevin O'Neal is due at my house any minute. Purely social, but I can't keep an ex-boss waiting."

He endured the students' gibes with relatively good grace, shaking his head ruefully when one of them called out, "I saw the latest poll today, Dr. Larimer. If you don't learn to keep your mouth shut, you may have to ask O'Neal for your old job back."

At the moment, Anthony thought as he tossed his briefcase into the trunk of his car, his *current* job was very appealing. His graduate seminar, "Soviet Policy Toward the Warsaw Pact Nations," was proving to be one of the most stimulating he'd ever taught. The Berkeley campus was beautiful in early

May, and if he hadn't been spending every spare moment of his time chasing around the state, he might have been able to enjoy it.

Kevin O'Neal had called him earlier in the week, saying that he'd be in San Francisco on business Wednesday and Thursday, and wanted to drop by Thursday evening. Anthony had promptly delegated the task of cooking dinner to Kris and Jessica, who promised the best Italian meal this side of Rome.

He pulled into his driveway at about six to find a blue sedan parked in front of the house, right behind Kris's sports car. Kevin O'Neal was already settled in the living room with a drink, looking over the newspaper, and impressive aromas were emanating from the kitchen.

The two men shook hands and talked about Kevin's trip to the Coast while Anthony fixed himself a gin and tonic. Once both were seated again, Kevin rifled through the paper, turning to the poll mentioned by Anthony's student.

"There's no way in the world you can lose the primary," Kevin said, "but I see you're giving it your best shot. Fifty-four percent against a trio of nonentities." He took a healthy swig of his drink. "Hell, Anthony. You could run Attila the Hun against those guys and he'd do better than *that.*"

Anthony put his feet on the coffee table and stared at his drink. "Do I really need to sit here and listen to this from *you?* I've heard it from Bill Dorset, Kate Garvey, and Sandy Cohen. I've heard it from Vince Collier, my brother Doug, and even my daughter. Last week my mother-in-law phoned from Massachusetts, and today one of my students told me I should learn to keep my mouth shut. But at least the reporters are happy. It gives them something to write about."

"Sandy's polls show the same thing as this one?"

"Sure." Anthony was about to tell Kevin to drop the subject when a measured look at his friend's face told him he was acting like a fool. He saw neither a critic nor a judge, just an old friend who really cared about him.

"I haven't been particularly easy to live with lately," he admitted. "Sandy accused me of unconsciously wanting to lose, but I don't think that's true. I seem to wind up sounding like a professor even when I don't mean to. I want to take clear-cut positions and answer questions honestly, but I'm not trying to make a crusade out of anything. Last week Sandy and I sat down and talked about the results of some focus groups he's been running. It isn't so much the clear-cut positions the voters are reacting to as the arrogance they think is behind them. A typical comment went something like, 'I think Anthony Larimer is a brilliant man, but he doesn't *listen*. Maybe he knows all about foreign policy, but he doesn't know all about *everything*.' I don't mean to give that impression, Kevin."

"You mean you *don't* know all about everything?" Kevin needled.

Anthony shook his head, smiling. He was beginning to realize just how much he needed this kind of conversation. "On the contrary. Between the campaign and my personal life, I've reached the conclusion that I don't know much about *any*thing, Kevin."

"Spare me the humility or I may lose my lunch." Kevin gestured toward the kitchen. "How long before those two get dinner on the table?"

"I don't know. Why?"

"I think we should go for a walk."

"We can't talk here? You think the room is bugged?" Anthony asked.

"No, but *you* are. And you don't want your daughter and niece overhearing anything."

"You're right. I'll go check." Anthony poked his head into the kitchen, returning a moment later with the news that dinner would be in about half an hour. "Back in the old days," he told Kevin, "I used to wonder if you could read minds. What made you call me on Monday?"

"One of our scientists developed a new machine." Kevin finished his drink and stood up. "It can pick up dreams and replay them on a television screen." The two men walked to the door, side by side. "Last night I focused it on the White House. Would you believe that Hendrickson has lurid fantasies about the chancellor of West Germany?"

Anthony laughed and said he didn't. The chancellor of West Germany was a sixty-one-year-old grandmother who needed to lose about forty pounds. "As a matter of fact," he added, "I don't believe in your machine at all, Kevin."

They were outside now, strolling down the front walk of the street. "Don't you?" Kevin's face was wearing a wolfish grin. "I admit the reception between Berkeley and Washington could be better—the Rocky Mountains get in the way— but I thought I picked up an image of you and Katie Garvey in bed."

Anthony flushed slightly. "Now how in hell did you know that?" he demanded.

"No comment."

"Dammit, Kevin . . ."

"Okay, okay." Kevin nodded toward one of Anthony's neighbors, who was working in his garden. "Ah, suburbia. Look how happy that man is, pruning his rosebushes. Cultivating his garden. What we need is the simple life, Anthony. We need to . . ."

"He's a nuclear physicist and he's working on weapons I don't even want to contemplate," Anthony interrupted. "You were saying?"

Kevin had the good sense to take mercy on him. "Katie was in Washington a few weeks ago. I bumped into her at a dinner party. She cornered me and started asking about your marriage. I figured her interest was more than professional."

Anthony's heart started to pound heavily. He suddenly felt like an adolescent with his first crush. "What did you tell her?" he asked.

"That you and Beth were very happy. That she worshipped the water she thought you could walk on. That the two of you had a very traditional relationship that probably would have changed if Beth had lived"—Kevin's voice dropped to a gentle murmur—"but of course she didn't. You can't spend the rest of your life looking for another Beth Shipley, Anthony. Times have changed. Women have changed. Even Beth would have changed."

Six months ago Anthony would have shoved that speech down Kevin's throat. Now he simply kept walking. It was a lovely, tranquil evening, complete with gentle breeze and fragrant flowers, and the peace and beauty all around him put him in the mood to talk. "I made a total jerk of myself with Katie," he told Kevin. "I chased her until I got what I wanted and then broke things off as soon as I realized what a decent person she was. I was afraid I'd get serious—I couldn't picture myself married to someone like her. Since then we've managed to work together fairly well whenever we get together, but she's been spending a lot of time on Mac Pendergast's congressional campaign, so I've only seen her a few times a month. But there's an undercurrent of tension whenever we're in the same room. I look at her and I can hardly keep my hands off her. It's been that way right from the beginning and it isn't getting any better. She has more class than I do—she's been patient and encouraging, but very, very cool. I figured if I came anywhere near her I'd wind up with terminal frostbite. Besides, I don't have the guts. Not after the things I said to her."

Kevin shrugged. "For some demented female reason, she actually seems to like you. I don't know what you said, but I think she might forgive you if you threw yourself at her feet and begged hard enough."

"I'll keep it in mind." Anthony shoved his hands into his pockets. "She has a strange effect on me. I've told her things I've never told anyone else."

The effect of this pronouncement was to stop the director of Central Intelligence dead in his tracks. "Oh?" he said calmly.

Anthony was aware that he should have explained about this months ago. "The State Department," he said. "Katie's as sharp as they come. She looked through old newspapers until the right incident caught her eye. Her speculations were right on target. I was angry about something else and I let her goad me into confirming them, but I wouldn't have done that if I hadn't wanted her to know. I also told her about Beth's pregnancies, that I've always wondered if they might have contributed to her illness. I blamed myself for wanting another child. . . ."

"It's an understandable reaction, but don't forget that Beth wanted the same thing. You like to be in control, Anthony, but you couldn't control whether Beth lived or died. Maybe guilt is easier for you to deal with than accepting that."

"Maybe." The twisting pain Anthony had once felt was gone now. "If so, my need to be in control has taken a few kicks in the stomach lately. Which brings us back to the election."

They'd slowly circled the block and were almost back at the house again. "Not quite," Kevin said. "We were digging up moles at the State Department. Exactly what did you tell her?"

"That you planted me in the Department without informing the secretary. That you made sure that the operation eight months later was legal but that I stuck around the Department for three more years and kept you unofficially informed. Since Katie is Hank's daughter, she must have a fairly good idea of how much we bent the rules."

Kevin agreed, adding, "I know you wouldn't have said anything if I hadn't made it clear you could trust her discretion, but for God's sake, Anthony, enough is enough. Don't start reciting chapter and verse on what happened in Asia."

That was the last thing Anthony planned to do. "All I want to do is forget about that," he said.

They started back up the walk. *"Now* we're back to the election," Kevin announced. "Are you telling me that you're ready to listen to the experts now? You *are* paying them an unholy amount for their advice."

"That's what I'm saying. We've bought almost no television

time for the primary—we're saving the money for the general election. Dorset's been after me to approve the kind of commercial I hate. You know, the candidate walking on the beach with his daughter and cocker spaniel, saying—"

"You don't *own* a cocker spaniel," Kevin pointed out with a grin. "You're allergic to dogs."

"So I'll buy one and take allergy shots. And he can cock his wretched little ears while I hold forth on the future of the planet and sneeze." Anthony opened the front door. "Alternate scenario: film clips of Larimer facing down the Russians, facing down the Washington press corps, facing down the California legislature. Who wouldn't vote for such a heroic character?"

"Don't look at me!" Kevin laughed. "I don't even live here."

As Anthony pushed the front door shut, Jessica called from the kitchen, "Five more minutes, Dad. We're doing the garlic bread."

Anthony and Kevin went into the dining room to wait. The wine was already uncorked, so Anthony poured out two glassfuls. "I've come to the reluctant conclusion that if I want to win the general election, I'll have to throw myself on the mercy of Dorset and Associates," he said. He glanced toward the closed kitchen door and continued in a softer tone of voice, "After the campaign goes into full swing around Labor Day, I'm going to be seeing a lot of Katie. I don't know what I feel and I don't know what I want from her, but I do know what it's going to do to me to be around her all the time. Do me a favor, Kevin. If you happen to see her in Washington, tell her I'm not such a bad guy."

"I think you'll tell her that yourself." Kevin raised his glass. "To the future," he said. "May it be even more fulfilling than the past."

"I'll drink to that," Anthony answered.

Postmortems had never been Kate's favorite way to pass a morning, especially grim postmortems. She'd spent election night at the San Francisco campaign headquarters of Congressman McDonald "Mac" Pendergast while Bill held Anthony Larimer's hand in Los Angeles. Hers was much the better assignment. Pendergast's race, a contest that had seesawed back and forth throughout the months of the campaign, had wound up a heartbreaker for his opponent. Kate had gone to bed at midnight, leaving behind an increasingly raucous celebration.

The next morning she was sitting on a plane to Los Angeles, frowning at the morning *Times*. It wasn't that Anthony had lost; that would have been impossible. It was that he hadn't won by nearly the margin he'd started with, so that his showing was perceived as a defeat. The final figure was a disappointing fifty-two percent of the vote, an amount that even Jack Handlin might have garnered. With Bob Woodruff sweeping to a seventy-eight-percent victory in the Republican primary and Eli Hendrickson's popularity higher than an incumbent president had any right to expect, the prospects for November looked dim. Even Kate's father, a professional optimist, admitted that the words *Republican landslide* haunted his dreams at night.

When Kate arrived at the office, Bill Dorset was sitting in the reception area, drinking a cup of coffee. He looked up, sober faced. "At least we won one last night," he said. "I spoke to Mac about midnight. He sounded happy with us."

"Ecstatic. We're heroes." Kate helped herself to a cup of coffee. "Of course, it helps to have a candidate who gives you a free hand with the advertising and can deal out nonresponse responses as fast as he gets the cards. How's Anthony doing?"

"Subdued."

"He's been subdued for weeks," Kate pointed out. "It didn't make him listen to you."

"He listened. He's tried, but he just couldn't do everything I told him to." Bill got up, cocking his head toward the door of his office. "Let's go inside. Sandy should be up any time now, and Vince and Anthony are due in half an hour."

Kate grabbed the thermal coffee pot and took it along with her. A stack of newspapers was sitting on the coffee table, morning editions from various cities in the state.

"Every single article mentions that Anthony dropped sixteen percentage points between early April and the election," Bill said. "November is a challenge I could do without."

"Does Anthony realize what a tough election he's looking at?" Kate asked. "And, more important, does he care?"

"It's the one bright spot in this whole fiasco. Seeing those figures on a television screen shook him up. I think that the polls have never been entirely real to him—or not as real as the scruples he's been grappling with."

Kate had never discussed her personal relationship with Anthony Larimer—or lack of one—but Bill could see that the two of them weren't entirely comfortable with each other. He'd noticed the way Kate suddenly became more formal whenever Anthony walked into a room and the way Anthony avoided Kate's eyes. It was one of the reasons that he and a few assistants had handled most of the details of the campaign thus far. The other was that Kate had been needed in San Francisco. Now, however, with the Pendergast primary out of the way, Larimer was the one who faced a tough election contest.

"Relax and listen to me a minute," Bill coaxed softly. "Whatever you think of Anthony as a candidate—and I admit he isn't the easiest guy to work with—he happens to be a first-rate human being. He cares about other people, and about the country as a whole, in a way that candidates too often don't. He tries to be honest and people think he's arrogant. He tries to explain the issues to them and he's labeled pedantic. Last night we sat in his hotel room and listened to Woodruff thank his supporters and accept his opponents' concessions, and Anthony turned to me and said, 'Bob's a decent man, Bill. But he's heartless. Maybe he's had it too easy all his life, but he doesn't seem to understand that people suffer, that they try their best and fail, that a society that does nothing but reward its most successful members is a soulless place to live.' I wish to heaven he could talk that way to a crowd, but he's never been able to pull it off. In small groups he's wonderful—you know how people take out their checkbooks for him—but it's not happening in more formal settings or on TV. That's *your* job, and I expect you to do it."

Kate sighed but didn't argue. Bill knew she'd worked with Anthony earlier in the campaign, going over tapes of his speeches and role playing audience questions and interviews, but the progress he'd made hadn't been enough. She wondered if there was too great a barrier between them for trust to develop. Most of the time she was businesslike but friendly with him, but every time she caught a glimmer of desire in his eyes, she froze up. It made her angry that he wanted her in bed but didn't consider her good enough to take seriously.

It might have been easier if she hadn't come to respect and even admire him. She'd stood and watched as he talked to two or three people, charging the air with emotion and inspiration. Jessica often traveled with him, and Kate had observed numerous moments of tenderness or humor between them, bespeaking his deep capacity for love. The girl was always so friendly that Kate felt closer to *her* than to Anthony by now. She remembered thinking that if she ever became involved with him, he'd threaten the comfortable fabric of her life, and she knew that was already happening. People thought that political consulting was a cynic's refuge, but Kate would never have stayed in the game this long without a very broad streak of idealism. She believed that good people could make a difference. She believed that good laws could make a difference. Compromise and maneuvering were merely tools toward a laudable end.

Slowly her world was turning upside down. Was her career a way of avoiding emotional entanglements? Was there something distasteful about the tactics she sometimes used? Anthony clearly thought so, and he wasn't the type of man she could dismiss. She didn't enjoy feeling confused, so most of the time she put such troubling questions out of her mind.

She managed a smile for Bill, assuring him that from now through November her primary concern would be electing Anthony Larimer to the Senate. He was nodding his satisfaction just as Sandy Cohen walked into the room, carrying a thick sheaf of papers.

Sandy's eyes were so swollen that they looked like they needed a pair of toothpicks to prop them open. "I've been up all night," he croaked. "I hope that the coffee is strong today."

Kate took a mug from one of the cabinets and poured him a cup. "What have you been doing?" she asked.

"Reading through the responses from the exit polling."

"But there were hundreds of interviews—"

Sandy interrupted Kate's incredulous objection. "Exactly. Remind me to find people who can write legibly next time. I may go blind."

Sandy had selected key precincts throughout the state and hired experienced people to interview voters as they left their polling places. He wanted to know who they'd voted for and why. If they were Republicans—or Democrats who hadn't voted for Larimer—he wanted to know how Larimer could get their votes. It wasn't strictly scientific, but Sandy was confident that the survey was well designed and would reflect the public mood accurately.

"It's a matter of psychology," he explained. "Anthony will be here any minute. I could see last night shook him up. I want to hit him hard while he's in a mood to listen."

"For once," Bill said, "I'm not going to stop you." The phone buzzed and he walked over to pick it up. "Right. Send them in. And, Liz, we'll need some more coffee in here." As Bill crossed the room, he looked back over his shoulder at Sandy. "Be as abrasive as you want," he said. "After all, Larimer is too much of a gentleman to hit someone weaker than he is."

The moment Kate laid eyes on Anthony, she felt a whole host of emotions she could have done without, chief among them worry. He looked as tired as Sandy, but even more than that, he looked horribly unsure of himself. In the five-odd months since she'd first seen his face on a television screen, she'd never noticed such quiet dejection on it.

Vince Collier was several steps behind. He slowly shook his head and waved his hand back and forth a few times. The subtle gesture said "Go easy on him" and necessitated a swift shift in strategy.

Anthony's eyes flickered around the room, not really acknowledging the three people already present. He slumped into a chair, declining Bill's offer of coffee.

When Sandy opened his mouth to talk, Kate held her breath. "I've got about two-thirds of our exit polls here, Anthony," he began. He tapped the stack of papers. "I'll have the rest by five, and I'll start analyzing the data tomorrow. But I've spent most of the night reading through what I have, and I can tell you this: You can win in November. You'll have to work your tail off, you'll have to keep your foot out of your mouth, and you'll have to show the voters a side of yourself you couldn't—or wouldn't—show them before, but Bob Woodruff doesn't have the election sewn up. Maybe thirty to thirty-five percent of the total electorate is solid in his camp, but the same is true for you. The people who voted against you know who you are. A lot of them voted the way they did to send you a message. There are things about you they don't like, but almost all of them can find something good to say also. That's more than a lot of candidates have going for them."

Kate could have hugged Sandy for being tactful for once, but Anthony merely muttered, "Since when did you become a cheerleader, Cohen?"

Sandy shrugged at Bill and kept his mouth shut. Kate, thinking that gentleness might have been the wrong strategy after all, decided to try the opposite. "Dr. Larimer," she said firmly, "we will permit you several days of sarcasm, depression, and general ill humor. You can lick your wounds while you make life miserable for everyone in sight. But once your time is up, I expect you to remember that you've just won a primary election and will be on the ballot in November."

When Anthony had no perceptible reaction to this lecture,

Kate's tough facade promptly crumbled. "Five months ago the only thing people knew about you was your name. Now the whole state knows exactly what you stand for. We have the same length of time to work on your image and get you elected. Republican sweep or not, I think you'd be a better senator than Bob Woodruff. All we need to do is convince the voters of that."

"You don't understand." From the intimate way that Anthony was looking at Kate, they might have been the only two people in the room. The physical attraction she felt for him had increased rather than waned over the last few months, but most of the time she kept her feelings well hidden. Now, however, with Anthony so very subdued, it was impossible to keep the concern and tenderness out of her eyes. "I realized a couple of weeks ago that all of you were right," he went on. "I've tried to make the changes you want. So what happens? I go *down* by two percentage points."

"That's one way of looking at it," Sandy responded. "On the other hand, any poll has a margin of error built into it. Three weeks before the election I had you at 54.4 percent. The actual figure was 52.3 percent. Maybe you didn't gain any ground, but in essence you held your own. You've got a first-rate team behind you and every one of us agrees with Kate. You can do something for this country, and for this state, that Bob Woodruff can't."

The barest hint of a smile nudged its way onto Anthony's lips. Kate watched it grow and then sat there, amazed, as the smile turned into a burst of laughter. It reminded her of the first time they'd met, when he'd convinced her he was half crazy and then dissolved into hysterics. "Hell, Sandy," he said, wiping away a tear, "if I listen to you for much longer, I may decide to run for *president!*"

Sandy grinned at him. "We do the difficult here, Anthony, not the impossible. The only one who could beat Eli Hendrickson this year is Franklin Delano Roosevelt, and unfortunately for the Democrats, he isn't running."

Now that the candidate had regained his balance, they were

able to get to work. During June and July they would concentrate on community organization and fund raising. Anthony couldn't afford to take off two full terms from teaching, so he'd arranged to teach over the summer and take off the first term of the new academic year, from early September through the beginning of January. He would therefore be able to campaign full-time during the crucial months before the election.

Bill sketched out several ideas for television commercials, all of which had the same general thrust: to portray the candidate as warm and caring and to convince the voters that he knew how to listen. According to Sandy the voters perceived Anthony as patriotic, well informed, and intelligent, but believed that Bob Woodruff had those same qualities, as well as approachability and a commitment to representing the people of California as well as himself. The fact that Bob had three terrific teen-agers and a wife whom everyone loved didn't hurt him any either. Anthony winced at a suggestion that his family, particularly Jessica, be given high visibility in the campaign, but promised to consider it. From what Kate had learned of the girl, she'd be the first to agree to the idea.

Sandy summarized the results of his polling, which left the ball squarely in Kate's court. "Well," she said airily, "they don't call me the Henry Higgins of California politics for nothing. We'll just have to work on that ornery, arrogant, pompous behavior of yours until we stamp it out."

Anthony grimaced, then stood up. "'Tell me, Dr. Larimer,'" he mimicked, "'do you think the federal government should construct the Crane River Dam and reroute water from the Sierras to the Central Valley?'" A mask slipped onto his face, the warm, folksy smile of Bob Woodruff. "'I've studied that issue carefully, Tony, and I believe that the rain near the Crane falls mainly on the plain.' Which is about as lucid as Bob ever gets on that particular issue," Anthony grumbled.

"We're working on a series of debates," Vince reminded

Anthony, "with a format where each candidate can question the others. I hope you'll be able to back Bob into a corner on a few of those issues. Politely, of course."

"Of course," Anthony agreed sarcastically. "It wouldn't do to be arrogant and aggressive. I might shock a little old lady in Red Bluff."

"What all of us need is a vacation." Bill Dorset got up, bringing the meeting to a close. "Let's get together in a few weeks, Vince. By then I'll have some concrete ideas for the media campaign, and Sandy will be able to give you a complete analysis of the polling he's done. Should we go ahead with the rock concert?"

"Yes. It'll get us a lot of ink, along with visibility among younger voters. Not to mention a hundred thou or so."

Appointment books were pulled out of miscellaneous pockets and a meeting date selected. Kate was about to leave when a husky "Uh, Katie?" from Anthony caught her attention.

Her guard went up when she noticed the look in his eyes, but she managed a breezy, "Yes?"

"Can I see you in your office for a couple of minutes?"

"Sure." Kate opened the door and waited for him to leave, then followed. Once they were in her office, she retreated to the safety of her desk, leaving Anthony no choice but to take the chair across from her. She knew perfectly well that if he touched her she'd promptly cave in and that afterward she'd be totally disgusted with herself.

"I just wanted you to know," he began, "that I'm sorry about the things I said a few months ago."

Kate felt a tug of sympathy—Anthony was pleating a piece of paper—but she wasn't about to rehash ancient history. "You apologized at the time. If that's all . . ."

"It's not all. You don't understand." His face was a little flushed. "I've known for over a month that I acted like an arrogant idiot. It seems to be one of my less admirable traits."

"And humility is one of your least convincing," Kate retorted. She refused to pick up where they'd left off.

"What's this all about? You want to go to bed with me, but you figure you need to eat a little crow first?"

When he stood up, Kate felt like biting her tongue. He looked nothing short of grim, and she realized that she hadn't given him much of a chance to explain his feelings before jumping all over him. "I'm sorry," she said quickly. "I guess I was just being defensive."

He studied her face for a long moment, still standing. Kate allowed him to see how very much she cared.

"I thought . . . maybe I could take you to dinner tonight. It would have to be early—I have an eight o'clock flight to Oakland."

Kate knew the answer to her next question but asked it anyway. "I take it this has nothing to do with business?"

"You take it right." He took a few steps forward; the next couple of sentences came out in a rush. "I can't make any promises. I don't know how I feel, except that I made a jerk of myself three months ago and I want you. . . ." He cut himself off. "You're so different from Beth," he muttered.

Kate felt a tight coldness in her chest. "Meaning I'm not suitable?" she asked stiffly.

"No! I don't mean that at all. It would just be an entirely different kind of relationship, that's all, and you know I'm not the most adaptable guy in the world. But I'm serious about this, Katie. I want to be with you."

Her anger quickly evaporated, giving way to a poignant smile. "Not adaptable," she said, "but honest and very decent. I'd like to have dinner with you. You've already heard my speech about getting involved with clients, so I want to remind you that I'm breaking the rules for you. I think—I'm serious, too, Anthony. I've hated the last few months."

"You shouldn't tell me things like that," he said hoarsely. "You don't know what it does to me."

"On the contrary," Kate teased, "I can see *exactly* what it does to you." Knowing Anthony, if she gave him too much encouragement, she'd wind up half naked on the carpet. "I'll pick you up at your hotel at five-thirty and we can eat near the airport." She pulled the top folder off a pile on her desk and pretended to start reading.

Out of the corner of her eye she saw Anthony's scowl at being dismissed like a pesky little boy, but he stifled his objections and agreed, then let himself out of the office.

Chapter 13

KATE WAS WEAVING HER WAY IN AND OUT OF LOS ANGELES traffic, changing lanes whenever she saw an opening, when the car in front of her braked sharply. She did the same, muttering under her breath. She must have been insane, driving Anthony to the airport during rush hour instead of eating at his hotel and taking him to the airport afterward.

Then again, she knew exactly why she was fighting the traffic. She was afraid that Anthony would find some excuse to drag her up to his room. Twice now he had coaxed or seduced her into bed, and it wasn't going to happen a third time. She needed a few answers first.

As they inched along, she glanced across at him. He was staring at the car ahead of them, his right hand gripping the door handle. "Nervous?" she teased.

He started. "What? Am I—no, not really." His denial was less than convincing.

"With your background, I would have expected nerves of steel," Kate said.

"Not with a woman driver on the Los Angeles freeways,"

he muttered. "I've known a lot of dark alleys where I felt safer."

Kate informed him that he was a male chauvinist, adding that she'd never had an accident in her life. He promptly apologized, trying to stifle a yawn. Traffic started to move again and Kate returned her attention to the road. A few minutes later she noticed that Anthony was asleep, his head lolling back against the headrest. He looked endearingly boyish and innocent that way.

It was past six-thirty when she pulled up to a hotel near the airport entrance and parked the car. The lack of motion woke Anthony up; he immediately glanced at his watch and frowned. "I wish I could stay in LA," he said, "but Kris is going away for a four-day weekend with a friend tonight, and I don't want to leave Jessica alone."

"That's okay." Kate reached for the door handle, half expecting Anthony to stop her. He didn't, even though he looked like he wanted to. She'd momentarily forgotten how much attention he could attract, but the stares as they walked into the hotel reminded her. Any notion she might have had about an intimate, meaningful conversation over dinner began to fade moments after they were seated in the coffee shop.

A man of about Anthony's age approached the table, politely explaining why Anthony was wrong on a number of issues. Kate studied the menu while Anthony listened, ultimately telling the man, "You've given me a lot to think about. Thanks for stopping by."

"I think he's disappointed that you didn't try to argue with him," Kate said as the man returned to his family.

"I'm trying to act like a politician." Anthony raised a hand to summon the waitress, who gave him a dazzling smile as she took out her order pad and volunteered the information that she'd voted for him the day before.

Once they were alone again, Anthony rested his elbows on the table and leaned forward. "You must have had a tough couple of months. The Pendergast election was a real horse race."

"But November will be a piece of cake." Kate didn't want to talk shop. "What made you change your mind about *us*, Anthony?"

Before he could get three words out, a woman and her teen-age daughter were standing by the table. "Susie would like your autograph," the woman said, shoving a paper napkin at him. Susie looked mortified.

As Anthony scrawled his name, the woman stared hard at Kate. "Are *you* anybody?" she finally demanded.

Kate shook her head, trying not to laugh. "No. Nobody famous."

"Well, sign it anyway," the woman ordered.

Kate wrote out "Katharine A. Garvey" and returned the napkin to its owner. By mutual agreement she and Anthony abandoned any further attempt to talk seriously. Anthony started to tell her about some of the stranger people he'd run across during the campaign, prompting Kate to reply that she'd seen her share of eccentrics roaming the corridors of the capitol. In between eating and coping with interruptions, they managed to have a very enjoyable time laughing at each other's stories.

Only when they were seated in the car again did Anthony answer Kate's question. "We have a few minutes," he began. "Let's sit here and talk."

With the chemistry between them working overtime, Kate had other things on her mind besides conversation. The tingling arousal that had started over dinner was growing into a hot-blooded ache, now that they were alone together in the car. She forced herself to disregard the effect he always had on her and agreed. "I'd like that."

"You asked me what made me change my mind. The truth is—seeing you and not being able to touch you. You've been friendly enough and very encouraging, but underneath that, I knew you were angry with me. A couple of weeks ago Kevin O'Neal stopped by to spend the evening and we talked things over. Maybe that's when I finally admitted to myself that there weren't any carbon copies of Beth floating around—and that even if there were, I might not want that anymore. Kevin mentioned that you asked him about me; otherwise I wouldn't have had the nerve to speak to you. I just know that I want you, Katie. Do you have any idea what it's doing to me, to sit here like this, knowing that in five minutes you'll have to take me to catch my plane?"

It wasn't precisely the explanation that Kate had hoped to hear. "You know, Anthony," she said gently, "for the past few months I've been watching you, learning from you, and coming to really care about you. But all you seem to think about is sex."

"I didn't say that." Anthony sounded disgruntled.

"Didn't you?"

"No. Of course I care about you. If I didn't, do you think I would have been afraid to approach you? I know you're not the kind of woman a man takes to bed and forgets."

Kate couldn't believe what she was hearing. "Are you saying," she asked coolly, "that if I'd had as many lovers as you undoubtedly have, you wouldn't be able to—to respect me?"

Anthony looked at his watch and muttered that he'd even miss his plane if that's what it took to straighten Kate out. "And don't start in with the feminist rhetoric," he added. "I'm thirty-nine years old and I was raised in a very strict family. I grew up with a different standard of behavior from the men you seem to meet. I think you realize that there haven't been all that many women since Beth, and if you're asking whether I'd marry someone who's been passed around to half my friends, the answer is no."

"You'll have to give me a list." Kate smiled sweetly at him. "I'll check off the ones I've been to bed with."

Anthony raised his eyes heavenward in exasperation, then slowly smiled at her. "I got further with you when I took instead of asked," he drawled. He picked up her purse and tossed it onto the floor near her feet, then slid over.

"Oh, no you don't," Kate warned as his thigh made contact with her own. "We're supposed to be talking. If you lay a finger on me, I'm going to hit the horn, Anthony."

Her threat made no impression on him. "Those are fairly

tough conditions," he said, "but I think I can live with them."
He held up his hands, then twisted them behind his back.

Kate grumbled that she should have known better than to
get involved with a straitlaced professor, but the truth of the
matter was that her objections, never very strong to begin
with, had weakened to almost nothing in the face of his lazy
smile and husky tone. A torrid chill raced along her veins
when he leaned over to taste the sensitive little hollow just
below her ear and then proceeded to nibble the lobe. The
weight of his body was pressing her against the door, but she
scarcely noticed it when the handle started to dig into her
spine. His chest was flush against her breasts, making them
swell with pleasure even through the intervening layers of
clothing. True to his word, Anthony wasn't touching her—at
least, not with his hands.

Kate already knew that his lips and tongue could tease her
until she was feverish with desire, but now he proved it all
over again. Tiring of her ear, he dropped a series of hard little
kisses along her jaw and then turned his attention to her lips.
She closed her eyes, all sensation focused on her mouth now.
His lips made a tentative pass back and forth, then settled
down for a thorough reconnaissance. As he explored and
probed, Kate slid her arms around his neck. A familiar
hunger suffused her body, leaving it pliant and responsive.

Only when her lips were parted in submission did Anthony
ease away from her. He waited until she opened her eyes,
then asked, "Am I allowed to use my hands yet, ma'am?" He
was smiling a little too triumphantly, but his voice was smoky
with passion.

Kate refused to give him the satisfaction of a yes. "You're a
dirty fighter," she complained.

"True. But it sure beats arguing." He bent forward and
started to kiss her again, but lightly, almost chastely. His
self-control was infuriating. Finally, defeated by frustration,
she said irritably, "I'm not going to blow the stupid horn,
Anthony."

His arms went around her almost instantly, holding her
possessively, while his tongue invaded her mouth with a

yearning roughness that stunned and then utterly conquered her. There was no finesse to their kiss—it was a devouring mutual explosion that refused to end. Kate couldn't get enough of him; her whole body was suddenly on fire.

By the time they surfaced for air, Anthony was breathing rapidly, a film of perspiration on his face. "Any more of this," he muttered, "and I'm going to . . ." His voice trailed off, but Kate got the message. She felt exactly the same way.

"When can I see you again?" he asked. "Next weekend?"

"You'll be at home *this* weekend?"

He nodded. "With Jessica. But I want you to myself, Katie. Someplace quiet and far away. Can you get away or not?"

Kate suspected that she was being oversensitive, but couldn't help asking whether he wanted to go away with her in order to keep her away from his home and his daughter. He stroked her cheek and answered tenderly, "Of course not, honey. But I'm not going to look over my shoulder every time I want to touch you. We could go up north, maybe to Shasta Lake. Have you ever been there?"

She had, and the idea of going back with Anthony was irresistible. "I'd love that," she said. "We could rent a boat and cruise around the lake. People can't stop you to argue politics when you're in a motorboat, can they?"

"No. Or when you're in a motel room," he teased. "If you can come Friday, I'll make a reservation . . ."

"Hold it." Kate gave him a regretful look. "I have a dinner on Friday that I have to attend, but I can fly into Oakland first thing Saturday and we can leave directly from the airport. And let me handle the room reservation, Anthony. The moment they hear your name they'll call the local paper."

He took her into his arms and kissed her gently on the lips. "Promise me you won't change your mind," he ordered.

"I promise." Kate wriggled out of his grasp. "You can still catch your plane if we hurry, Anthony."

He picked up her purse and fished out her key. "I'll probably go crazy between now and next Saturday," he said, putting the key into the ignition for her.

Kate smiled to herself and started the car, thinking that if she had any say in the matter, he'd go crazy *on* next Saturday and not before.

Kate's plane landed in Oakland at a quarter of nine. She and Anthony had spoken twice in the last eight days—brief, intense conversations that had nothing to do with politics. She'd discovered that he was something of a romantic at times. He liked to whisper all the different places on her body he planned to kiss, and exactly what he imagined each caress would do to her. She only hoped his phone wasn't tapped.

He was standing with an elderly couple as she walked out of the jetway, trying to disengage himself from what appeared to be a lecture. Kate walked over, smiling formally despite the jeans and short-sleeved sweater she wore, and said to him, "Thank you for meeting my plane, Dr. Larimer. I hate to drag you away from potential constituents, but if we're going to be on time for your meeting, we really have to go."

Anthony introduced her to the couple at his side, asked for their support in November, and then escaped toward the baggage claim area. "I'm beginning to think that even Shasta Lake isn't far enough," he said, once they'd collected her suitcase and were seated in the car. "Maybe we should go up to Oregon."

"That's another two or three hours. Do you really want to wait that long?" Kate twisted around and gave him a tantalizing little nibble on the corner of his mouth.

Her lips were captured in a hungry, probing kiss that made her wonder just how far she could tease him today without being consumed in the flames. "I'll probably get a speeding ticket as it is," he muttered as he pulled away and started the engine.

"I can see you plan to drag me straight to bed," Kate remarked.

"You'd better believe it," Anthony answered.

To Kate's way of thinking, such overbearing male arrogance deserved harsh punishment. She was just as eager as Anthony, but the thought of tempting and taunting him until he was ready to explode was far too delicious to resist. As he pulled out of the airport, she raised a playful hand to his face and brushed her fingers across his lips. "I've been thinking about this all week," she murmured. "The feel of your skin, the way you kiss me, the way you move inside me. Just talking about it turns me on. Did I tell you I got a king-sized bed?"

"No," he answered curtly.

Kate's hand trailed down Anthony's arm and drifted to his leg, moving lightly up and down the tautened thigh. "Cut it out, Katie," he finally growled.

"Don't you like me to touch you?" she asked. "You look so cute in jeans and a golf shirt that I could eat you up. Let me see now. Where should I start?" She leaned over and nibbled her way up the muscles of his exposed arm.

"*Katie . . .*" he threatened.

She sighed and straightened up. "All right. I'll behave myself—for the moment. Why don't you tell me about the papers you've been grading?"

Anthony had mentioned that several of his seminar students had done outstanding work, and now he elaborated. His enthusiasm was contagious, involving Katie so deeply in a discussion of the papers that she almost forgot the reason for her presence in his car. Almost, but not quite. She sat close beside him, deliberately touching him every now and then, well aware that he wasn't ignoring her provocation nearly as successfully as he appeared to be. When they pulled into a gas station for a cold drink, he looked at her with a hungry intensity that left her weak in the knees. The better she knew this man, the more potent his effect on her seemed to be.

"You know what I'm thinking?" he said.

"For heaven's sake, Anthony, there's nothing but miles of fields all around." Kate giggled and scrambled out of the car. Anthony caught up with her just as she reached the soda machine.

"I did notice the blanket in the back," she teased, "but it's going to be for picnics, not for making love on. You'll have to wait."

"I don't *have* to do anything." Anthony glanced around to make sure that no one was watching before pulling her into his arms. "You're deliberately driving me crazy," he accused. "Give me one for the road."

Kate wound her arms around his neck and nuzzled his lips. "All right," she sighed, "but it will probably just make things worse." Her body and her tongue were maddeningly elusive, moving sensuously and clinging for long moments, only to suddenly dart away. After a minute or so of this treatment Anthony placed a firm hand at the base of Kate's spine to keep her body close to his, then twined the fingers of his other hand through her hair to coax her head up.

"There's a term for what you're doing," he said.

"Is there?" Kate asked innocently. A wave of heat shimmered through her body. "Maybe I should get two rooms, just for the sake of propriety. I noticed a pay phone near—"

Anthony cut her off with the sweetest kind of punishment, kissing her until his demanding mouth and thrusting body were the sum total of her universe. When he finally eased away from her, he seemed well pleased by her glazed expression. "Two rooms?" he repeated.

It took Kate a moment to figure out what he was talking about. "Who said anything about two rooms?" she asked.

They bought a couple of sodas and returned to the car. For about fifteen minutes they drove in silence, but eventually Anthony asked Kate about the Pendergast election, and her answer led them to a discussion about his own prospects in November. The conversation kept them occupied during the tedious drive north. About an hour out of Redding, Kate offered to drive; by now they could see Lassen Peak and several smaller mountains to the east, and over one hundred miles ahead, 14,000-foot Mount Shasta. In the summer haze, it was almost possible to confuse the snowcapped mountain with the sporadic white clouds that drifted along the horizon.

Kate had chosen a small, quiet motel on the outskirts of Redding, the nearest sizable city to Shasta Lake. Anthony waited in the car while she checked in and asked about a place to eat lunch. Of course, she thought as the clerk handed a key to the customer ahead of her, Anthony hadn't seemed all that interested in eating, even though it was past twelve-thirty.

Once her own key was tucked away in her purse, she picked up a couple of brochures from the rack by the desk and went back outside. Her features were schooled into a disappointed frown as she slid behind the wheel. "The room isn't ready," she said. "They only have one room with a king-sized bed, and the people who slept there last night haven't checked out yet. The woman isn't feeling well. The clerk promised they'd be out by two-thirty."

"Two hours?" Anthony made it sound like a lifetime. "Let's get a different room—go someplace else. I can't wait another two hours, Katie."

Kate contrived to look vastly offended. "Anthony, I'd like to see more than the inside of a bedroom this weekend. I've just put in a crippling couple of months on the Pendergast campaign and very soon I'll be working day and night for *you*. I need to relax. I don't see why we can't pick up a picnic lunch, drive out to the lake and rent a boat, and spend the next few hours on the water." She paused, then sniffed, "I'm sure your glands can survive the strain."

He studied her irritated expression and then reached for her, but her rigid anger stopped him cold. "What is it you want? Candlelight and music?" he demanded.

"It might be nice." With the outside temperature close to 90° the car was quite warm, so Kate started the engine, switched on the air conditioning, and made a U-turn out of the parking lot. "In the five months that we've known each other, you've never even taken me out for a decent dinner or a movie. You snap your fingers and I'm supposed to fall into bed. Is it too much to ask . . ."

"Okay, okay." Anthony ran his fingers through his hair, muttering something about the peculiarities of womankind. Pleased by his reaction, Kate drove to the deli-style restaurant recommended by the desk clerk and coaxed a brooding Anthony to come inside with her and pick out some lunch.

She had second thoughts about her tactics as they drove
north—Anthony was very miffed indeed—but decided that
he'd forgive her as soon as she permitted him to seduce her.
They rented a small powerboat and some water skis and then
returned to the car for their bathing suits, towels, and the
blanket, changing in the rest rooms. Anthony was buying
suntan lotion when Kate emerged. His lips tightened omi-
nously when she sashayed up in a yellow string bikini, a towel
draped over her shoulder, but he didn't say anything until she
slipped an arm around his waist and teased that he had gained
some weight.

"Maybe a pound or two," he mumbled, removing her hand
from his body.

Kate ran her fingers over his stomach and around his
middle, as though testing the truth of his claim. He caught her
hand, noticed that a couple of teen-agers were staring at
them, and stalked off to the car.

They left their clothing in the trunk and then walked down
a flight of wooden steps to the dock. Once Anthony had
maneuvered the boat away from the jetty and into the open
channel, Kate settled back in her seat and closed her eyes,
savoring the feel of the cool breeze on her heated skin.

The modern-day Shasta Lake, fed by three major rivers,
had been created by the construction of a six-hundred-foot-
high dam at the southwest end of the lake. Though Shasta's
primary purposes were flood control and water supply, the
residents of the surrounding area preferred to put recreation
first on the list. In dry years, when the level of the lake was
unappetizingly low, due to the release of water to Southern
California, residents who depended on tourism for their
livelihoods would complain vociferously to their federal
representatives that the south's demand for water was ruining
them economically. Anthony Larimer, who tended to side
with big agriculture on such matters, had made more than a
few enemies up here.

Rainfall had been unusually heavy the past winter, and the
water level was near a record high. The 370 miles of shoreline

twisted and turned to produce an endless number of little
inlets and coves along the four main forks of the lake. The
surrounding land was heavily wooded with evergreens and
dotted with mountain peaks, some of them over 4,000 feet
high.

When Anthony accelerated sharply, Kate opened her eyes
and looked around. They were in the main channel now, the
tip of the boat thrusting high into the air and then dropping
down. The sensation of speed and power seemed to improve
Anthony's mood. He smiled and raised a hand to trace the
curve of Kate's neck, and she smiled back. Occasionally they
passed a houseboat or powerboat as they cruised along, but
the lake was so large that they could pretend it was their own
private playground.

Anthony was heading for the easternmost fork of the lake,
the Pit River. He slowed down as the channel narrowed and
began to look for a place to stop for lunch. When he came to a
little creek that offered a stretch of sunny rock along its shore,
he turned left and cruised to a likely-looking tree to tie up the
boat. Then he tossed the picnic lunch and the blanket onto
the rocks, got out himself, and extended a hand to Kate. He
had such a devilish glint in his eye that she was afraid he was
going to push her into the water, but he didn't.

They walked inland a little ways, spreading the blanket
down near some trees so that it was half in the sun, half in the
shade. "I didn't realize how hot it was when we were out in
the boat," Kate said, starting to apply suntain lotion to her
face and shoulders. When she was finished she handed the
bottle to Anthony, asking him to do her back for her.

"You enjoy living dangerously, don't you?" he grumbled.
Kate gave a contented little moan as he spread the lotion over
her back with brusque, impersonal strokes.

"Well, you wouldn't want me to get burned." When
Anthony abruptly declined her offer to return the favor, she
stretched languidly and then sat down cross-legged on the
blanket. "It's gorgeous here—a perfect day," she said. "Let's
eat."

The tension between them gradually mounted as their sandwiches and drinks slowly disappeared. They'd exchanged only a handful of words during lunch and now they were sitting side by side, silently facing the water, Anthony's eyes on the opposite shore rather than on Kate. She stood up, announcing that she was hot, and trotted to the shore to wade in a few feet. Although the water was cold, she was warm enough not to mind. She quickly ducked down to her shoulders and then jumped up again, a bold blond goddess with water streaming down her body, her bikini even more revealing now that it was wet.

"You should try that," Kate said when she returned, reaching down for her towel. She deliberately brushed her breasts against Anthony's shoulder on the way back up.

He took a long swig of beer, gave Kate a menacing look, and then took her advice. His short swim in the lake might have cooled his skin, but it did nothing to slake his passion. Kate took in the picture he presented—the muscled, lean body in modest blue trunks that did nothing to hide his desire for her—and gave him a cheeky grin.

"It's much too early to go back yet," she said. "Besides, you haven't tried water skiing." She picked up a towel and started to slowly dry him, paying special attention to his chest and thighs. Touching him so freely aroused her almost as much as it aroused him. He was standing so stiffly that she knew he was struggling not to take her into his arms.

"Is something the matter?" she asked ingenuously. "You seem a little—preoccupied."

"I understand that you're paying me back for the last couple of months," he growled, "but that doesn't mean I have to like it. No more, Katie."

"But your suit is soaking wet," she answered blithely, and proceeded to pat it dry—inch by tormenting inch. Finally, only too aware that she'd pushed him right to the wall, she dropped the towel and pecked him on the lips. "Time to go," she announced.

He stayed right where he was. "You realize," he said, "that

I have absolutely no intention of permitting that indecent bikini of yours to continue to cover your beautiful body. Take it off, Katie."

"In *public*, Anthony?" Kate managed to sound scandalized. "The room will be ready—"

"To hell with the room!" Anthony scooped Kate up in a single deft motion and slung her over his shoulder. With his free hand he grabbed the blanket, then marched off into the woods.

"I'm not a sack of potatoes," Kate hissed. "Put me down."

Her writhing attempts to escape accomplished nothing, but then, they were meant only to arouse her captor. When Anthony set her down among the evergreen needles, firmly holding her wrist, she airily assured him that she had no intention of running away.

He dropped her hand, his eyes narrowing. "Oh, yeah?"

Kate removed the blanket from his arm and spread it neatly on the ground. After a gentle tug at the string ties behind her back, her damp bikini top was clinging loosely to her breasts; a tug at the strings behind her neck and it slid to the ground. She removed the bottom with equal efficiency. Anthony stood there, motionless, his hands on his hips, his legs spread slightly apart, looking annoyed with her.

She dropped to her knees at his feet, her hands upraised. "What do you think you're doing?" he demanded.

"Taking off your bathing suit." He didn't cooperate as she maneuvered the wet trunks over his narrow hips and down his powerful legs, but he didn't exactly object either. Just looking at him, standing there naked like some vengeful god, made Kate ache for his possession. She ran teasing fingers up his calf to his thigh, and then higher. He was already fully aroused, and when her lips followed her hand to coax him out of his black mood, he resisted for all of fifteen or twenty seconds before groaning out a hoarse "Oh, *God*, Katie—I can't take any more of this" and dropping down beside her.

As he molded her body against his, Kate could feel him trembling, his heart beating quickly and heavily. The heat of his hardened body, the male scent and salty taste of his sweat-slick skin, made her dizzy with desire for him. Her own pulse rate soared as their lips met, tasted, probed. One burning kiss and she was lost, shaking as much as he was. As he pulled her underneath him, her hands stole around his waist, her thighs obediently parting in response to a hard, arrogant leg.

He brought her to the brink of satisfaction, abruptly pulling away just before sheer ecstasy blocked out everything else in the world. Breathless and confused, Kate opened her eyes and stared at him.

He brushed a few stray locks of her hair away from her flushed face and smiled complacently down at her. He was in complete control now, not only of her body, but of the situation.

"The room was empty, wasn't it, Katie." It was a statement, not a question.

She nodded, unable to say a word.

"And you didn't give a damn about going out to dinner or a movie, did you?" he continued.

Kate shook her head.

"Aloud, Katie," he demanded. "I want to hear you admit it."

"No, Anthony," she managed.

"In fact, you've been having a terrific time teasing me all day today, haven't you."

"Yes," she whispered. Anthony's hand wandered to her breasts, brushing methodically back and forth until Kate could barely catch her breath. Then he took her all over again, moving his body with sensual slowness, watching intently until she closed her eyes and moaned his name.

She was arching her neck for his kiss when he abruptly stilled. "Katie!"

Startled, her eyes flew open. "Anthony, please . . ." she whispered.

"When I'm ready," he drawled. "First admit that you're crazy about me."

She was in no fit state to resent his lazy arrogance. "You know I am."

"And for the next day and a half, we'll make love whenever and wherever I say."

"Yes, Anthony." She hesitated, then added, "If that's your idea of punishment—"

"And furthermore," he interrupted, "you're very, very sorry that you put me through all the torments of hell today, aren't you?"

Kate shook her head, a satisfied smile tugging at the corners of her mouth. "No, I'm not, Anthony."

"But you're going to make it up to me?" he asked, smiling back at her.

"Definitely, Anthony. Whenever and wherever you say," she promised.

"And you promise never to do it again?"

"Not a chance, Anthony." Kate giggled. "And if you're all through questioning me, could we finish making love? *Please?*"

His mouth came down hard on hers, ending both his questions and her answers. After eight days apart and five frustrating hours together, it took less than a single passionate minute before a throbbing explosion tore through both of them, leaving them weak and fulfilled in each other's arms. Afterward, Kate ran a lazy finger down Anthony's chest, tracing the arrow of hair that dipped below his navel, and sighed, "That's what I get for getting mixed up with a spy. A merciless, torturing interrogation."

Anthony took her hand and planted a kiss in the palm. "If all my duties with the Agency had been this pleasant, I never would have resigned."

After dinner at a superb French restaurant in Red Bluff, Kate dragged Anthony to a foreign film in Redding. She'd heard that it was erotic, but her informant had underestimated how much so; halfway through the movie Anthony put his arm around Kate's waist and stood up, taking her along with him. "Whenever" had obviously arrived; to her relief, "wherever" turned out to be their room and not the back seat of the car.

Wanting to spoil him, she got up early on Sunday and went out for breakfast and a newspaper. Any notions she might have had about spending the day sightseeing were abandoned when she realized that he had no intention of letting her out of bed once she got back. As they drove home that afternoon, she felt a contentment that was entirely new to her. Even saying good-bye to each other at the airport caused no wrenching pain; Anthony would be in Los Angeles in another week to deliver a speech. She was surprised by how quickly she invited him to stay at her house. All her scruples about her professional reputation had been pushed into the background. His genuine pleasure in accepting her invitation was enough to keep them there.

Chapter 14

"NOBODY COULD ACCUSE YOU OF NOT FOLLOWING OUR ADVICE, Anthony." Bill Dorset was uncorking a bottle of California Chardonnay as Anthony Larimer, Kate Garvey, Sandy Cohen, Vince Collier, and George McClure settled into chairs around his conference table. The strategy session that was about to begin was the latest in a series of meetings that had taken place throughout the summer and early fall. Slightly over a month remained before the election.

Bill's secretary brought in a tray of hors d'oeuvres and everyone tried to relax, despite a situation that was more conducive to ulcers. As Bill poured the wine, he continued, "It's one of those situations where the breaks are going against you. Sandy, you want to run down the latest poll?"

Sandy Cohen passed out photocopied summaries of the data. "You can see that our basic problem isn't going away. Woodruff has solid conservative support with nobody on his right to drain away votes, whereas Anthony has two minor party candidates on the left who are continuing to attract about seven to nine percent of the vote. In the latest poll Bob is ahead forty-two percent to forty percent with ten percent undecided, but that could change back again by next week. The fact is, Anthony, you're between a rock and a hard place. Those undecided voters are middle-of-the-roaders who feel that both you and Bob are good candidates. If you move to the left to try to pick up liberal voters who decide not to waste a vote on a minor party candidate, you're going to lose support from the center, and vice versa. Hendrickson's campaign for a Republican Congress is just one more headache for us. I'm afraid it's coming down to what you most dislike—a sort of popularity contest."

Anthony cupped his wineglass in both hands, his elbows resting lightly on the table. "Bob was better in that first debate than I expected him to be. The guy could charm a cobra and weasel through a mesh screen." He looked at Kate. "I've gone about as far down the road as I can manage with sincerity and responsiveness. Jessica's practically a full-time professional candidate's daughter by now; we're spending a fortune on media time to run commericals that make me look like a cross between Dag Hammarskjöld and St. Francis of Assisi; and if my schedule gets any heavier . . ." He hesitated, then murmured, "You know how tired I've been at night, Katie."

Though Kate's relationship with Anthony was hardly a secret, a light flush crept into her cheeks at his personal reference. Occasionally Bill had taken her aside and asked her to coax Anthony into reconsidering his position on some subject or issue, but the fact that they were lovers was never openly discussed. Anthony was even quite demonstrative in public by now, and although Kate wasn't entirely comfortable with that, she enjoyed his expressions of affection too much to object.

Knowing that it was foolish to be embarrassed, she gently agreed. "Yes, I do. And frankly, I'm out of suggestions. Even if it were possible for you to change your style any more than you've already changed it, you would come across as phony and opportunistic. People expect a certain reserve and formality from you by now."

"What we need," Vince Collier announced, popping a cheese puff into his mouth, "is a major foreign crisis. It's the one area where Anthony can run circles around Bob, but the voters don't pay attention to foreign affairs until the Russians are pointing missiles at us from Cuba."

"Maybe I could order the California National Guard to invade Siberia and provoke a little trouble," George McClure drawled. "It might help Anthony more than the speeches I've been making for him."

"At least speeches won't get you committed to the nearest mental hospital," Vince reminded him. "We'll have to come up with something else."

Kate sighed and asked dramatically, "Where is Vladimir Rvanski now that we need him?"

The question provoked a much-needed round of laughter. "As a matter of fact," Anthony answered, "I heard that Rvanski was working as an aide to Spelnikov, the one whose villa he stormed into. The official explanation is fairly convoluted—something about divergent viewpoints accommodating and correcting each other in a dialectical process of revolution. I'm waiting for someone to reveal that Rvanski is actually Spelnikov's illegitimate son, but I suppose that only happens in bad novels."

"But the two men knew each other beforehand?" Bill asked.

Anthony shrugged. "Nobody knows, but it seems likely. The one I feel sorry for is Borlin. He's slaving away at some minor job in the Kremlin now."

"Moving back to California"—Sandy ruffled a sheet of his polling data for emphasis—"we've got an election to win in November."

"True," Bill agreed. "So let's take a look at the next four weeks and see if there's anything we want to change."

They proceeded to do exactly that, running down the list of Anthony's campaign appearances, discussing strategy for the second and final debate against Woodruff and the minor party candidates, and deciding to produce a new television commercial that would emphasize Anthony's expertise in foreign affairs. Two hours, two platters of hors d'oeuvres, and two bottles of wine later, everyone was ready to spend the night reading. They would meet again at seven at a dinner for the party's presidential candidate. Both Anthony and George McClure were scheduled to speak.

Kate didn't attempt to start a conversation with Anthony as she drove him back to her house; he didn't seem as if he was in the mood to talk. Instead she mused about the past few months, which in many ways had been ideal. She was working very hard and enjoying every minute of it. Two-thirds of Anthony's campaign time was spent in Southern California, which meant that she saw him often. Many times she would hop on a plane or drive to wherever he happened to be speaking and spend the night with him. She and Jessica were fast friends by now, keeping each other company when Anthony was busy with voters. After all the lurid tales Kate had heard about adolescent children destroying her friends' romances, she was surprised that Jessica so clearly approved of her. The girl was unusually mature and intelligent, and Kate talked to her and explained things to her as though she were an equal, which might have accounted for her attitude. It was also true, however, that neither Kate nor Anthony had ever mentioned marriage. Their relationship constituted no threat to the girl.

Kate and Anthony had grown much closer over the past four months, but they never talked about the future, even to each other. Either they focused on the past, primarily on Anthony's marriage or Kate's childhood, or they talked about the campaign. Kate believed that she loved Anthony, and yet it would have suited her perfectly if the campaign could have gone on forever, with no further commitments beyond the minutes and hours she gladly managed to spend with him. With November seventh only a month away, she could hardly ignore the fact that life would go on afterward, but when she started to worry about that, she always told herself that things would somehow work out. Whenever she suspected that they wouldn't, she simply threw herself into her work and pushed the thought aside.

For once the traffic moved briskly, and it wasn't very long before Kate pulled into her driveway. Anthony got out of the car and she did the same, following him around to the trunk.

"Did you want me to look over your speech?" she asked as he took out his suit carrier.

He shook his head. "You've heard it all before. What I need is a couple of aspirins and a shower. I'm beginning to wish it would start raining—anything would be better than this heat."

He looked rather wilted, but Kate didn't think the weather was to blame. "It's frustrating to do everything you can, to really believe in yourself, and to still find yourself fighting to stay even," she said.

"Tell me about it." They walked into the house in silence. After Anthony had hung up his bag in Kate's closet, he lay down on the bed, hands behind his head, staring at the ceiling.

"If you'd told me nine months ago that winning would become this important to me, I wouldn't have believed it. I must be more competitive than I realized, because I can't honestly stand up there and tell the voters that Bob would be a lousy senator. He wouldn't be."

Kate sat down by his waist. "But you'd be better."

"Of course." He pulled her down for a gentle kiss, but it failed to grow into anything more passionate. He merely released her, rolled off the bed, and disappeared into the shower. A moment later Kate heard the sound of running water.

She hated to see Anthony so dejected. Smiling to herself, she decided that the least she could do for him would be to try to improve his mood. She stripped off her clothing and let herself into the bathroom, finding that Anthony was already rinsing shampoo out his hair, almost done with his shower.

"Will you keep me company for a few minutes?" she asked as she opened the glass door to the stall.

"If you want me to." He stepped aside to share the spray with her and handed her the soap.

They didn't speak as Kate lathered her skin and rinsed off,

but when Anthony reached out to turn off the water, Kate covered his hand with her own and murmured, "Let me scrub your back."

Anthony shook his head. "Honey, I'm not in the mood—"

"I understand," Kate interrupted. "But a massage will relax you. You'll see."

Anthony shrugged and turned around with no discernible enthusiasm, but soon admitted to Kate that the slightly rough cloth she was using felt very pleasant against his back. When she expanded the area of her massage, he made no protest, but smiled briefly and made a sound that indicated something between acceptance and genuine approval. Kate made her hands slick with soap to more easily knead his calves and then his thighs, but for once the act of touching him didn't particularly arouse her. It was cramped in the small stall, and since Anthony was under the spray of water and Kate wasn't, it was rather cold. More to the point, however, she was concerned only with *his* pleasure right now, not with her own.

She noticed that her efforts were beginning to affect him and continued to arouse him with gentle, intimate hands, well satisfied when he moaned in contentment and closed his eyes. But relaxation gradually gave way to something far more urgent. Kate straightened up, only to have Anthony pull her into his arms and kiss her with a burning ardor, an ardor she responded to with a sweet kind of warmth but little passion. She wanted to soothe him and take care of him, nothing more.

He didn't seem to notice her mood, but backed her against the hard, tiled wall of the shower and placed firm hands beneath her bottom to gently raise her up. Kate guided him into her and put an arm around his neck for balance. She matched the rhythm of his movements, entirely content to use her knowledge of his body to bring him to a quick, shuddering climax. Afterward she held him close for several long moments until his breathing slowed and his head cleared.

Anthony turned off the water, which was tepid by now, and opened the glass door. As he and Kate toweled themselves dry, he smiled at her and murmured his thanks. She noticed that he seemed a little embarrassed, probably because his first concern as a lover had invariably been for her, not for himself.

"It was my pleasure, Dr. Larimer," she assured him. "Do you feel a little better now?"

He didn't pick up on her playful mood, but solemnly replied, "You know I do." He paused to tuck a finger under her chin. "You don't have any idea how much I look forward to the times when we're alone, Katie. Sometimes I'll be standing there, answering some inane question, ready to lose my temper, and I'll see you wink at me from the audience, or remember that in a few hours I'll be holding you in my arms, and suddenly it all seems more tolerable."

Kate hugged him. "It's been a tough campaign, and the next month will be even tougher," she said as they stood in each other's arms. "But I'll be there whenever I can, even if it's only for fifteen minutes at breakfast or to warm up your bed at night."

"And afterwards?" Anthony asked.

He'd never asked that before, and the question made Kate uncomfortable. "Afterwards you'll go to Washington, of course. We intend to win this one."

She was relieved when Anthony didn't pursue the subject. Instead he walked her into the bedroom, but rather than starting to dress, as she expected, he picked her up in his arms and set her down on the bed.

"Anthony, we really don't have time . . ." Kate began, only to be cut off when his lips settled against her mouth.

"I owe you one," he whispered.

Kate shook her head. "No, you don't. I wanted to relax you. You have a speech to give tonight."

He fondled a breast, watching the dusky peak harden in response. "Are you saying it was all in the line of duty?" His hand moved to the other breast to arouse it just as effectively.

A delightful warmth suffused Kate's body even as she teasingly answered his question. "Of course. I make love to all my candidates in the shower. Didn't you notice that clause in the contract you signed with Bill?"

Anthony bent his head to kiss her breast, nuzzling a nipple between his lips. "No wonder all of your clients are so pleased with your services," he murmured. His hand slid between her legs, gently caressing her, sending sensuous little shock waves through every part of her body. "But tell me, Katie, do all of them pay their bills?"

Kate could sense his amusement, even through the haze of desire that had enveloped her. "Sometimes"—she lost her train of thought for a minute, distracted by the fluttering movements of his fingers—"sometimes they don't. And we—they—Anthony . . . ahh . . . honey . . ." Whatever she'd planned to say was forgotten. He was setting her flesh on fire, short-circuiting her thought processes.

"I wouldn't want you to label me a deadbeat," Anthony said as his lips wandered lower. "I always settle my debts."

After that Kate couldn't get another word out, and as for Anthony, his lips and tongue were otherwise engaged. She arched her body to his mouth, lost in the pleasure he was giving her, moaning softly as he worked his exquisite magic on her.

Lost causes are never particularly appealing, but the fund raiser that night was well attended despite the near-certainty of a Hendrickson victory in November. Kate smiled her way around the room, predicting a Larimer victory and ignoring the occasional look or comment suggesting that *of course* Kate Garvey would say that about her lover. She was used to it by now. When she noticed Anthony and Bill Dorset standing with a network anchorman who was also one of the reporters for an hour-long weekly newsmagazine, she made her way over in time to pick up the end of an impassioned speech from Anthony. ". . . but I haven't been as successful as I'd have liked in communicating those kinds of things, Jack. Bill keeps telling me that the minute I find myself in front of a large group, I automatically start to lecture."

Anthony slipped an arm around Kate's shoulders and continued, "Katie, do you know Jack Walsh? Jack, this is Kate Garvey, of Dorset and Associates. Jack is putting together a segment on the California Senate race for the newsmagazine."

"We've met," Kate said, and was about to remind Jack Walsh of when and where when he announced, "Three times, to be exact. Once when I was covering one of your father's campaigns, once when I was a Washington correspondent, and once at a party in San Francisco." His eyes flickered over her body, which was slender and alluring in a simple but elegant black strapless gown. "I'd like to claim an outstanding memory, but the truth is, you're not the slightest bit forgettable."

"And *you're* just as charming in person as you are on TV," Kate answered. People were drifting toward their tables and she suggested that they do the same. "It was nice to see you again," she added to Jack.

The meal and the after-dinner speeches proceeded with predictable tediousness. After Anthony was finished with his five-minute stint in the spotlight, both Kate and Bill offered the requisite words of praise, but all of them knew that the fire and emotion he exhibited in intimate settings had been largely absent. He'd sounded concerned and well informed, but he hadn't brought the partisan audience to its feet.

As the evening drew to a close, Jack Walsh strolled up to Kate, putting a friendly arm around her waist. "Can I steal you away for a few minutes?" he asked.

"I always have time for media stars," she told him.

They sat down at a deserted table. "I've had an interesting evening," Jack said. "In private, your candidate is nothing short of inspiring. But what comes across in public is a watered-down version of the man. I'd like to do an interview with him for the TV show, an honest look at what makes him tick. I want to know about how working for the CIA affected him, what he hopes to accomplish with his life, his relationship with his daughter, his feelings about his wife's death. I asked him if he'd talk about those things and he said no, only about the issues. I gather he's a very private person. I also gather that you two are very close friends. Can you change his mind for me?"

"As one of his political advisors I wish I could say yes, Jack, but he's not the type to spill his guts for national TV. He won't even give responsive answers to routine questions from the press about those things."

Jack took out an appointment book and thumbed through the pages. "We'll be filming the candidates for the next ten days or so, then rushing the segment through postproduction in time for the election. You have until the fourteenth to work on him, okay?"

Kate said she would do her best, but when she broached the subject with Anthony that night, she knew she was wasting her time. "I'm not a movie star, Katie," he grumbled. "I've permitted my family to be put on display, I've had to read analyses of my character by people who barely know me, and at the moment reporters are more interested in my relationship with *you* than in what I can contribute as a senator. I've had enough."

"Talking to Jack would make you less mysterious," Kate cajoled. "More sympathetic and approachable. You want to win the election. . . ."

"Not that much," he stated flatly.

Although Kate dropped the subject, it didn't leave her mind. Random strands from the last few hours were weaving themselves into a pattern. They needed something dramatic to capture the voters' attention, something Anthony would *have* to talk to reporters about. He would probably kill her, but her primary job was to get him elected, and she intended to do it to the best of her ability.

Early the next morning Kate drove Anthony to the airport for his flight to San Diego, kissing him good-bye just as though she wasn't about to throw him to the wolves. She then made two phone calls, the first to Bill Dorset, the second to her father. She crisply informed Bill that she was taking the nine-o'clock flight to Washington and would return the next day, but allotted Hank Garvey a few minutes of political chitchat before coming to the point.

"I'm flying to Washington in a little while," she said. "I

need to speak to Kevin O'Neal. I want you to ask him over for dinner tonight. If he's busy, get him there for cocktails or after-dinner drinks, and if he still puts you off, threaten to investigate him if he doesn't show, but just get him there, okay?"

"You couldn't just phone him?" Hank Garvey asked, tongue firmly in cheek.

"I'm more persuasive in person, and it isn't the kind of situation where I can stroll into his office. I'll be landing at about five, but don't bother to meet my plane. I'll rent a car."

Her father agreed, his amusement very evident. He didn't ask what Kate was up to because he knew she wouldn't tell him.

Kate's mother, Frances, let her into the house at about six-thirty that evening. The two women kissed hello, cheeks barely touching, lips pecking the air. Kate inquired after her mother's health, listened to her account of a recent bout with flu, and followed her into the living room. Hank Garvey and Kevin O'Neal were seated together on the couch, but stood up as soon as the women appeared.

Kate hugged her father hello and kissed Kevin on the cheek. "Thank you for coming," she said.

"I hope you realize that I'm giving up dinner with my brother-in-law and his third wife for this," he drawled back.

"In that case, I'm sure my daughter won't keep you," Frances Garvey told him. "Of course, Kevin, I've been cooking ever since Hank phoned to say we'd have company. I've made the most wonderful pâté, with chilled asparagus soup to follow and veal for the main course. And for dessert . . ."

"Sold." Kevin stood up, nodding toward the hallway. "May Katie and I use your den, Hank?"

"Only if you promise not to bug it or search it," Hank laughed.

"I never make promises I don't intend to keep," Kevin shot back. "Katie?"

Kate installed Kevin in her father's favorite easy chair,

pulling over the desk chair for herself. She didn't waste time with small talk, but began at once. "Anthony has real problems. The election is going to be much too close for my peace of mind, Kevin."

"If you're asking me to knock off Bob Woodruff," he said with a grin, "I'm afraid I'll have to turn you down."

Kate pretended to consider it. "It's a tempting prospect, but no. I think I'll have to be more subtle than that. I want you to leak Anthony's role in the State Department case thirteen years ago."

In the best poker-faced tradition, Kevin never batted an eyelash. "I'd like to oblige," he said, "but Anthony's activities then were . . . questionable. You know I didn't follow the book on that one."

Kate cocked an eyebrow at him. "Really? Anthony took a job at the State Department. He came across something that made him suspicious, so he went to you. Naturally, you informed the attorney general and the President just like you were supposed to and cooperated fully with the subsequent FBI investigation. Nothing questionable about that or about the operation itself. You can even claim that the secretary of state knew in advance—since he died two years ago, he can't very well argue the point."

"My dear," Kevin laughed, "even though your version is mildly creative, we could use a few more like you at the Agency. Tell me the rest of your scenario."

"I'll have to back up a bit," Kate answered. "You know how closemouthed Anthony is about his personal life." She waited for Kevin's nod and then continued. "All along we've felt that if we could just get him to talk for the cameras the way he talks to me and Bill, it would win him a lot of support. But he can't or won't do it. I'm trying to create a situation that people will ask questions about, questions Anthony will have to answer. Jack Walsh is out in California right now, shooting tape for a story on the Senate race. I want to push Anthony into holding a news conference in the hope that he'll say the things I'd like him to, but if not, I'm prepared to set up an interview with Walsh and feed him the kinds of questions that will force Anthony to open up. It may be hopeless, but it's my best shot."

Kevin was sprawled in the chair, apparently quite relaxed. "The mole's wife remarried and moved to Europe, so that's no problem," he mumbled to himself. "If I play it right . . ." He straightened and looked at Kate. "If any of this gets out, I'm going to have my head handed to me on a plate. Mucking around in domestic politics is bad for my health."

"No one even knows why I'm here. Dad will eventually figure it out, but you're not worried about him, are you?"

Kevin shook his head. "Hank wouldn't knife his future son-in-law in the back—or me, for that matter."

"You're a little premature." Kate acknowledged to Kevin what she had realized the night before. "Anthony is going to know I set this up the minute the story breaks. He'll be furious, Kevin. Talk about heads on plates . . ." She shrugged. "He'd never approve of this. He'll probably tell me to get lost."

"Then why ask me to do it? Is it worth it?"

Kevin was asking questions that Kate had struggled with all day. "All I could think about during the trip east was whether I was going to wreck my relationship with Anthony in order to get him elected. Leaking a story to the press in the most favorable way possible is fairly standard procedure, but this isn't an ordinary story and I'm going behind Anthony's back to leak it. Knowing him has changed me, Kevin. When I think about the stuff I pulled to get him to run, I kind of wince. He's a very complex mixture of moral principles and pragmatic flexibility."

"It made him a first-rate agent. We were sorry to lose him. It's the ones with no principles who wind up resigning from the Agency to make a fortune training enemy guerrillas. The next thing we know, the people they've trained are blowing up US property and citizens all over the world. But go on."

Kate found it difficult to express her feelings. "I'm all tangled up inside," she admitted. "Last month, or even last week, I couldn't conceive of giving up my job, but flying to

Washington today I realized that I'd lost some of my enthusiasm. There are questions I never used to ask myself about
what's right and wrong, and for months now Anthony has
been making me ask them. Maybe it's perverse, but if I didn't
love him so much, I guess I wouldn't be sitting here now. At
first I told myself that I was just doing my job, but both of us
know that this goes way beyond that. I'm operating on
emotion rather than logic. All I know is that I believe in
Anthony and I'll do whatever I have to to help him win."

In the end Kevin made no promises. He and Kate joined
Kate's parents for a very pleasant, very political dinner,
which broke up at about eleven o'clock; the next morning
Kate was on a plane back to California.

She said nothing to Bill that afternoon and nothing to
Anthony that weekend. Bill knew better than to ask questions, and Anthony was so keyed up from campaigning that
he didn't seem to notice how edgy Kate was. The story broke
the following Wednesday, making the front page of every
paper in California and all the TV news shows.

The Agency's chief gadfly, a man whose private newspaper
had once published a list of American agents in Eastern
Europe, had printed an article stating that Anthony Larimer
had once been involved in illegal domestic counterintelligence work and that he had been employed by the Central
Intelligence Agency while working at the State Department.
The article further charged that Agency personnel had directed and carried out an operation resulting in the death of a
Soviet double agent, without the knowledge or approval of
the president. When Kate opened the morning paper and
read the story, she was puzzled and then shocked, but she
quickly realized that Kevin O'Neal hadn't held on to his job
this long by being stupid.

Bill was on the phone to Anthony when Kate walked into
his office an hour later, and judging from Bill's end of the
conversation Anthony was trying to calm him down. Kate
made herself comfortable in the chair opposite his desk and
waited for him to finish.

"He says not to get excited." Bill, whose face was blotchy

with aggravation, slammed down the phone. "Grossly exaggerated, he says. He has to wait for the official government statement before he can comment."

"That sounds reasonable." Bill scowled at Kate's casual reaction. "In nine years I've never seen you so . . . flappable," she drawled.

"What the hell are you so calm about?" Bill shot her a suspicious look. "This isn't a surprise to you, is it? Exactly what were you doing in Washington, Kate?"

"No comment," she replied. "Just keep watching the papers, Bill. Things will work out."

The next day Kevin O'Neal issued a statement in Washington categorically denying that Anthony Larimer had ever been on the CIA payroll while working in the United States. In the strongest language possible, the statement insisted that the operation to identify and "terminate" the threat to American security had been implemented by the FBI with the support of the CIA and with the full knowledge and approval of the president. Naturally, Anthony Larimer had cooperated completely. When a reporter asked O'Neal whether he would make documents relevant to the case public, he answered that the details were classified but that he would of course make them available to the appropriate congressional committees. Within hours, both the former president and the former attorney general had issued statements backing up this version of events.

Up till that point, Anthony had refused to comment on the matter, but afterward, under heavy pressure from all of his advisors, he agreed to let Vince Collier set up a news conference at a San Francisco hotel on Friday. Both Kate and Bill flew up from Los Angeles to attend, joining Anthony and Vince in a private suite shortly beforehand.

Kate knew immediately that Anthony was just as angry as she'd feared. He curtly asked Vince and Bill to leave the room, then laced into Kate with all the fury of a husband who's just caught his wife in bed with someone else.

"I've spoken to Kevin three times over the last few days," he began, "and I finally have a clear idea of how the State

Department story got into the papers. Kevin is damn good at guarding his flank—not many people could manage to feed their worst enemies a fabricated version of events just so they could deny it later—but Hendrickson will run him through with a dull sword if he ever finds out the truth. Kevin's career would be finished."

Kate didn't believe there was any chance of that. "I asked Kevin for a favor," she replied evenly. "He wouldn't have agreed if he didn't think he could get away with it."

"A favor!" Anthony sprang out of his chair and started to prowl around the room. "You asked him to put his neck on the line for *me*. Needless to say," he added sarcastically, "it never occurred to you to ask me whether I *wanted* the story leaked. You arrogantly decide that it will help my campaign, so you hop a plane to Washington and start twisting arms— and all of us know what an expert you are at *that*. Then you come back, make love with me, talk to me like nothing has happened, and send me back to Berkeley. My God, Katie! Does winning mean so much to you that—"

"Anthony, please." Kate's tone was beseeching. "I know you're annoyed that I didn't consult you first, but . . ."

"Annoyed? I'm not annoyed. I'm bloody furious." He stopped pacing and glared down at Kate. "You really get a kick out of manipulating people and situations, don't you?"

Since Anthony was attacking and not asking a serious question, Kate merely flushed and looked into her lap. She felt that there was no point trying to explain until he'd had a chance to cool down.

When his hand shot out and jerked her chin up, her pulse rate soared with alarm. "Answer me, dammit!" he growled. "Does winning mean so much to you that you would open up a can of worms that could lead to a major domestic scandal?"

Kate was trembling by now. Her face was a little sore where he'd touched it, and he looked like he wanted to do far worse. "You said Kevin was careful about—about the *appearance* of keeping within the law. I knew that he'd covered himself in case there were ever questions. We needed something dramatic, and . . ." Kate's voice trailed off in the wake of the disgusted expression on Anthony's face. "I wouldn't have done it if I didn't love you," she added weakly.

He gave an incredulous snort. "Love me! Are you serious? You don't know the meaning of the word. It goes along with openness and trust and honesty. Thanks to you, Miss Garvey, the press is waiting out there, and right this moment I'm so fed up I'd like to tell them the truth. But of course I can't do that, can I? Not without sticking my best friend's neck in a noose!"

He turned on his heel and slammed out of the room, leaving Kate pale and a little sick to her stomach. When Vince and Bill walked back inside, they found her doubled over, choking back tears. Vince came over and put a gentle hand on her shoulder, telling her, "Don't take it so hard. I don't know what you were up to in Washington and I don't particularly *want* to know, but if the idea was to smash through his defenses, I think you succeeded. Let's go sit inside and see if I'm right."

The news conference itself was being held in a large meeting room just down the hall. As they walked outside, a blessed numbness started to supplant the shock that Kate felt. She felt almost protected as she sat down between Bill and Vince, especially when Bill leaned over and asked her if she were all right. She nodded that she was, even though she wasn't.

"Things will work out," he said with an encouraging smile. "Anthony is essentially a pragmatist, Kate. He won't stay angry. I've seen the way he looks at you, remember?"

Kate didn't bother to answer. Anthony had just walked into the room and was adjusting the microphone. His prepared statement reiterated the government's official explanation: As a trained intelligence officer, he'd become concerned after noticing certain irregular activities on the part of his superior. He'd gone to Kevin O'Neal, who had promptly contacted the president and also the attorney general, who, as head of the Department of Justice, approved certain types of surveillance techniques and also supervised FBI activities. The subsequent counterintelligence operation had been carried out under orders from the president by a special FBI team. Then the questions began.

"Why did you go to O'Neal on a matter of domestic security?" a Washington reporter asked. "Shouldn't you have gone to the secretary of state or possibly the attorney general?"

Anthony's face was expressionless, but Kate knew him too well not to sense the internal struggle taking place. His professional instincts and his sense of privacy told him to stonewall, but his desire to be honest pushed him the opposite way. When the barriers started to drop, her surprise was so great that it managed to penetrate her numbness.

Anthony took a sip of water and ran his hands through his hair in the gesture she knew so well. "Look," he began, leaning toward the mike, "Kevin O'Neal wasn't only my boss when I was in Asia, he was my friend. When I signed on with the Agency, it was because I wanted to serve my country. I was a middle-class kid, and even the training I'd received hadn't prepared me for what I was going to face. You have to understand that I can't talk about those four years. I've passed them off as being fairly routine—reporting on activities of certain people, for example—but that wasn't entirely true. It was much more dangerous than I'd expected. There were a number of close calls before I almost got myself killed. Kevin O'Neal was the guy who kept me going."

Kate had never witnessed such a quiet group of reporters. The normal buzz of voices and shuffling of papers were absent as they strained to hear every word.

"I went to work at the State Department because it seemed to be a sensible way to use my expertise to contribute something." Kate knew that the statement was the truth; it simply wasn't the *whole* truth. "And I came across activities that didn't fit in."

Someone shouted, "Give us details!" and Anthony shook his head. "I can't. I'm sorry. If you were in my position, what would you have done? You wouldn't have gone to the secretary of state—the man I suspected was a close personal friend of his. You wouldn't have reread the National Security

Act of 1947 for guidance. You'd have gone to someone you knew and trusted. Kevin O'Neal brought in the appropriate people at the appropriate times. I want to stress that the late secretary of state was totally cooperative."

That was true, too, Kate thought, since the man hadn't known about the operation until it was over. There was a quick, loud buzz until Anthony recognized another reporter. "You've been accused of working for O'Neal the entire time you were in the State Department. Is that true?"

"I wasn't on his payroll, but I can't honestly sit up here and claim we didn't talk. Of course we talked. We were close friends by then. If that makes me disloyal or a criminal, I'll have to plead guilty." Anthony paused, sipping his water, but his eyes never left the reporter who'd asked the question. "When my wife was dying, Kevin O'Neal was the one I called at four o'clock in the morning when I thought I'd fall apart if I didn't speak to someone. There's very little I wouldn't do for him, and that includes involving myself in the Odessa situation in a way I would have preferred not to." Anthony held up his hand at the sudden undercurrent in the room. "I know—you want to know what I mean by that. I was asked to play for time and I did—you know that. But people's lives were at stake. It scared the hell out of me. I either trusted Kevin's judgment or I trusted my own. In the end I did the first, just as I had on other occasions, and he was right, but it was . . . very difficult for me."

Kate translated *difficult* into *agonizing*. "When I was asked to run for the Senate," Anthony continued softly, "I had my share of doubts. I didn't know whether I wanted to give up teaching. I was concerned about my daughter. I've had problems doing the kinds of things that candidates are supposed to do to get elected. After eight years in government service I was tired of ambiguity and compromise. The world is so complex that the dictionary definition of morality tends to become meaningless. If I save the lives of two American officials by destroying the reputation of a man whom we label an enemy, but who considers himself a patriot, am I a hero or a monster? I didn't have to ask myself those kinds of questions as a professor. I approached my research with total intellectual honesty and taught my classes the same way. But all of you know that in politics sometimes you have to vote for something you don't like in order to pass a bill you think is even more important. Sometimes the national interest conflicts with your constituents' interests. And I've learned the hard way"—Anthony smiled—"not to be too outspoken . . ." Laughter rippled through the audience and he continued, ". . . and not to think I have a monopoly on the truth. I'm probably not supposed to say this, and I hope the governor will forgive me, but the man I admire most in California politics is Allen Marks. Now, we all know that Allen is a Republican, and as such, sometimes misguided"—there was more laughter—"but he says what he thinks and he acts on his beliefs. I'll grant you that most of the time he's a pragmatic politician with one eye on the polls and the other on his principles, but there are issues he simply won't compromise on even though it might cost him votes. If I could be that kind of senator, I would consider myself successful. Allen's example helped me decide to run, but I don't suppose that either he or Bob Woodruff will thank me for the endorsement if I win."

Those closest to Anthony Larimer had been exposed to the potent combination of charm and sincerity he could wield, but most of the audience was clearly knocked sideways. What followed was one of the longest and most extraordinary news conferences that Kate had ever attended. Questions about Anthony's position on various issues alternated with more personal questions concerning his background and attitudes, and he answered all of them but one. The question he dodged, from a Los Angeles features writer, was "You're often seen in the company of Los Angeles political consultant Katharine Garvey, the daughter of Connecticut senator Henry Garvey. Are you planning to marry?"

Anthony's smile abruptly faded, his answer a clipped "You'll have to ask Miss Garvey. She's sitting at the back of the room." He immediately recognized another reporter, who asked a question about social-security benefits.

About ninety minutes after delivering his opening statement, Anthony looked at his watch and lifted up the pitcher of water at his elbow. "This is about empty," he announced, "and so am I. I'm not trying to kid either you or the voters—I wouldn't have sat here for this long, answering the types of questions I've refused to answer in the past, if my political advisors hadn't been after me about it for months. They tell me that since I have no record as a public official to run on, it's only reasonable that I . . . explain myself, I suppose. Ladies and gentlemen, if I had to do this only once every six years, it would be too often. Thank you."

Anthony ignored the subsequent clamor of voices and walked briskly out of the room. Kate was not so lucky. A barrage of questions about her relationship with Anthony rained down on her head, making her feel flustered and trapped. In desperation she singled out a reporter she knew quite well and told him, "It's no secret that Anthony and I are friends, but first and foremost I'm a political consultant, and more than anyone else I pushed him into holding this news conference. He's—he's not too pleased with me at the moment." She looked away, her cheeks stained pink, and mumbled, "I don't have anything else to say."

When the reporter tried to ask a follow-up question, Bill threw a protective arm around Kate's shoulders. "Back off, Jerry," he told the man. "It's been a tough few days for all of us, but especially for Kate." He hustled Kate out of the room and down the hall, taking her to the suite where they'd gathered before the news conference.

Anthony and Vince were already inside, talking to other top campaign officials. The consensus was that Anthony had been superb. The news conference would be featured on all the evening news shows, as well as on Jack Walsh's magazine show: Walsh had taped the entire ninety minutes. Bill wanted to use Anthony's answers in a couple of new television spots, to be run in the crucial last two weeks of the campaign.

Kate sat and listened, feeling very removed from the conversation. She only knew that Anthony had spared her a hard, cold glance when she walked inside and refused to look at her since. Somehow she'd held on to her composure, but every minute was a struggle. The only consolation was that she'd done her job and accomplished her goal.

Chapter 15

THE ULTIMATE EFFECT OF THE LARIMER NEWS CONFERENCE, though not as decisive as everyone had hoped, was measurable all the same. Anthony enjoyed a dramatic rise in support in the poll immediately following, but when Bob Woodruff hit back with the force and skill he was so capable of rallying, the gap started to diminish again. Woodruff continually reminded the voters that he was supported not only by President Hendrickson but also by Senator Allen Marks, the man whom his opponent admired so greatly.

Anthony's schedule for the final three and a half weeks of the campaign was an exhausting round of speeches, plane flights, and interviews in every major city in the state. Kate and Bill put together two highly emotional thirty-second TV spots that credited the candidate with intelligence, sensitivity, and plain old-fashioned guts, but said nothing about his stand on any of the issues.

Three times during campaign trips to Los Angeles, Anthony stopped in at Dorset and Associates to discuss the latest poll or strategy, but he was never anything more than coolly impersonal to Kate. Her repeated attempts at conciliation were ignored. She wasn't the type to fall apart—she kept herself busy and tried to push her personal problems to the back of her mind—but by the end of the third week she was running on nerve alone. She was trying to cope with the fact that on November seventh the campaign would be over, leaving her with no idea of what she would do for the rest of her life. She'd lost her taste for her work, and the obvious alternative, a job on Capitol Hill, was impossible. She didn't want to run into Anthony Larimer. Sacramento was too small to appeal to her, which left a job in city government. She decided to explore the possibilities after the election.

She wasn't eating and she wasn't sleeping, but at least she wasn't crying either. Whenever she succumbed to a bout of wistful fantasizing about herself and Anthony with two dark-haired children, she angrily reminded herself that for her entire adult life she'd been independent, that she'd never wanted to marry, and that there was no longer any reason for her to change.

She wasn't fooling herself, but until four days before the election she believed that the composed facade she tried to display was fooling everybody else. That was the day that Bill called her into his office half an hour before a scheduled meeting with Anthony, Vince, and Sandy and sat her down on the couch.

"You look terrible," he said bluntly. "You're working yourself into the ground, Kate. Is there anything I can do?"

Kate shook her head instead of answering him. All the strain of the past three weeks suddenly seemed to catch up with her, making her feel that if she tried to speak, she'd break down completely. She looked up, startled, when Bill mumbled a heartfelt curse. He never used that kind of language, even when everyone else did.

"This isn't doing either of you any good," he said. "Anthony's upset and you're upset. Can't you talk to him?"

Kate managed a shrug. Maybe Anthony hadn't been at his

best over the last few weeks, but at least he was holding his own. "It's too late anyway," she said. "With the election next Tuesday . . ."

"I'm not talking about the damn election! I'm talking about two people I care about, two people who happen to be doing an excellent job of making each other miserable."

Kate heard nothing but an accusation and reacted almost violently to it. "It's not me!" She was hoarse and close to tears. "I've tried to be friendly, but he won't bend an inch. What am I supposed to do, get down on my knees and beg for forgiveness?"

Bill immediately looked contrite. "Okay, honey, just relax. I'll get you a cold drink, okay?"

He took a bottle of cola and poured some into a glass for Kate. Her hand was trembling as she took it from him. She couldn't possibly get through the meeting ahead with the same self-contained air that she'd feigned during all the others.

Bill sat down next to her and apologized for upsetting her. "After twenty-four years of marriage and raising two kids, you'd think I'd have learned that people have to work things out on their own," he added, giving her knee a gentle pat.

Kate brushed away a couple of stray tears and told him she'd be all right. She had five minutes to get herself under control before Sandy walked in with the latest poll, and really didn't succeed. When Vince and Anthony followed a few minutes later, she didn't even look up.

"The difference between the California poll and our own poll is negligible," Sandy announced once everyone was settled. "You're a little ahead of Bob, with eight to nine percent undecided. People may not make up their minds until they walk into the voting booth. I wish I could be more encouraging, but it's just too close to call."

Vince proceeded to state the obvious: Anthony needed the strongest possible finish, with lines in his speeches that would wind up quoted on the evening news. Kate was on her second glass of cola by now. She was following the conversation only with difficulty, her mind more blank than preoccupied. When the meeting broke up and the four men started toward the door, it never occurred to her to move. She didn't notice Bill take Anthony aside for a moment, or the door gently closing, leaving Anthony alone in the room with her.

When he sat down next to her on the couch, she didn't fully understand why he'd returned. He slipped an arm around her shoulder and bent his head to kiss her, but Kate didn't respond at first. Only when his lips started to move gently back and forth, his tongue exploring the space between her lips to coax them farther apart, did she come alive. She stifled a sob, clutched at his jacket, and kissed him back with a wildness that owed everything to distress and nothing to passion. When Anthony carefully drew away, her face was wet with tears.

"What was that for?" she whispered.

Anthony took a handkerchief out of his pocket and dried her face. "I don't know. Maybe just to see how you'd react."

Kate turned away, feeling a painful tightness in her throat. If he was trying to punish her, he was succeeding beautifully.

"Listen to me, Katie." Anthony tucked a couple of fingers under her chin, turning her face up to his. "I'm angry and I'm confused. Angry because you put me in an absolutely untenable position. I had no choice but to back up Kevin's version of the truth, to protect both Kevin and myself, and maybe not even in that order. It's one thing to stand up there and shade the truth when national security is involved, but in this case the only things at stake were reputations and careers. Neither you nor Kevin had any right to leak that story without my permission, but you knew I wouldn't give it, so you didn't ask. I find that hard to forgive."

Kate couldn't be less than honest with him. "Maybe I shouldn't have done it, but I was too emotionally involved not to. Even if I could turn back the clock, I'd do it all over again, Anthony. But I promise, in the future I'll never go behind your back."

"I wish I could believe that, but you have one hell of a track record." Anthony seemed more weary than angry now. "Until this afternoon I had no idea you were taking this as hard as I was. What confuses me is that I can't stop thinking about you and I can't stop wanting you."

Kate raised a hand to stroke his face, but he seized it before she could touch him, kissing her palm and then forcing the hand into her lap. "I'm so wound up I can't think straight right now," he said. "I'm in no shape to make decisions about the future. We'll talk after the election, okay?"

"Okay. But I'll be here if you want me." Kate wanted to add "I love you" but didn't, because he'd never once said it to her and she couldn't bear the rejection of not hearing it now. "You've got three more days," she reminded him. "Go out there and knock 'em dead."

Anthony smiled and shook his head. "Never use show-biz jargon to a spy, Katie. He might take you seriously."

She stared at him, paling slightly. "You never . . ."

The smile turned into a grin. "No. But there's a very beautiful blonde in Los Angeles who's sorely tempted me on more than one occasion." He gave Kate a lingering kiss on the lips, which improved her mood immensely, and then strode briskly from the room.

Eli Hendrickson was reelected president of the United States hours before the polls even closed on the West Coast. He carried along many of the party's candidates on his generous coattails, but the election was not the all-out sweep that the Republicans had hoped for and the Democrats had dreaded. By nine o'clock Pacific Time, four or five Senate races were still "too close to call," depending on which network you were watching. The Larimer-Woodruff contest was one of them.

In a ritual that never seemed to change, the supporters of each Senate candidate gathered in downtown Los Angeles hotels, doing their best to celebrate. From time to time one of the candidates would step up to the microphone and deliver a couple of dozen rousing words to those present, who would then cheer, yell, or blow noisemakers. As the hours dragged on, local television reporters started interviewing the same people for the third or fourth time. After one such interview

Vince Collier returned to the three-room suite where Anthony Larimer and those closest to him were watching election returns and grumbled that he was going to make a recording of his answer and play it for the next newsman who approached him. He claimed he was losing his voice.

When the telephone in the suite rang, it was usually for Sandy Cohen—one of his people calling in results from a key precinct. By midnight Sandy was knee-deep in numbers, but he seemed to have a perfect grasp of the situation.

The problem was breakdowns in California's computerized vote-counting system, another election-night ritual. Kate remembered a state assembly race when the computers hadn't been fixed until twenty-four hours after the polls closed, and hoped that the same thing wouldn't happen tonight. As soon as Sandy had the numbers he needed, he would no doubt be able to forecast the outcome. In his eleven years as a polling expert he had never made a mistake. But in the meantime the lead in actual votes counted kept switching back and forth, depending on which areas of the state had just sent in results.

Kate passed the evening watching the returns, sipping Amaretto, and talking with various members of Anthony's family. When the candidate himself wasn't downstairs bucking up the faithful, he was sitting in an easy chair, staring at the television set. He was obviously extremely tired and in no mood to talk, but once or twice he smiled at Kate in a way that she hoped was personal rather than professional. She felt that a private conversation would have to wait until the election was decided and Anthony's future settled, but that didn't make the waiting any easier.

At one-thirty Anthony went downstairs for one last speech to thank his supporters. He explained that his advisors had told him that it might be many more hours before some crucial figures came in from San Francisco and Orange County and admitted that he was all but asleep on his feet. Kate stood and watched him on television, and when he didn't come back to the suite afterward, she assumed that he had gone directly to his room to try to get some rest. He knew that they would wake him up as soon as they were sure of the outcome.

Although the party downstairs eventually broke up, most of Anthony's family and key campaign aides stayed together in the suite. At two-thirty the call Sandy Cohen had apparently been waiting for finally came. He jotted down the numbers, whipped out his calculator, and retreated into his own private world for the next fifteen minutes. Then he looked up, a huge smile on his face, and announced, "That's it, Bill. That was the Bay Area on the phone. The minor party candidates did significantly worse than the exit polls indicated—even our *own* figures were off—and it's enough to nail it down. I wanted to be positive before I told you that you've got yourself a senator."

Relieved smiles quickly gave way to one of the most emotional celebrations Kate had ever seen. Everybody seemed to be talking, laughing, and hugging, all at once, united by their love for Anthony and their belief in his ability to make a difference.

After exchanging a kiss with Bill and then with Sandy, Kate looked around for Jessica Larimer and noticed her standing in the arms of her grandfather. Her two grandmothers were only a step or two away, actually embracing each other. As Kate started over, Jessica suddenly burst into tears, turned away from her bewildered grandfather, and ran straight into Kate's arms, sobbing her thanks. Kate was nothing short of astonished by this.

"Hey, Jessica, there are a lot of people to thank besides me," she said, stroking the girl's back. "You should start with yourself. You worked as hard as any of us, missed a lot of school, and still made straight *A's.*"

Jessica sniffed and straightened, rubbing the tears out of her eyes. "If it hadn't been for you," she said, "he never would have shown people what he's really like. The only thing is, he's kind of a male chauvinist, Katie." She gave a teary little giggle. "Kris and I have been trying to educate him, but she'll have to stay in Berkeley to finish her degree when we move to Washington. I'm glad I'll still have an ally around."

The uncertainty in Jessica's voice told Kate that the girl was fishing for information. She was deeply touched by Jessica's implied approval of her, but couldn't provide the reassurance she seemed to want.

"That depends on your father," she said gently. "For now, why don't you go up to his room and give a knock on the door. If he's awake, you can tell him what Sandy just said."

Jessica shook her head. "You go, Katie."

"Walk me outside," Kate murmured.

When the two of them were alone in the hall, it was Kate's eyes that filled with tears. "You are one prize package, Jessica Larimer," she said huskily. "Didn't anyone ever tell you that a fifteen-year-old girl is supposed to loathe on sight any adult woman who comes near her father?"

Jessica wrinkled her nose. "That kind of stuff is for psychology articles," she said crushingly. "Dad went through a horrible time when Mom was dying. It took him almost a year to even ask a woman out. I was lucky, I guess, because Kris came to live with us while she went to college, and even though she's only six years older than I am she's been like another mother to me. But Dad was awfully lonely—until he met you. And I think he knows that."

Kate smiled, stroked the girl's hair, and quickly turned toward the elevators. When she got to Anthony's room, she hesitated, her heart beating so strongly that she could feel it in her throat. Her first knock was almost inaudible, the next two much stronger.

Anthony answered the door, the room behind him dark except for light filtering in through the gauzy curtains. It took Kate a moment to realize that he wasn't wearing a stitch of clothing. His only concession to decency was a towel around his waist.

"I could have been a reporter," she said, "with a photographer right behind me."

"You know the way I sleep. Why should I get dressed just

to answer the door?" He pulled Kate into the room and shut the door behind her, tossing the towel onto a chair. "Besides, I knew it was you. I could tell from the way you knocked."

He sat down on the edge of the bed, then yawned and stretched lazily. "I couldn't sleep for more than a few minutes," he said. "What took you so long?"

Kate stared at him, bewildered. "In the first place," she informed him, "you have no right to be so relaxed when you don't even know the outcome of the election. And in the second place, Sandy just decided you're going to win it. Hendrickson pulled in a lot of Republican votes, but Sandy says that enough liberal support swung to you at the last minute to make up for it. They finally got the computers working in San Francisco, and his elf phoned in the numbers a few minutes ago."

"That's very nice, but it still doesn't explain what took you so long." Anthony swung his legs onto the bed and lay back against the pillows. "Do a nice, slow strip for me, Katie. And then come make love to me."

Kate had the distinct impression that she'd missed something here. "Don't you think we should talk first?" she asked.

"I think I've talked enough for the last eight months to hold me at least until morning." He smiled. "Take off your clothes and come to bed, Katie. I've been lying here alone, waiting for you, for too long already."

The statement was very promising. Katie removed her suit jacket and draped it over the back of a chair. Slipping off her skirt, she said, "I wanted to wait until the results were in. But you don't even seem excited about winning the election."

"I'm ecstatic about winning the election. The blouse, darling."

Darling. That was even more promising. Kate took her time with the buttons, not because she wanted to be seductive, but because so many thoughts were chasing through her mind. "I told Jessica she should come up," she said, "but she wanted me to do it. You have a wonderful daughter, Anthony. She's—"

"I know my daughter is wonderful," he interrupted patiently. "We've talked about how wonderful she is on numerous occasions, but right now the subject of my daughter holds absolutely no fascination for me. Do you think you could stop fiddling with the slip and take it off?"

Kate lifted it over her head and added it to the pile on the chair. She was suddenly aware of the way Anthony was gazing at her, intense and a little amused. She rolled down her panty hose and walked to the edge of the bed, clad only in a black lace bra and matching panties now.

"Your family is thrilled." The room felt a little warm to her. "Your mother even hugged your mother-in-law. The Democrats even have a shot at holding on to the Senate, which would make my father happy. . . ."

"It would make *me* happy if you'd just shut up." Anthony stretched out a hand, running his fingers back and forth over the lace of Kate's bra. A familiar weakness invaded her legs at his touch; the four weeks since he'd made love to her seemed like an eternity. "Take off the bra, Katie," he ordered.

Kate did so, but when she started over to the chair to add the bra to her other clothing, Anthony looped a finger through the lace of her panties and tugged her back again. His hand seemed to scorch her skin as it stroked her hip and thigh. Her bra wound up on the floor, the panties following a moment later.

Anthony made room for her on the bed, then lifted the covers for both of them. As Katie slid in beside him, she whispered, "I love you," but he didn't answer back.

A ragged stab of disappointment tore through her body. Blinking back tears, she remembered his earlier request— "Make love *to* me," not "*with* me"—and started to comply. She kissed his neck, then trailed her lips to his face, nuzzling his mouth, his cheek, his closed lids. Her fingers stroked the hard muscles of his arms before moving to his chest and stomach. When she started to caress his thighs, she thought to herself that she'd almost forgotten how beautiful his body was, but there was sadness behind the passion she felt. He murmured her name and drew her a little closer to him.

She bent her head to flick her tongue across his nipples and felt him stroke her hair, then twine his fingers through the tousled locks to keep her mouth from moving any lower. "I thought . . ." she began.

"Shh." He pulled her up until she was sprawled half on top of him, her breasts pressed against his chest. "Some things are better shown than said, better felt than heard," he softly told her.

Their lips met in a tender kiss that quickly deepened, yet there was no wildness or loss of control in the embrace. Anthony slowly explored her mouth with his tongue, savoring the Amaretto-flavored sweetness inside. Kate, her own tongue languidly probing in return, gradually slipped into another world, a world where emotional and mental fatigue had combined with desire to produce a sensation of drifting, of floating in an endless void. Every sense was heightened, every movement slowed.

Anthony's hands seemed to creep down her body, branding her skin as they moved lower. She was gently pushed onto her back, her breasts teased and caressed until she moaned deep in her throat and blindly sought his lips. She felt too weak to do anything more than run her fingers through his hair and respond to the demands of his mouth. The tenderness slowly gave way to passion; her lips parted wide for a kiss that burned with desire. Kate was still floating, but the void was surrounded by fire now. The flames moved closer, licking at every part of her body, but especially where his hands so insistently stroked her. When his fingers skittered away to graze her legs, she twisted around in frustration. Her hands sought his hips in an effort to bring him closer.

Instead she found herself turned onto her side, a muscled leg snaking between her thighs, her hips raised up to receive him. They came together so naturally that being apart seemed like some abnormal state of affairs. Kate slid her arms around Anthony's neck and melted against him, totally responsive to his wishes, wanting only to follow where he led. She could feel the rapid beating of his heart and hear his labored breathing; she could sense the tension in his movements as he forced himself to slow the pace of his lovemaking. Only a fool could have missed the tenderness in the body that so ardently claimed hers, or the love in his touch as he stroked her dewy skin.

When Kate understood what he was showing her, something inside her snapped. She stopped drifting; her submissiveness disappeared. She suddenly felt wanton and irresistible and wonderfully alive. Anthony never knew what hit him when the clinging little kitten in his arms turned into a demanding wildcat. For a second he was so stunned that he stiffened and didn't respond, but Kate's passion soon destroyed his control. They took each other with an urgent need that couldn't be bothered with gentleness. At the end Kate was barely able to think or breathe, much less move, as wave after wave of pleasure wracked her body. Only slowly did she realize how heavy Anthony felt sprawled on top of her. He was laughing and trying to catch his breath, both at the same time.

Kate tried to wriggle out from under him. "You're not supposed to *laugh*," she said, pretending to mind.

He obligingly rolled onto his back. "Why not? I'm happy. I'm wildly in love, I just won a very tough election, and making love at forty is better than it ever was at twenty or thirty. This has to be the best night of my life."

Kate felt an inward glow that should have lit up the world, but all she could think to say was, "You're not forty."

"Next month. Do you think I'm over the hill?"

Kate smiled at him. "Not from what *I've* just seen," she drawled.

Anthony sat up and clicked on the bedside light, then looked down at Kate, who was stretched out on her side. "There's champagne on ice in the bathroom," he said. "Go bring it."

Kate was too comfortable to move. "Why me?" she asked.

"Because I like to see you walk around naked. Move, woman!"

Kate didn't keep arguing. She fetched the champagne and two hotel glasses from the bathroom counter and set them down on Anthony's night table so he could do the honors. Once they'd had a chance to take a couple of sips, Anthony said to her, "I want to make sure you understand what we're celebrating."

Kate thought she knew, but teased, "The election, of course."

"Nope. Even if I'd lost, I'd still be drinking champagne with you. We'd be quiet and a little depressed, but we'd still have something to celebrate." He paused, then asked gently, "Do you feel the same way, Katie?"

Kate's lighthearted mood evaporated. She suddenly needed to be sure of where she stood with him. "Are you telling me that you're not angry anymore? That you want us to be together?"

He scowled at her. "Spare me the psychobabble about 'being together.' This is an old-fashioned proposal. I want you to marry me. As for being angry . . ." He downed the rest of his champagne and put the glass on the night table. "Dammit, Katie, if you ever, *ever*, go behind my back in an attempt to manipulate me into doing what you've arrogantly decided is best for me, I swear to God I'll turn you over my knee and tan your sweet little bottom till you cry for mercy."

Kate considered the threat, then said airily, "It's not such a harsh punishment. You *could* have threatened to divorce me. Still," she promised, "I've reformed." She held out her glass to him, giggling. "Give me a refill, honey. This is terrific stuff."

He filled both glasses to the halfway point and then held out his arm, inviting Kate to snuggle against the crook of his neck. She felt so safe and secure lying in his arms that she asked the one question that really frightened her. "Anthony," she began uncertainly, "do you—do you love me as much as you loved Beth?"

The withdrawal she'd half expected never came. "It's totally different," he explained gently. "I grew up with Beth. We married over the objections of both families and then went halfway around the world with no one but each other to turn to. Both those experiences brought us close together, and yet you know more about my work and my reactions to it than Beth ever did. What I said before about making love—I meant it, Katie. Both of us were novices when we met, and by the time we got rid of our inhibitions and learned to really please each other, we were so caught up in trying to have children that too much of the joy went out of it. And when she got sick . . ."

He paused for several seconds, then continued, "But you asked me about love, not sex. I loved Beth very much. It's taken me a long time to accept the fact that you're nothing like her and never will be. This afternoon, once the campaign was finally over and there was nothing I could do to affect the outcome, I took a long drive around some of the back roads near my house, just thinking about the future. I suppose it was a matter of recognizing what I'd already decided, more than receiving any startling revelations. I realized—I love you the way you are. If I've never told you before, it's only because, until last Friday, you always held a part of yourself back from me and I couldn't be sure of my feelings until I felt an emotional commitment from you. I share things with you that I never shared with Beth. I always felt like her protector, but I feel like your equal, your partner. Both of us have changed over the last eight months, but I wouldn't expect—or want—you to change in a way that would make you more like Beth. I need you to be Kate. As for how much I love you . . ." He shook his head. "How can I answer something like that? Beth and I had eighteen years together, but, God willing, I'll have twice that many with you." His voice dropped to a husky murmur. "I love you very much, Katie, but more next month than today, and more next year than next month. Is that good enough?"

"Yes," Kate said, and meant it. She couldn't be jealous—not when Beth was gone and she was here. "I want you to know something, Anthony," she went on. "It wouldn't have mattered if you'd lost. I'd have moved to Berkeley and had your children and . . ."

His laughter cut off her words. "My darling Katie," he said, "children or no children, you'd have gotten yourself a job in San Francisco, and between your working and commuting and just hanging around the city, I'd have been a very lonely man. When the voters throw me out of office someday, I'm going to go back to teaching. And you have my word that when I do, it will be in a major city. I intend to keep you happy."

Kate blushed sheepishly, thinking to herself that she was getting a very realistic man. But then, one of the advantages of marrying someone with a successful eighteen-year relationship behind him was that he understood better than she did how to make a marriage work. "If you want to keep me happy," she teased, "you'll have to offer me a job."

"You have so many talents, I don't know how to use you. You can handle the political end of the office if you want to, but you'd also do a first-rate job on legislation." He bent over and nibbled her earlobe. "Then again, Miss Garvey, maybe I'll just lock you in an office with nothing but a bed in it and assign you the job of keeping the senator happy. Whenever the spirit hits me, I'll come in, relock the door, and ravish you." His mouth wandered to her lips, parting them for a playfully dominating kiss that tasted of champagne and contentment.

Kate was about to retaliate by tickling him until he asked for a truce, but the ringing of the telephone interrupted their game. "One of the advantages of having you for a wife is that you run interference so beautifully," Anthony announced. "Whoever it is, get rid of him fast."

Kate picked up the phone, her soft "Hello?" answered with "This is Bob Woodruff. May I speak to Anthony, please?"

"It's Kate, Bob." Kate mouthed his name to Anthony, who grinned and shook his head. "Anthony's asleep, but both of us want to thank you for a good campaign."

"I called to offer my congratulations. Even my own pollster tells me it's over. But the formal concession statement will have to wait till morning—I'm not going to deliver it in the middle of the night, when no one is watching. By the way, I understand that best wishes are in order."

"Best wishes?" Kate was genuinely puzzled. "Where did you hear that?"

"You're not getting married?"

"We are, but . . ."

"Haven't you been watching the tube?" Bob Woodruff sounded astonished. "The networks only predicted Anthony's victory twenty minutes ago. I mean, I know the man is cool, but not to watch the returns of his own election . . ."

"Sandy beat the networks by a good half hour. But what was on television that we missed?"

"His daughter. A reporter asked her if she was looking forward to living in Washington, and she said yes. She got this teasing look in her eyes and said she was especially looking forward to meeting Senator Garvey, because she thought he was about to become a member of the family. But then she blushed and refused to say another word."

Kate couldn't help but laugh. "A future politician," she said, then added, "You sound very cheerful for a man who just lost a heartbreaker, Bob. It was very gracious of you to call."

"Naturally I'm disappointed. I even admit to smashing a few glasses and kicking the wall. But under the circumstances, it's not too hard to be gracious. The President called earlier in the evening with a pep talk. In the unlikely case I didn't win, he mentioned that he wanted me to come on board as a Special Assistant for Congressional Relations. So tell your future husband that he hasn't seen the last of me."

"I'll do that." Anthony was listening intently by now, trying to figure out the other end of the conversation from Kate's responses. "And, Bob, we hope that if you decide to run for the Senate again, it will be for Allen's seat when he retires and not against Anthony. We wouldn't want to face you again."

"The feeling is mutual. And I fully intend to try again. We'll see you in Washington, Kate."

After she hung up, Kate repeated the conversation to Anthony, who smiled and shook his head. "This afternoon I told Jessica that I wanted to work things out with you, and I guess she assumed I'd succeeded." He hesitated, a suspicious frown suddenly supplanting his smile. "Then again, maybe she was trying to make sure that I'd actually propose by making provocative statements to the press. If the two of you ever team up, you'll be downright lethal."

Kate twisted around and twined her arms around his neck. "Nothing that a former hot-shot intelligence officer shouldn't be able to handle," she teased, nuzzling his lips. When he tried to deepen the kiss, she pulled away a little, repeatedly nibbling at his lower lip, only to dodge away every time he tried to capture her. By the third or fourth escape Anthony's eyes were smoky with frustration.

"The way you affect me," he muttered, "sometimes I wonder." With singular determination he took the phone off the hook, letting the receiver dangle, and pulled Kate into his arms.

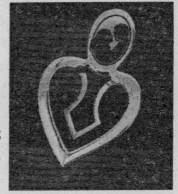

Silhouette Intimate Moments

more romance, more excitement

$2.25 each

Let Tapestry™ historical romances carry you to a world of love and intrigue... <u>free</u> for 15 days!

"Long before women could read and write, tapestries were used to record events and stories . . . especially the exploits of courageous knights and their ladies."

And now there's a new kind of tapestry...

In the pages of Tapestry romance novels, you'll find love, intrigue, and historical touches that really make the stories come alive!

You'll meet a brave Norman knight . . . a handsome Count . . . a rugged American rancher. . . and more. And on each journey back in time, you'll experience tender romance and searing passion!

We think you'll be so delighted with Tapestry romances, you won't want to miss a single one! We'd like to send you 2 books each month, as soon as they are published, through our Tapestry Home Subscription Service.℠ Look them over for 15 days, free. If you enjoy them as much as we think you will, pay the invoice enclosed. If not delighted, simply return them and owe nothing.

A world of love and intrigue is waiting for you in Tapestry romances . . . return the coupon today!

HISTORICAL *Tapestry* ROMANCES

Silhouette Intimate Moments

Coming Next Month

Widow Woman by Parris Afton Bonds

Cass Duval Garolini had come back to New Mexico untouchable and unapproachable. Cade Montoya was determined to make a dent in her heart, but he was hiding a secret that threatened to destroy them both.

Her Own Rules by Anna James

Diana Manning's assignment threw her back into the arms of Nick Fremont, the man who had once broken her heart. She could keep personal feelings separate from business . . . or so she told herself.

Russian Roulette by Möeth Allison

Kat Dobrinin wasn't ready to fall in love again, especially to a man who reminded her painfully of former ties. Sasha Gordon was as unwilling as Kat to fall in love, but fate decreed that they spend their future together.

Love Me Before Dawn by Lindsay McKenna

Tess Hamilton was designing a prototype airplane and Shep Ramsey was the man chosen to test its wings. For months Tess had been obsessed with her work, but now Shep had entered her heart and if her calculations should fail Shep would forfeit his life.